Praise for Emily Liebert's Novels

Those Secrets We Keep

"Emily Liebert's evocative new novel reveals how the secrets we keep can entangle us—and how only the deep power of friendships can set us free. Settle in for a vacation at the lake with these unforgettable women. Within a few pages, you'll practically feel the warm sand beneath your toes." —Sarah Pekkanen, author of *Things You Won't Say*

When We Fall

"Brimming with detail and emotion, *When We Fall* paints an absorbing picture of the gilded lives of the hedge fund elite, as the arrival of a young widow sends shock waves across an affluent suburban enclave. Add in a crumbling marriage, a lethal frenemy, a love interest, and a dizzying cascade of wealth and entitlement, and Emily Liebert's latest will keep you turning pages long past bedtime."
—Beatriz Williams, *New York Times* bestselling author of *The Secret Life of Violet Grant*

"A fun, insightful read. Liebert is a welcome addition to the world of women's fiction." —*New York Times* bestselling author Jane Green

"Fans of Jane Green and Jennifer Weiner will appreciate the realistic concerns of Liebert's heroines." —*Booklist*

You Knew Me When

"[Liebert] has a knack for crafting realistic, witty dialogue. An emotionally honest novel full of nostalgia for old friendships, the struggle of reconciliation, and the everlasting power of female friendships." —*Booklist*

those secrets
we keep

EMILY LIEBERT

NEW AMERICAN LIBRARY

New American Library
Published by the Penguin Group
Penguin Group (USA) LLC, 375 Hudson Street,
New York, New York 10014

USA | Canada | UK | Ireland | Australia | New Zealand | India | South Africa | China
penguin.com
A Penguin Random House Company

First published by New American Library,
a division of Penguin Group (USA) LLC

First Printing, June 2015

REGISTERED TRADEMARK—MARCA REGISTRADA

LIBRARY OF CONGRESS CATALOGING-IN-PUBLICATION DATA:

Liebert, Emily.
    Those secrets we keep / Emily Liebert.
        pages cm.
    ISBN 978-0-451-47187-1 (softcover)
    1. Female friendship—Fiction. 2. Pregnancy—Fiction. 3. Chick lit. I. Title.
    PS3612.I33525T48 2015
    813'.6—dc23   2014047497

Printed in the United States of America
10   9   8   7   6   5   4   3   2

Set in Spectrum MT
Designed by Alissa Theodor

For my husband, Lewis, the secret to my success.
Ten years of marriage and I still love you more
with each passing day.

acknowledgments

Thank you to my extraordinary agent, Alyssa Reuben. I depend on your endless support, cheerleading, and—above all—your friendship.

Kerry Donovan, my eagle-eyed editor, your guidance and expertise transform my novels. And for that, your friendship, and so much more, I'm truly grateful to have you on my team.

To my publicists, Kathleen Zrelak and Diana Franco—thank you for always going above and beyond.

I'm grateful every day for my best friend, Melody Drake; my in-laws Mary Ann Liebert, Peter B. Liebert, and Peter S. Liebert; my brother, Zack Einhorn; my grandmother Ailene Rickel; and my parents, Tom and Kyle Einhorn.

Thank you to a very special group of people who always stands behind me: Kerry Kennedy, Sara Haines, Shari Arnold, David Goffin, Devin Alexander, Jake Spitz, Jane Green, Sarah Pekkanen, Zoe

Schaeffer, Hyleri Katzenberg, Robin Homonoff, Emily Homonoff, Jessica Regel, Debbie Mogelof, Marni Lane, Allison Walmark, Danielle Dobin, Amy Kallesten, Jen Scott, and Karen Sutton.

I saved the best for last. Thank you to my love, Lewis, and to our sons, Jaxsyn and Hugo—I love you to the moon and back.

those secrets
we keep

chapter 1

Sloane gripped the steering wheel with clenched fists as her mind darted furiously from one direction to the next. Had she remembered to pack absolutely everything Maddie would need at sleepaway camp? She'd included enough clean underwear for four weeks without laundry and had reminded her to reapply sunscreen every two hours and always after swimming. Naturally, her daughter had rolled her eyes in response to what Sloane perceived as responsible parenting. Still, aside from time spent at Grandma's house, it was Maddie's first time away from home for more than a few days. Sloane couldn't help but feel anxious.

Her unease had tripled since she'd left Maddie at camp, even though her daughter had shown no signs of separation anxiety. As she'd pulled away from Maddie's cabin, watching her daughter's wide smile grow smaller in her rearview mirror, Sloane's stomach had roiled. It felt like another loss. Not the same kind of loss as the one she'd been struggling to recover from lately, but a significant loss nonetheless. She wasn't sure why.

In springtime, when she'd filled out the enrollment paperwork, she'd been so full of anticipation for everything Maddie would experience on her own during summer camp. All the friends she would make. The new skills she would learn. And Maddie had seemed happy, possibly even overjoyed at the prospect of four weeks without her mother and father to answer to. Four weeks of freedom.

Shouldn't Sloane feel the same way? No lunches to pack. No negotiations over appropriate attire for a pre-tween-aged girl to wear to school. And no threat of boys calling past ten o'clock at night to discuss "homework."

Yet, as soon as the gate to Camp Pinewood had closed behind her car, she'd felt vacant. Fretful. Now she and Eddie would have the summer to themselves. They could go out to see a movie without having to secure a babysitter. They could eat dinner naked on the back porch if they wanted—not that they'd ever do something like that. They could have sex with the bedroom door open. Weren't those the sorts of things that were meant to be going through her mind? Weren't those the sorts of things that married couples whose only child would be absent from their lives for a whole month were supposed to anticipate with great excitement? Yet Sloane had to acknowledge that she felt quite the opposite. Her daughter's departure had brought on a rush of unsettling emotions. Empty. Unfulfilled. If she was being honest, all the emotions were familiar companions. Things hadn't been right for Sloane for some time.

Her mother had insisted on meeting for lunch as soon as she got back to Brookline. Sloane tried to seize on the idea of lunch with her mother as a distraction for her morose thoughts, but she would no doubt receive the third degree about how Maddie had taken to her new surroundings. She'd have to be careful not to let her misgivings show, lest her mother think there was anything wrong with Camp Pinewood. She'd indicated more than once that she thought four weeks was an awfully long time for a nine-year-old to be away from home but in typical fashion had conceded, albeit reluctantly, with a hearty dose of guilt, that it was Sloane and Eddie's decision to make. *"Who am I to say? I'm just her grandmother. What do I know?"*

Of course the very last thing Sloane felt like doing at the moment, on the heels of a three-hour drive, was being on the receiving end of her mother's barrage of questions. Thankfully, her mom had invited Sloane's aunt to join them. With any luck that would divert the focus from her.

Sloane pulled into the parking lot of an off-the-beaten-path vegan restaurant, which must have been selected by her aunt. Apparently, they had the best tofu curry this side of South Asia. Period. Who could argue with that? She pushed in the front door and immediately homed in on her mother flailing her arms in the far corner to wave her over to their table. A blind man could have spotted her.

"How's my baby girl?" Sloane's mother swooped in, kissing her forcefully on either side of the mouth as she crushed her cheeks between her fleshy palms.

"I'm fine, Mom. That hurts." She shuffled into the booth and reached for a napkin to eradicate the tangerine lip stain she'd undoubtedly been branded with. Twice.

"You need to put some meat on those bones." Her mother surveyed her with one eye half-closed, taking in everything from her faded purple Crocs with their flattened backs to the Red Sox baseball cap she was wearing to conceal her day-three-without-washing chestnut brown hair. "Did you lose more weight?"

"I don't know, Mom." She did know. And she had. Ten pounds in the past month alone. Quite unintentionally. "I'm just stressed-out, I guess."

"You kids these days and your stress."

"I have a lot on my mind is all." Sloane spread her menu in front of her face, intending it as a makeshift barrier. As if that would discourage her mother's third degree. Margaret Allen was not one to be discouraged. Ever. As a devout Catholic—somewhat ironic in light of her overbearing and overfeeding tendencies; she would have made a great Jew—as well as a lifetime busybody, her claim to fame was that she hadn't missed a Sunday at church in thirty-six years. Not even when she'd given birth to Sloane's younger sister, Amy, on a Saturday afternoon. God couldn't have forgiven that?

"I'm listening."

"I'm not really in the mood to talk about it now." Sloane fidgeted with the frayed corner of her menu.

"Well, fine. Then how's my granddaughter? Did she cry when you left?"

"No, Mom. She's nine."

"So? You bawled for three hours when Daddy and I dropped you at day camp."

"I did not."

"You most certainly did." She nodded, as if she'd never been as sure of something in her entire life. "Do they feed her at this camp?"

"No, they starve them."

"Very funny. Maddie is skinny enough. I hope she doesn't lose weight." She paused. "I'm going to send her a care package with some of my brownies."

"They don't allow them to receive food in the mail, Mom."

"That's ridiculous!"

"It's the rule." Sloane shrugged.

"Well, it sounds like *jail* to me."

"It's not jail, Mom. Believe me, jail doesn't cost a fortune."

"Well, hello, ladies!" Sloane's aunt floated toward them, her commanding voice drawing the attention of almost everyone in their vicinity, despite the fact that Annabel Winston was a woman whose presence needed no verbal introduction.

Today, she was bedecked in a caftan that looked more suitable for Woodstock circa 1969 than present-day Brookline, Massachusetts, with its swirling rainbow of colors and coordinated handkerchief-inspired headband—if you could really call the tattered piece of fabric tied across her forehead a headband. During Sloane's childhood and well into her teenage years, her aunt had represented everything her mother wasn't. She would descend upon their modest New England saltbox house bearing exotic gifts, such as the worry dolls from Guatemala she'd instructed Sloane to place under her pillow before going to bed to ensure a good night's sleep.

Annabel Winston did not cook. She most certainly did not clean. She didn't help with homework or wipe tears away when knees were bruised. But she did regale Sloane and Amy with tales of her mysterious and, typically, unpredictable travels around the globe.

All the while, Sloane's mother would endure being sidelined, often rolling her eyes as her sister elaborated, possibly to the point of untruth. But Sloane and Amy didn't care and their mother's nagging cynicism served only to shine a brighter and more flattering light on their aunt.

"Hello." Her mother's lips pursed into a thin line as Annabel proffered three kisses on alternating cheeks and then signaled for her to slide over so she could squeeze into the booth next to her.

"Now let me get a look at my gorgeous niece. Stand up, stand up." She gestured by lifting both hands in the air.

"Aunt Annabel," Sloane moaned, but she couldn't hide a smile. She got out of her seat and stood in the aisle, where she did a quick rotation at her aunt's direction—one index finger held high, winding in a circular motion.

"Every inch as stunning as ever. You must have inherited my genes." She nudged her sister in the side. "Right, Margie?"

Sloane laughed. Her mother absolutely despised being called Margie and had been known to bite the head off anyone who dared to mutter any version of a nickname without explicit permission.

It never ceased to astonish Sloane how very different her mother and aunt were. Same parents. Same DNA. Same Roman nose and olive complexion. Same zaftig thighs. But the similarities ended there. Nothing like Sloane and her sister, Amy. While they'd certainly pursued diverse interests growing up—Sloane had been head cheerleader and Amy had been head of the debate team—they'd always preferred the same clothing, food, friends, sometimes even boys. Amy had been the smarter sister, no doubt. Sloane had been the prettier one, but not by much.

"So, what's good here aside from the tofu?" Sloane's mother lifted her reading glasses, which hung around her neck on a thick, glossy gold-link chain, onto the bridge of her nose out of habit, even though they all knew she could decipher the menu just fine without them.

"What do you have against tofu?" Sloane's aunt arched a bushy eyebrow.

"Well, for starters, it tastes like a soggy sponge."

"Oh, would you stop! It's good for you. And it wouldn't hurt you to lose a few pounds."

"I could say the same to you," Sloane's mother grumbled. "On the other hand, my daughter here is fading away to nothingness from all of the *stress* in her life."

"Is that so, dear?" Sloane's aunt turned to her, a look of genuine concern swathing her rugged face. "What's troubling you?"

"It's nothing really."

"It's never nothing." She contemplated this. "Is it . . ."

There it was. The proverbial dot dot dot. As if saying her name would make it a final period.

"Amy?" Sloane filled in the blank and her aunt nodded somberly. "No. I mean, I don't know. Maybe." She noticed her mother shift uncomfortably in her seat. She'd already compartmentalized things and closed off this particular topic of discussion. Apparently, she and God had worked it out. "I'm probably anxious because I just dropped Maddie at sleepaway camp for the whole month of August, and with Eddie working . . ."

"You're concerned you'll be a bored housewife?" her aunt blurted, not bothering to consider a tactful response. Nothing revolutionary on that front.

"That's not exactly how I would have put it." Sloane laughed. "But I guess kind of." Nor was it nearly the whole truth.

Sloane had quit her job as a third-grade teacher nine years earlier when Madeleine was born. It was hard to believe almost a decade had passed since she'd nuzzled her colicky little miracle and watched the rest of the world fade into the distance. She'd gone from the workforce to force-feeding a newborn—who'd spit up nearly everything she'd ingested—without so much as an inkling of regret.

"That's entirely understandable." This coming from the woman who'd sooner be burned at the stake than bored.

"My friend Hillary and I have been thinking about taking a little trip or something, but I can't go too far with Maddie being away from home. I've been meaning to ask if you have any ideas. Someplace we can both . . . clear our heads."

"Not only do I have an idea." Annabel hesitated for effect. "I have the *perfect* idea!"

"I'm all ears." Sloane felt a rush of enthusiasm at the mere suggestion of an escape.

"My Lake George house!"

"I thought you were selling it?"

"I am. But it can wait until September. I'll take it off the market for a few weeks while you stay there."

"Are you sure?" Sloane nearly leapt across the table to hug her.

"Never been more sure. Gerome and I are leaving for Europe next week with no immediate plans to come back." She winked at Sloane, who knew that her aunt said such things only to get under her mother's skin. "So it's yours. You can leave tomorrow!"

"Tomorrow? That's amazing! I'll have to ask Hillary. It's okay to bring her?"

"Bring whomever you'd like, my dear."

"Won't Eddie join you?" This was Sloane's mother trying to insinuate herself back into the conversation.

"No," she answered abruptly, and then, thinking better of alerting her mother to any marital complications, cleared her throat. "I mean, maybe for a little, but you know he can't take much time off from work, especially on such short notice."

"He works for his father, for crying out loud!" Sloane's mother countered. "Like he's going to fire his own son."

Sloane ignored her. "I really can't thank you enough, Aunt Annabel. You have no idea how important this is to me."

"Listen, I'm just happy you'll get some final enjoyment outta that old place. She holds a lot of memories."

"She sure does." Sloane couldn't help but think back to one glorious summer she and Georgina, her best friend from college, had spent there. Those were the days.

"And . . . that house is famous for its healing qualities." Her aunt nodded sagely as she spoke.

"Is that so?" Sloane was dubious. While a getaway certainly sounded like a much-needed short-term antidote to her tumultuous emotions, it seemed highly unlikely that the house itself was capable of a permanent cure. Not that she was entirely sure what she was trying to cure.

"Oh yes. Enter broken. Leave fixed. Mark my words, my dear." She stared off into the distance. "Mark my words."

chapter 2

Back at home, Sloane dialed Hillary's number as fast as her fingers would allow. "Hill?" she said as soon as she answered. "It's me."

"Hey! How are you?" Sloane could hear the shuffling of papers in the background.

"I'm good. Great, in fact." She could barely contain her exuberance. "And I have amazing news!"

"That sounds auspicious. I'm all ears."

"What would you think of coming with me to my aunt's vacation house in Lake George for three weeks? It's steps from the lake. Nothing too fancy. Still, it would be so relaxing. We could go to Shepard's Park Beach and pick up wraps at Sammy D's Cafe—and—"

"Sloane?"

"Yeah?"

"Take a breath."

"Right."

"It sounds fantastic! When are you planning to leave?"

"Tomorrow."

"Oh, wow! I don't know. . . ."

"Oh." Sloane's body drooped into a slump. "I know it's really last-minute."

"Just kidding! I'm in!"

"You are? Woo-hoo!!" Sloane pumped her fist in the air, evoking Arsenio Hall, and then, thankful there were no witnesses, laughed at herself for the awkward throwback gesture. "We're going to have the best time ever! Three whole weeks away from everything!"

"Is Eddie coming at all?"

"I don't know. I haven't even told him yet. I was thinking it would be more of a girls' thing, like we talked about." Sloane bit her lip, praying that Hillary was still on the same page.

"Of course! It's just that three weeks is a long time. Maybe Greg could come for the last week? Only if it's okay with you. It's such a nice offer, I wouldn't want to impose. I know he'll ask, though."

"I'm sure we can arrange something." Sloane attempted to mollify Hillary's concern in a way that would not kill her own heady buzz.

"Maybe Eddie can come too and then the boys will have each other."

"Maybe." Sloane erased the thought from her mind, storing it away to be considered at a later date. "So, I'll pick you up in the morning? I'm so excited we're getting to do this."

"That sounds excellent! I may call you later for packing advice."

"Absolutely!" Sloane just barely managed to withhold a squeal. "And, Hill?"

"Yeah?"

"Thank you."

"For what?"

"For coming with me. It means a lot."

"Well, thank *you* for inviting me. I could definitely use some time away. No doubt about that."

Sloane tucked one last bikini into her suitcase and let it thud shut. She heard the front door open and then the sound of Eddie's footsteps ascending the staircase. He'd woken up early to go for a long run. She sucked in a gulp of air and murmured under her breath while exhaling, "Almost there. Almost there."

Eddie came into the bedroom, his whole body hunched in an unfamiliar pose. When he saw Sloane's suitcase, he closed his eyes meditatively, as if when he opened them it might not be there anymore. She'd broken the news of her getaway to Lake George as soon as he'd returned home from work the evening before. She'd said she needed time and space—something new to break up the tedium that had become her life. Although she'd left that last part out.

He'd been confused, rightfully so, and they'd spent the night in an awkward tango, talking about anything besides Sloane's impending departure. Every now and again she'd catch him out of the corner of her eye, staring at nothing, until he'd notice her watching him and smile halfheartedly.

"I guess you're really going." He collapsed onto the black Eames chair in the corner of their room, next to the window, resting his elbows on his legs and hanging his head in between. Just outside, the swollen gray clouds threatened to burst over their already lush lawn as the sun backed farther away from the woeful mood indoors.

"I am." She lowered herself onto the edge of their unmade bed.

"So that's it?" He looked up, his eyes bloodshot.

Sloane wasn't sure what to say. It upset her to see how unhappy he was over her decision to take a vacation by herself, yet she couldn't tell him it was all going to be okay. Nor could she reassure him that she felt the same way about him as she had when they'd first started dating in their sophomore year. Eddie had been the captain of their high school football team and the guy every girl, including her sister, wanted to call her boyfriend. He'd been tall for his age and naturally well built, with the same olive complexion as Sloane's and strikingly wise brown eyes that she was certain could see right through her and into the depths of her soul. Sure, she'd been popular, but that hadn't been what had attracted Eddie to her. He'd told her that when she was around him, he couldn't stop smiling. That she made him feel like a better version of himself. Little did he know at the time, she'd have gone out with him no matter what he'd said.

That was the thing about Eddie. He didn't get how desirable he was, not back then and not now. To this day, they'd be walking down the cereal aisle at the supermarket and—despite Sloane's presence next to him—women would come up to him and ask, for example, if he thought Cheerios were healthier than Special K, batting their eyelashes all the while. Admittedly, Eddie looked like he could be a personal trainer, but they were still blatantly flirting and he was entirely oblivious to it.

Why, Sloane had often wondered over these past several months, did she no longer see her husband in the same light as those other women did? She had at one time. She had for a long time. Through college. Through the first decade of their marriage. They'd been considered a sort of "golden couple"—all their friends had been envious of them because they couldn't keep their eyes and hands off each other. And then things had changed all of a sudden. It felt like within the last year.

The problem was, Sloane couldn't put her finger on what had changed. If only it were that easy. Then she could have gotten started on making things right again. But she felt lost and unsure. Why had they suddenly started growing apart? Why had she begun to feel anxious so much of the time? Rationally, she was well aware that she had what most women her age longed for—what they spent the first half of their lives working toward: a devoted husband, financial stability, and a healthy, beautiful child. So what was wrong with her? She'd asked herself a million times. She'd even thought about going back to work, but that didn't seem like the answer.

Her mother was right. She really had nothing to complain about. It was just that Eddie's naturally relaxed nature made it so easy to push him away when she was feeling like this. Part of her felt guilty for that and another part of her wanted him to push back.

It had gotten to the point where, on the nights that Eddie would call at five o'clock to apologize for having to work late, Sloane felt shamefully relieved. Relieved to eat Chinese takeout on the couch with Maddie while they watched *The Bachelor* or some equally mind-numbing show. Relieved that she could pretend to be asleep by the time Eddie got home, because the idea of having sex with him suddenly seemed like a chore.

They never fought. They never yelled. They never so much as

raised their voices at each other. Still, lately Sloane couldn't stop asking herself whether she was sure this life was meant to be her destiny. Whether Eddie was meant to be her destiny.

"It's not *it*. It's only a trial separation."

"A *trial separation*?" Eddie leapt to his feet. "I thought you just needed a few weeks to unwind? To relax, since . . . you know."

"Since Amy died?" He thought this was about Amy. Was it? Was that when the distance between them had started taking root? "I do. I mean . . . I don't know, Eddie. Things haven't felt right between us in a while. I told you that."

"I know, but I didn't think you meant it in that way."

"In what way?"

"Like that the problem was our marriage."

"I'm not sure what it is." In part, it was the truth. But maybe not the whole truth. She didn't know exactly what it was, but she did know that it had to do with them. Or her. "It's not your fault."

"I don't care whose fault it is. I love you, Sloane." He walked toward her and knelt at her feet, taking her hands in his. "I don't want you to go. I'll do whatever it takes to fix things."

She couldn't look at him. He didn't deserve to be the target of her uncertainty. All she wanted was some space to try to sort things out, somewhere he wouldn't be an easy target for her to lash out at in frustration.

"I love you too, but I need to do this. For myself. That may sound selfish to you, but it's something I need right now, Eddie."

"You could never be selfish." Except that she knew he was wrong there. She could be selfish, even with her husband. She had been. So many times. He was just too devoted to notice. Often, she thought

Eddie saw her the way he wanted to see her, through the rosiest-colored glasses. She could steal the pillow out from under his head and he'd think she was fluffing it for him.

"I wish that was true." Sloane shook her head. "I have to go. I'm supposed to pick up Hillary in fifteen minutes." She pulled her heavy suitcase off the bed, and immediately—like the gentleman he was—Eddie swiped it from her grip and followed her down the stairs to the same front door he'd walked through only minutes earlier, under the mistaken impression that his marriage was safely intact.

"Can Greg and I still come down for the last week?" They stood facing each other as he waited on her answer.

"That should be fine." Sloane wasn't sure how she felt about this particular detail, but now wasn't the time to deliberate on it.

"Good." He appeared temporarily reassured and leaned in to hug her. "I love you so much, Sloane. More than you'll ever know."

"I love you too." She said it for the second time before waving good-bye.

If only she were positive she still meant it.

chapter 3

"Sloanie? It's me!"

"Georgina?" It was difficult to make out her voice through the intermittent static coming through the phone.

"Who the fuck else?" Sloane winced. Despite her delicate appearance, Georgina had the filthy mouth of a drunken sailor.

"Georgina, I'm in the car with Hillary."

"Who's that?"

"My friend Hillary. I've told you about her a zillion times. And you're on speaker."

"Mmmm. Don't remember the name."

"Can I call you back another time?"

"I know you're not suggesting that this Hillary character is more important than *moi*?" Sloane could make out the familiar sound of Georgina taking a long drag of what was likely her tenth cigarette of the day. "Plus, I'm on my way out to dinner in a few."

"Where are you?"

"London. Where else would I be?"

"Well, let's see. . . ."

"Oh, lighten up, would you? What has you so grumpy?"

"Nothing." Sloane heard the snappy tone to her voice. But it was definitely not something she wanted to get into with Georgina at the moment. "Anyway, as I said, Hillary and I are in the car, so I really can't talk now."

"Where are you going?" Why did Georgina always have to know everything?

"She's coming with me to my aunt's lake house for a few weeks."

"That sounds splendid! *Love* that place. What a summer that was, huh?"

"I know. We're really looking forward to it."

"Well, count me in!"

"What?"

"You heard me. I'll book my tickets tonight. I can be there tomorrow."

"Hold on, I don't even know . . ."

"What?" Georgina chortled, likely figuring that Sloane was teasing her. "You can't very well tell me that you're going to *our* house with someone else and not even invite me to come chaperone, silly girl."

"Right, the thing is . . ."

"The thing is nothing. This is absolutely perfect! I've been looking for an excuse to blow this Popsicle stand as soon as possible. The timing could not be better."

"Why? What's wrong now?"

"Nothing. Why does something have to be wrong in order for me to want to vacation with my best friend?" Georgina was instantly defensive, clueing Sloane in to the fact that she was not being entirely forthcoming. "It's just that Brits are so stuffy. And the incessant rain is insufferable. Not bad Indian food, though. You know I can't live without my naan."

"Of course not." Sloane rolled her eyes.

"Okay then, kiss, kiss. Gotta run." She let out a faint shriek. "Lake George! What a blast from the past. I hope you're ready to have some good old-fashioned fun."

"Wait, Georgina. . . ." But before Sloane could say any more, the call was already disconnected.

Immediately she thought about calling her back. And concocting some kind of white lie to discourage her from wanting to come. Yet, even after knowing her for all these years, Sloane still couldn't put her foot down when it came to Georgina. She felt like she was right back in college declaring that she absolutely could not go out to the bars because she had a very important paper due the next day. At which point Georgina would plead, pout, and employ whatever brand of manipulation she deemed necessary in order to change Sloane's mind. Sometimes, when Sloane was being particularly stubborn, Georgina would start sifting outfits out of her closet and draping them on her futon as a means of motivation. If that didn't work, she'd swear on her cat Lucy's life that as soon as they'd returned from Newbury Street, where Georgina would let Sloane have only one beer—two, tops—she would stay up with her all night while she finished her paper, even if Georgina had to write it for her. As if.

Inevitably, Sloane would relent. Depending on her mood, she might sit stiffly on a barstool with a scowl on her face, sipping one beer—and one beer only—through gritted teeth. Or she'd throw caution to the wind, allow Georgina to get her drunk, and then set her alarm for six o'clock the next morning so she could piece together fifteen pages of utter nonsense to the tune of a head-pounding hangover. While Georgina snored beside her, wheezing like a busted ceiling fan, her silken red hair splayed across the pillow in the shape of a fan.

They'd first met freshman year at Boston University when they'd both landed the only two sought-after single rooms on their hall, next to each other and connected by a door you could lock if you so desired. After day one, they'd never even bothered to close the door, save for when Georgina was having sex. To Sloane's dismay and often disgust, the walls had not been soundproof. She'd been forced to wear padded headphones and retract herself under the covers like a turtle in its shell whenever Georgina brought a guy back to her room.

Still, as soon as Georgina had introduced herself at orientation, Sloane had—in some small way—wanted to be just like her. The five feet nine inches of endless legs. The swanlike neck. The abundant blush red mane cascading down to where the small of her back sloped into her tightly rounded rear end. And the creamy complexion, dusted with a spray of freckles across the bridge of her pinched nose, which served as scenery for a pair of midnight blue eyes so captivating that her sardonic wit became almost insignificant. Almost.

Sloane had never considered herself quite "beautiful." Still, she'd been head cheerleader, homecoming queen, and voted "Most Likely to Pursue a Career in Modeling" in her high school yearbook—

a designation that had not been based on her brain capacity. A designation that Sloane's aunt had said was "an insult to woman-kind." Sloane, on the other hand, had secretly delighted in it, especially since Eddie had been voted "Most Likely to Marry Sloane Allen."

Every now and then, when Georgina really wanted something from Sloane, she'd say things like "What I wouldn't give for your olive skin." Or "Being taller than every guy sucks. I wish I was cute and little like you." And Sloane's all-time favorite, "You know you should be thankful for your plain brown hair. Red clashes with everything." They were as close to actual compliments as Georgina was capable of and Sloane knew she meant them with the best of intentions, even if they were part of a grander scheme.

Sure, Georgina could be self-centered, often unable to see the world beyond her own petty problems. But, when it came right down to it, whenever Sloane had really needed her the most—like when Thomas Coffly had called her a "dumb bitch" for refusing to go out with him, in the middle of the quad for everyone to see, or when she'd failed her English literature class so miserably she'd thought she was going to have to repeat a year of college—Georgina had been there. Offering to demolish Thomas Coffly. And promising to give junior year a "second go" right along with Sloane.

Until last year. When Amy had lost her battle with ovarian cancer. Sloane had never needed her best friend more in her life. It still felt like yesterday. The hysterical phone call from her mother. The high-speed chase to the hospital. Sloane had sworn to herself she'd beat cancer to the ICU even if it meant running four red lights and nearly taking out two stop signs, which it had. And then sitting on the side of Amy's bed, grasping her icy, limp hand for the last time. Brushing the hair off her face and rubbing her own nose against Amy's—they'd called it an Eskimo kiss as kids. It'd been their thing. One of many.

The end had come quickly. Sloane had remained by Amy's side until the nurses wouldn't let her stay any longer. Eddie had practically carried her to the car, catatonic with grief, pain, and fear. The fear that the throbbing emptiness at the core of her being would remain raw and hollow forever. Then the anger had come on its heels. The anger at cancer. The anger at the doctors who'd been unable to save her sister. The anger at herself for not somehow knowing that Amy had been sick before she had. And, finally, worst of all, the anger at Amy. Amy, who'd done nothing but lose everything. A loving husband. Three perfect children. Her future.

Sloane's mother and father had turned to God. But Sloane had been angry at him too. Though she'd been wise enough not to say as much to her parents. Of course she'd also been angry with them for being able to find solace in their faith. As far as Sloane was concerned, there should have been no solace to be had. For anyone.

Georgina had definitely not been there for that, physically or emotionally. Even worse, she'd been essentially unreachable. And now she was pretending like everything was fine between them. How dare she ignore the disappearing act she had pulled? How dare she marginalize Amy's death in that way? How dare she fail so profoundly as a best friend? Since her sister's death, Sloane's mother had told her to talk to Georgina. To tell her how she was feeling. But how was she supposed to do that when she couldn't even get her on the phone, much less to return an e-mail?

"You okay?" Hillary's soft question cut into her thoughts.

"I guess."

"You don't want her to come?"

"Honestly, I'm not sure." Sloane tried to give her a cheerful smile, but it felt fake.

"Well, we're going to have fun regardless."

"Oh, that's not what I'm worried about. Georgina is nothing if not fun."

"What are you worried about, then?"

"Let's just say . . ." Sloane took a deep breath. "Georgina is a lot to handle. Her showing up is definitely going to change things over the next few weeks. For better . . . or for worse."

chapter 4

"This is it!" A wave of nostalgia hit Sloane as her Volvo station wagon rumbled down the familiar cobblestone driveway winding its way through the wooded landscape to her aunt's Adirondack home in the Bolton Landing area of Lake George. "Strange, I don't think there used to be gates."

"It's gorgeous!" Hillary stepped out of the car to survey the area and swept her wispy blond bangs off her face with her sunglasses.

"Don't get too excited. The exterior can be deceiving." Sloane hadn't been to the house since the summer after her junior year in college, but she remembered it like it was yesterday. Or so she'd thought. "It does look like there have been some minor touch-ups and a new coat of paint for sure. Anyway, it's more cottage than mansion on the inside, I swear."

"I'm sure it'll be perfect," Hillary reassured her.

"There's a long story to go with the property, which I'm sure my aunt would be thrilled to regale you with one day." Sloane fished in her purse for the keys. "Something about a multimillionaire who'd purchased it as a vacation home for his family and then squandered all of his money, forcing the bank to foreclose way before it was finished."

"Really?" Hillary tilted her head up toward the sun as she gathered her fine, shoulder-length hair into a ponytail. "I love when a place has history."

"Me too. Apparently my aunt got an unbelievable deal on it, but didn't have the cash flow at the time to do much with the interior. According to my mother, one of her 'no-good boyfriends' had drained her bank account and fled the country."

"Nice."

"That's my aunt for you!" Sloane shrugged. "Leave your stuff in the car, and we can come back for it once we look around." She led Hillary toward the front door and struggled to shimmy it open. "I guess some things never change."

"Oh wow!" Hillary followed Sloane into the foyer, which spilled directly into a vast gourmet kitchen with white marble countertops and new stainless steel appliances. "This doesn't look like a cottage to me."

"You're not kidding! She said there'd been some nips and tucks, but I had no idea it was a complete overhaul." Not that Sloane was surprised. Her aunt was notorious for withholding substantial chunks of startling and often vital information. Like the time she'd said she was "popping in" on Sloane's parents to say good-bye before jaunting off to India for eight weeks of travel with her flavor-of-the-month boyfriend. And "popped in" she had. With two feisty pit bull puppies for them to look after while she was busy jaunting. Needless to say, said pit bulls had not taken up residence in the Allen home. Her mother had put her foot down and made sure of that. "Let's see what else she's done."

Hillary trailed Sloane around the first floor, into the commanding great room complete with a pool table, a wet bar, a wood-burning fireplace, and a series of French doors that opened onto a deck overlooking the lake. Next they passed through the two spacious bedrooms on the main level, both with new furniture, rugs, and remodeled en suite bathrooms. On the second floor there were three more bedrooms with panoramic views of the lake and mountains, an office, and a media room featuring a wall-sized movie screen.

"This is really amazing." Hillary stepped onto the back porch off the master bedroom and above a large beach.

"You're telling me." Again, Sloane was pleasantly shocked by just how much work her aunt had done. She hadn't even alluded to such large-scale renovations when she'd extended the invitation or talked about putting the house up for sale. While the layout seemed the same, somehow each and every room had been upgraded drastically.

"So, where are we in relation to everything?" Hillary asked, stretching herself out on one of the many lounge chairs, also pristine, and with the price tags still dangling beneath them. Sloane did the same.

Finally, she could feel the tension that had been coiled into knots on either side of her neck gradually start to unravel. This was exactly what she needed. And Hillary was exactly the person she needed to experience it with. Someone who wasn't energized by seeking out thrills. Someone who could sit comfortably, reading a book, chatting or not. Someone who would listen but not judge, if Sloane dared to share all the trepidations that had been eddying in her mind for the last year—by now, the heavy weight of them threatened to shatter her brain into a flurry of jagged pieces. Someone who was not Georgina.

Listening to the peaceful sound of the gentle waves lapping against the shore, Sloane wondered how it was possible that she could have two best friends who were so inherently different. Hillary, on the one hand, was an esteemed family counselor at a fancy private school in Boston for children with highly evolved brains and highly dysfunctional families. Georgina was just highly dysfunctional, in her own romanticized way of course. Hillary and her husband, Greg—a philosophy professor at Emerson College—didn't have any kids of their own, though they'd been trying for quite a while. Georgina had never given a moment's thought to either marriage or spawning a child of her own, which Sloane considered a good thing, seeing as she was barely more emotionally evolved than a child herself. Hillary liked to keep things close to the vest, which Sloane respected, even though it made it difficult for people to dig beneath the surface and really get to know her. Georgina, on the other hand, often regaled people with her whole life story within minutes of meeting them, if she deemed them worthy of her time.

Sloane sighed and pushed the thought of Georgina's impending arrival out of her head. At least she'd have twenty-four hours of peace and quiet before the storm hit.

"This area is called Bolton Landing, which is about ten miles from the head of Lake George."

"Do you know how long the lake is?" In the five years Sloane had known Hillary—they'd met one day when they'd both been first and last timers in a Bikram Yoga class together—she'd always been insatiably curious. It was one of the many things Sloane enjoyed about her. To Hillary, knowledge was fortifying. And no one was a more considerate or attentive listener than she was. In that way and a handful of others Hillary reminded her of Amy, which—in and of itself—was a profound comfort.

"A little over thirty miles. But it's narrow. No more than three miles wide at any point. We're basically in between Albany and Montreal, if that helps put things in perspective."

"Right." Hillary closed her eyes as the sun blanketed her pale face, but Sloane knew she was still listening intently.

"There aren't many people who live here all year. That said, I think there are close to fifty thousand or so in the summer. It's gotten much more touristy, but we're in a great spot. There are tons of cool restaurants and shops."

"Oh, we have to leave the house?" Hillary laughed. "Bummer."

"Just wait until Georgina gets here. She won't let you sit still for more than twenty seconds."

"She sounds like a real character, from what you've said."

" 'Character' doesn't even begin to scratch the surface!"

The fact was plain and simple now that Sloane stopped to consider it. Georgina and Hillary were polar opposites. In many ways, she realized, it was what had drawn her to Hillary in the first place. She was reliable, easy to get along with, someone who delighted in your ups and remained a stalwart companion through your downs. The antithesis of Georgina, who was a whirlwind of excitement and nonstop fun, but also childlike at times and flightier than a commercial airliner.

Perhaps there was a slight chance it could prove enjoyable to spend time with the two of them at once. After all, Hillary would be there to provide a buffer between Sloane and Georgina. But more than anything, Sloane still worried there would be an awkward dynamic as soon as Georgina arrived at the house. There was no doubt in Sloane's mind that Georgina would try to marginalize Hillary from the start. She'd never been particularly adept at sharing.

"Well, I'm looking forward to meeting her. You must be so excited to see her. Hasn't it been forever?"

"It has. And I am. I think."

"Still pissed, huh?" Sloane had confided in Hillary how Georgina's missing-in-action performance after Amy's death had been acutely damaging to the state of their friendship.

"Wouldn't you be?" Sloane sat up and turned toward Hillary, who mirrored her action.

"I would."

"I mean it was undeniably wrong of her. After all the years we've been friends, she should have been there for me."

"It was."

"Do you think I'm overreacting?"

"Not at all, but I don't know your relationship with her well enough." This was the family counselor in Hillary speaking. "If it were me, I'm not sure I'd want a friend, much less a best friend, who conducted herself in that way. As I said, though, I don't know Georgina or your history together well enough to judge her conduct."

"I hate to say it, but this is kind of who she is. Although never with anything nearly as important. Putting aside the fact that Amy was my sister, she and Georgina were friendly in their own right. Not in the same way, but . . ."

"Maybe she's coming to apologize."

"Ha! You definitely don't know Georgina."

"Oh?"

"Okay, now I'm making her sound like a total bitch." Sloane hesitated before continuing, trying to put her finger on the right way to explain her oldest friend. "She's a good person. And I know she cares about me. She just can't get out of her own way sometimes. She doesn't exactly come from a stable family life. Her mom is a glorified hippie and her father was barely ever around. Instead he was always up another woman's skirt."

"It's always the parents' fault." Hillary smiled genuinely. "Shall we go get the bags out of the car and then have some lunch?"

"Now, that sounds like a plan."

"Excellent—I'm starving." She stood up and walked into the house.

"Hill, I'll be there in a few minutes. I need to make a quick phone call," Sloane called after her, and then walked slowly down the steep staircase leading to the beach below. She moved toward the shore to dip her toes in the water and to carve out a moment to take in the gorgeous landscape and indulge in the sweet summer air.

Now that she'd had time to digest the fact that Georgina called out of the blue, Sloane couldn't decide whether to be ecstatic or irritated that Georgina would be descending on the house. The only thing she knew for sure was that the next three weeks were going to be wildly unpredictable. And perhaps that was what she needed. Unpredictability. The good kind. As in, not the kind where you find out that your sister is terminally ill when, all the while, you'd been living under the flagrant misconception that things like that didn't happen to people like you. Other people's sisters and brothers died. Other people lost children and parents and significant others and friends. Not you. She'd never had any inkling something so horrible could hit her so close to home.

Until it did. And then her world came to a screeching halt, and from that moment on, the heavy burden weighing down on her felt like a steamroller flattening a flea and it seemed impossible to bear for even another second. But she did. She pressed on. Somehow. Somehow each and every morning, she opened her eyes to a new day. A new day without Amy.

Sloane punched her sister's home number into her cell phone from memory. She'd taken it off her speed dial a week after Amy had passed away for fear she'd forget it. Why that had mattered she wasn't sure. But she was hell-bent on those seven digits being permanently etched on her brain.

"Hello?" Her brother-in-law, Trent, answered on the first ring.

"Hey. How are you?" It was always her first question. And she always kicked herself for it afterward. How was he? Well, let's see. He had lost the love of his life and was faced with raising their children without her. So probably not doing so well.

"Okay. You know. Taking it day by day." Each time they spoke, he sounded marginally better, and on any given day that reality could imbue Sloane with either hope or fear. Hope that Trent would be able to move on in the wake of Amy's death. And fear that Trent would be able to move on from Amy's death. What if she was the only one for whom it never got any better?

"Of course. How are the kids? Is Carter liking soccer?"

"Oh yeah. He's a real star. I think he inherited that from me."

"I know he inherited that from you! Amy was a strong swimmer, but soccer was definitely not her game."

"I know."

"And Ella and Jane? What are those sweet girls up to?"

"At the moment, I'm terrified to tell you they're trying to make all of us lunch on their own."

"Well, you'll have to let me know how that turns out!" Sloane laughed. Amy had always loved cooking with her girls, teaching them the basics as soon as they could grasp a mixing spoon. She'd set her sights on Carter too, insisting she would not raise a son who couldn't make a bowl of pasta and a plate of eggs.

"As long as they don't set the house on fire, I'll consider it a success."

"So, you know I'm in Lake George for a few weeks, but if you need anything, you have my cell and the house number, right?"

"Yup. You e-mailed it to me. And texted."

"Right. But seriously, call with anything. Please. And I'll give the kids a ring before bedtime whenever I can."

"Thanks."

"That's what I'm here for. Only a car ride away."

"I'll talk to you soon, then."

"Yes, you will."

"And, Sloane?"

"Yup?"

"Try to relax and have some fun." He paused. "You deserve it."

chapter 5

"Honey, I'm home!" Georgina burst through the front door of the house without knocking and had dropped her three suitcases in the middle of the foyer by the time Sloane reached her.

"Georgina! We weren't expecting you for another few hours."

"Now, is that how you greet your best friend in the entire world?" Georgina squealed at her, throwing her arms open. "Get over here, you!" Sloane couldn't help but laugh—Georgina was squeezing her like a ripe piece of fruit, practically jumping up and down mid-embrace. If nothing else, Georgina's excess of frenetic energy was contagious. "Look at how gorgeous you are."

"Yeah, right." Sloane crinkled her nose. Her mass of thick brown hair was piled into a disheveled bun on top of her head, slicked back with sunscreen, and—just that morning—she'd discovered an unsightly enormous blemish in the middle of her chin. No doubt from the additional stress surrounding Georgina's looming arrival, not to mention everything else on her mind.

"All except for that ulcer on your face." Georgina smiled imp-ishly, pointing directly at it.

"Thanks. I can always count on you to make me feel good about myself." Sloane rolled her eyes.

"Nothing a hot compress won't fix." She took Sloane's hand in hers. "Don't worry, lovey. Mama Georgina is here to make it all better."

"I can only imagine."

"Um, P.S., this place looks a bit different, huh?"

"I know. Can you believe it?" Sloane led Georgina into the kitchen and motioned for her to sit on a nearby barstool. "Do you want something to drink? We've got cranberry juice, OJ, water, and coffee."

"Any champagne?" Georgina kicked off her black leather ballet slippers and heaved her legs onto the counter.

Sloane winced. "Make yourself at home."

"I will, thank you." She raked her long, slender fingers through her sleek red mane, which Sloane noticed she'd had cut to fall at the center of her back. "Now, about that booze."

"It's eleven in the morning. Don't you think it's a little early for liquor?" Sloane knew what Georgina's answer would be, but she couldn't keep herself from giving her a hard time.

"Okay, for starters, it's never too early to start drinking when you're on vacation. Second of all, haven't you ever heard of a mi-mosa?"

"Fair enough." Sloane nodded. "I'm sure my aunt has some champagne somewhere." She searched through a series of cabinets until she happened upon a bottle that looked to be fairly new. "How about this?" She held it up.

"Chilled would be ideal, but as long as it bubbles, it's fine with me." Georgina hopped out of her seat to help. "So, where's this friend of yours?"

"Her name is Hillary, and she's in the shower. As I said, we didn't think you were going to be here until two, so we were going to head into town and pick up something to make for dinner."

"I just couldn't see flying all this way commercially, so Daddy sent his private jet. At least he's good for something."

"Isn't that nice?" For as long as Sloane had known Georgina, she'd been independently wealthy from inherited family money. As a result, she'd never held down any kind of steady job postcollege or shouldered any kind of real responsibility. Instead, after they'd graduated, Georgina had taken off to travel the world—bounding from one location and one boyfriend to the next. She never stayed anywhere or with any one man for too long. What would be the fun in that? "No wonder you have so much stuff."

"Oh, that's just some of it. I couldn't carry it all in myself. What? No butler to go with the fancy face-lift?"

"You know we're only here for three weeks, right?"

"Yeah, yeah. Details." Georgina waved her hand in the air dismissively.

"Oh, hey, you're here early." Hillary entered the room, wearing a pair of khaki shorts and a white T-shirt, her towel-dried hair framing a makeup-free face. "I'm Sloane's friend . . ."

"Hillary." Georgina barely looked in her direction.

"I guess that's kind of obvious, huh?" She held out her hand to shake Georgina's and then pulled it back once it became evident she'd been left hanging.

"Kind of."

"Well, welcome! We're so excited you're joining us." Sloane hid a smile. Hillary had no idea whom she was talking to and that her seemingly innocuous comment "*you're* joining *us*" would, beyond any doubt, send Georgina into a quick tailspin.

"Is that so?" She turned toward Hillary at last. "I wasn't aware you were playing hostess."

"I'm not. I'm just glad you're here is all." Hillary walked toward the brewing coffeepot and reached for a mug to pour herself a cup. "Anyone else?"

"Sloane and I are having mimosas."

"No, I'm not." Sloane shook her head.

"Don't be such a party pooper."

"Sorry, but I don't want to be wasted by noon."

"No one said anything about getting wasted." Georgina slapped Sloane on the rear end, while pirouetting around the kitchen. "But I think it's a fabulous suggestion."

"Is that a British accent I detect?" Hillary cradled her coffee mug in her palms and took a careful sip of the piping hot liquid, dodging Georgina as she whisked past. "Sloane told me that you're living in London, but I didn't realize you were from there originally."

"That's because she's not. She's from Allentown, Pennsylvania." Sloane rolled her eyes and gritted her teeth. Then she tried to summon a sympathetic enough look that would convey to Hillary her apologies for Georgina's stony behavior.

"Where I lived for all of five minutes." She stuck her tongue out at Sloane, who knew that Georgina hated it when Sloane told people where she was born. In her words, it was "so very pedestrian."

"Where did you grow up?"

"Here and there."

"What she's trying to say is that the accent is put on." Sloane infused a lighthearted quality in her voice. She couldn't help but goad Georgina for acting as if she hadn't pulled a disappearing act over the last year, but at the same time she didn't want to make the next three weeks any more difficult than they already would be as she navigated the tricky waters of Georgina's jealousy where sharing a friend was concerned.

"Oh, darling, you can pick up certain inflections once you've been residing someplace for long enough. Right, Hillary?"

"Beats me. I've only ever lived in the United States of America."

"Well, you can." She lifted a lone champagne glass from the cabinet. "You sure you're not joining me, Sloanie?"

"I'm sure." Sloane shook her head for emphasis.

"I'll have some," Hillary interjected, and Georgina whipped her head around.

"I like your style." Georgina handed her a glass and popped the cork on the bottle of champagne, spilling it into their glasses.

"Fine, I'll have some too," Sloane relented. "If you insist."

"Oh, I do." Georgina kissed Sloane on the cheek in a move that caused some of the mimosa to drip out of her glass onto their bare feet. "Now, let's have a toast, shall we?"

"To warm champagne and a relaxing and peaceful respite with my two best friends." Sloane held her drink high in the air.

"Amen to that." Hillary did the same.

"Relaxing and peaceful, my ass!" Nevertheless, Georgina clinked her glass with theirs. "You know what they say, ladies. What happens in Lake George . . ." She paused for effect and offered them both a sly grin. "Well, I'll let you fill in the rest."

chapter 6

"My *two* best friends," Georgina sniffed to herself. "Absolutely ridiculous." She sat cross-legged on the chocolate brown sisal rug in one of the guest bedrooms, the contents of her suitcases littering every inch of clear floor space. She suspected Sloane had carefully considered her words, purposefully intending the statement to rankle Georgina. And it worked like a charm. Georgina had been Sloane's *one and only* best friend for long enough to recognize her calculated digs.

So clearly Sloane was still pissed about the Amy situation. About how Georgina had failed her once again. Sloane could go ahead and add it to her running list of the many, many occasions on which she'd been disappointed by, let down because of, or frustrated in light of something Georgina had done to her.

There'd been the time, second semester of their junior year in college, when Sloane had been involved in some cheesy theatrical production off campus. She'd been going on for months about how this particular company was so exclusive that they accepted only those with exceptional dancing skills. So exclusive they hadn't even made Sloane try out. Still, Georgina had known it was *very* important to Sloane that she come watch all three performances. Mainly because Sloane had told her no less than ten thousand times.

She'd gone to the first show. It hadn't been her top choice of plans for a Saturday night, but that was what best friends were for, right? She'd even brought a bouquet of wildflowers. So what if she'd plucked them from some stranger's front yard? Then she'd gone to the second show, slipping out only twice in two hours for a cigarette break. Of course Sloane had called her out on it. Twice.

When it had come to the day of the third performance, Georgina had casually mentioned that her then-boyfriend, Ricardo—a Spanish-speaking line chef at the best tapas restaurant in the Copley Square section of Boston—had asked if he could take her to see his favorite band, since they were playing at the hottest new club downtown. It'd been his only free Saturday night for three months. Surely Sloane could understand that.

And, initially, she had. Although not before saddling her with a weighty guilt trip. The next morning and for four days to follow, it had been an entirely different story. Sloane had vacillated between giving Georgina the cold shoulder and dropping a series of not-so-subtle hints to the tune of "I hope the band was worth it," and "Maybe Ricardo will be the one to drive you to the airport when you go home for spring break."

Then there'd been the time that Sloane had left school for the weekend on a Thursday night—who could even remember now where she'd been going? Probably to visit Eddie at UMass Amherst.

Before she'd left, she'd handed Georgina her midterm English paper in a neatly sealed manila envelope, labeled with the teacher's name, the time of the class, and the room number. Sloane had told her that she'd already informed the teacher of her absence and let her know that a friend—*Georgina*—would be by at the end of class to drop it off. At least Sloane had had the sense not to say she'd be there at the start of class at eight in the morning. Sloane had repeated the directions to Georgina, even making her parrot them back for good measure, until she was wholly satisfied that there was no confusion whatsoever. Georgina, in turn, had assured her that the job would be carried out to Sloane's satisfaction.

What Georgina hadn't predicted was the stomach-scraping, green-in-the-face, unable-to-walk-away-from-the-toilet case of food poisoning she'd been inflicted with that night. The very last time she'd ordered in from Tandoori Kitchen.

When Georgina had finally fallen asleep—with throw-up congealed to her hair and breath so offensive she'd dreamed of squeezing a tube of toothpaste directly into her mouth, in the manner of an Easy Cheese spray can—it had been five in the morning. The previous evening, she'd set her alarm clock to chime at nine a.m. on the nose, to make absolutely certain she was standing at the door to Sloane's English lit class at ten, not a second later, with her paper in hand. Unfortunately, Georgina had slept straight through the shrill hoot of her alarm, and hadn't cracked a crusted eye open until eleven. At which time she'd leapt out of bed in a panic, darted directly across campus in her pajamas and Sloane's Snoopy slippers, only to find a sign taped to the classroom door saying, "Any midterm papers that have not been collected will receive an automatic fail. Have a great weekend!"

Georgina had hung her head in shame and then puked on the hallway floor. By the time she'd skulked back to her dorm room, desperately trying to choreograph her impending conversation with Sloane, she'd already had six phone messages, one more irate than the next.

The first five had been long-winded diatribes detailing how Georgina had ruined her life. How she was the worst, most irresponsible person in the entire world. And where was she now? Why was she not answering her calls? Was she still in bed? Was she even in her *own* bed? Was she deliberately dodging Sloane!?

The final message had been one sentence and one sentence only. *If you do not call me back in the next five minutes, I will disown you as a friend.*

So Georgina had made the call she was dreading. Because it wasn't enough to be harangued via voice mail. She hadn't even bothered to tell Sloane about the food poisoning. Sloane had been way too far gone to accept any excuse short of spontaneous amputation of all four of Georgina's limbs.

Victim and victimizer. Those were their roles. And oh, how convenient it was to glide right back into them.

Georgina crawled onto the bed, covered herself with the plush white comforter, and coiled her body into the fetal position. Maybe she had been a crap friend at times. But *no one* cared more about Sloane than she did. No one loved her as unconditionally, save for her family and Eddie. Especially not this Hillary chick. She'd known Sloane for all of what? Ten minutes?

She'd wait for Sloane to bring up Amy. There was no sense in disrupting the tentative peace between them prematurely. That and

Georgina wasn't sure what she was going to say when the subject did eventually rear its ugly head. Which it would. Because she knew Sloane.

It wasn't as if she could tell her the truth. The real reason why she hadn't been there for Sloane when Amy died. She couldn't tell anyone. Not yet. Perhaps not ever.

Georgina let her heavy eyelids fall closed. Sleep wouldn't numb the pain. But it would allow her to forget. If only for a few peaceful hours.

When she finally woke up with a crick in her neck and a patch of drool dampening the crisp cotton pillowcase, the room was pitch-black. Georgina stretched her arms above her head and patted her hand across the nightstand until she felt the lamp, and fumbled with the switch to turn on the light. She was craving a cigarette in the worst possible way, but she hadn't taken a drag since boarding the plane to Lake George. If only she had one handy now. Sure, Sloane would act judgmental, and, most likely, so would Hillary. But, at the moment, she really didn't give a flying fuck.

Her personal belongings were still strewn about the floor as if a tornado had swept through, leaving a flurry of Topshop, Whistles, and Miss Selfridge in its wake—Kate Middleton's closet had nothing on Georgina!

She swung her legs around, dangling them off the side of the bed. She could make out the faint din of Sloane's and Hillary's voices coming from downstairs. Georgina would be damned if she missed out on anything. Not that there was much action to be had with the two of them. She was going to have to captain this party boat if she expected it to be any livelier than a Circle Line sightseeing ferry.

First she weeded through a pile of clothing, tossing lace bras, silky thong underwear, and tank tops haphazardly, finally settling on a pair of too-short-for-her-age cutoff jean shorts that she could still rock like the twenty-one-year-old she imagined herself to be and a white voile tunic with shisha embroidery. She'd purchased it from a street vendor during her travels through India; she'd thought it looked identical to a Tory Burch she'd seen in *Cosmopolitan*. Next Georgina shimmied into the stylishly wrinkled garment and searched around until she found a brush to run through her tangled hair, finally resorting to a messy topknot instead. She glided into the bathroom, splashed a handful of cold water on her face, and pinched the apples of her cheeks to achieve the slightest rush of color. Georgina had once heard Julia Roberts confide to Ellen DeGeneres or Oprah Winfrey, one of those American talk show host ladies, that she did the very same thing as soon as she heard her husband, that cameraman guy—Danny? Dave?—come home. She'd said it was important to look good for your man, especially since she still had a crush on hers after however many years they'd been married. Longer than most Hollywood couples, that was for sure. Not that Georgina had a man to impress in Lake George, but it never hurt to be safe. For all she knew, a stunningly gorgeous—and single— man, who'd gotten lost on a road trip, could knock on their front door at any given moment and ask to use their telephone. Because of course his cell had run out of juice. And her blushing cheeks might be just the thing to lure him.

She bounded down the staircase and into the kitchen, where she found Sloane and Hillary sharing a bottle of white wine and a plate of cheese and crackers. Sloane looked naturally pretty and elegant in a yellow maxi dress with a navy blue sash tied under her bust. Hillary, in turn, appeared every bit as preppy as Georgina had surmised she would in a khaki knee-length skirt and a mint green collared golf shirt, her delicate features framed by her fine blond hair.

"Hey, sleepyhead!" Sloane smiled, earmarking the page she'd been perusing in a thick hardcover recipe book.

"We thought we might be rolling solo tonight." Hillary poured a third glass of Chardonnay and slid it in Georgina's direction.

"No such luck, I guess." She bristled. Hillary wasn't going to get rid of her that easily. She pushed the drink back toward her. "I'm going to need something harder than that."

"If you can find it, it's yours." Sloane cast an eye over the refaced cabinets, sweeping her hand in the same motion.

"Excellent, let's see what good old Aunt Annabel has a taste for." Georgina went from cupboard to cupboard, opening each one to survey the merchandise. "Aha! Jackpot." She knelt down under the center island, pulling bottles out and placing them on the mahogany-stained hardwood floor beside her. "Vodka, no." She shook her head definitively. "Whiskey. No way." She pushed them aside. "Rum. For another night." Finally, she jumped to her feet, wielding a bottle of caramel-colored liquor with a ball-shaped cork. "Patrón Gold. That's my girl!"

"Tequila? Nasty." Sloane scrunched her nose and stuck her tongue out.

"*Au contraire*, my friend. You don't know what you're missing." She climbed onto the counter to reach three shot glasses on the highest shelf.

"Be careful," Hillary warned in a maternal tone.

"Not my first rodeo, doll. I'd scale Everest for a nip of the good stuff." Georgina hopped down, filling the shot glasses to the brim. "Now, who's joining me?" She winked at them and held up one of the glasses.

By the time ten o'clock rolled around, Sloane was sprawled on the sofa in the great room, with Hillary nodding off in the lounge chair opposite her, and Georgina still gamboling in between them. The half-eaten vegetable pizza, crumbled garlic knots, two empty bottles of wine, and significantly emptied bottle of tequila cluttering the coffee table served as evidence of their evening's endeavors.

"I don't think I've had this much to drink since college." Sloane slurred her words.

"That's embarrassing." Georgina plopped onto the couch beside her.

"I don't think I've had this much to drink ever." Hillary's whisper was barely perceptible. "Is the room moving?"

"Only if you want it to be." Georgina laughed. Fine, so maybe it had been mean to introduce them to Señor Patrón and suggest they sleep with him on the same night. Their virgin encounter with swilling straight tequila. But it wasn't like she'd forced them to join her in imbibing. They were both grown adults perfectly capable of making decisions of their own volition. She'd remember to remind Sloane of this in the morning when she was blaming Georgina for everything.

"Oh, okay." Hillary yawned. "Gosh, that stuff makes you exhausted."

"So I guess we're not going out on the town?" Georgina had surrendered to that notion about two hours earlier when she'd tipped the remains of the second bottle of Chardonnay into Sloane's and Hillary's empty glasses. "Never know who we might run into."

"Who?" Hillary looked around the room, visibly tipsy.

"Not here, drunkie." Georgina rolled her eyes. She had to give Hillary credit for rising to the occasion. She hadn't been sure she'd had it in her. "His name begins with an L." She turned to Sloane, whose cheeks reddened into a heated blush, although she didn't speak.

"Larry?" Hillary's eyes widened.

"Who the hell is Larry?" Georgina laughed.

"My tax attorney." Hillary sighed. "I sure hope he's not coming." She hiccuped. " 'Scuse me."

"Doubtful."

"Leonardo?"

"Leonardo who?" Georgina smiled sardonically. "Let me guess. Da Vinci?"

"Don't be silly." Hillary giggled. "He's dead. I meant DiCaprio."

"Ah, yes, because it's very likely he'll turn up here. Perhaps he'll sail in on the *Titanic* with Kate."

"The *Titanic* sank in 1912. And who's Kate?"

"Winslet," Georgina grumbled. "*Anyway*, Sloane knows who I'm talking about. Right, Sloanie?"

"Luke." She croaked his name under her breath.

"Who's that?" Hillary sat up, intrigued.

"Sloane hasn't told you about Luke? Oh my. Where to begin?"

"Georgina." Sloane shot her a dirty look.

"What? I think your second-best friend ought to know about your great love. Don't you?"

"Great love?" Hillary was a captive audience.

"Aside from Eddie, naturally."

"Uh-huh." Hillary nodded, keen to hear more. "So who is he?"

"Well, if you insist." Georgina paced the room. "Sloane had a steamy affair with him the summer we spent here in college. She and Eddie were on a break of sorts, kind of like Ross and Rachel in *Friends.* I was there when they first met. Fireworks. *Serious* fireworks."

"Wow."

"He's no slouch. Hot as an Arizona summer. And his net worth makes Donald Trump's look like an empty piggy bank."

"What from?"

"Family money." Sloane answered this time. "But can we *please* stop talking about this? I'm sure he doesn't live here anymore and I'm going to bed." She stood up, balancing herself on the arm of the couch.

"You never know," Hillary sputtered, wobbling to her feet to follow Sloane.

"Exactly," Georgina agreed. "And we'll never know if we don't find out." She smirked, dropping the subject for the time being and allowing them to stumble upstairs.

chapter 7

The next day Sloane shambled into the kitchen in her nightshirt and slippers to find Hillary perched on a barstool reading the *Lake George Mirror*, her hands clasped around a glass of juice.

"Good morning." Hillary smiled sympathetically, and Sloane noticed that she'd already taken a shower and gotten dressed. "Or should I say 'Good afternoon'?"

"What time is it?" Sloane rasped, clearing her throat and spitting a wad of phlegm into a paper towel. "Sorry."

"Just after twelve."

"Oh, wow." She shuffled toward the coffeepot and helped herself to a cup. "I can't remember the last time I slept this late."

"Eddie phoned a couple of hours ago. I told him you'd call him back."

"Thanks." Sloane hoisted herself onto the barstool next to Hillary, crossed her arms on the counter, and buried her face in them.

"How are you feeling?" Hillary rubbed Sloane's back gently, while she moaned. "I take it not so well, huh?"

"Not as well as you, clearly." Sloane lifted her head, which felt more like a barbell wobbling around on her needle of a neck. "Correct me if I'm wrong, but we drank a shitload last night, right?"

"Yup. You could say that." Hillary took a sip from her glass of orange juice. "Want some? Vitamin C can only help."

"No, thanks." She put her hand on her stomach. "Not quite ready."

"Maybe a piece of toast? It'll absorb the booze."

"In a bit." Sloane tried to pry her eyes farther open with her fingers, but it was no use. They were practically swollen shut. She hadn't dared to look at herself in the mirror yet. "So why are you all bright eyed and bushy tailed? I thought you drank as much as I did."

"Three Advil before bed and then again when I woke up at four in the morning. And water. Lots of water. I drank two liters last night alone. Then I went for a short jog this morning to sweat out the toxins."

"You're killing me." Sloane massaged her throbbing temples.

She'd gone for a run already? It'd been all Sloane could manage to get out of bed and down the stairs. And that alone had been a gamble. Still, here sat Hillary, her wet hair slicked into a neat chignon, and her flawless complexion glowing without a trace of makeup. Hillary didn't possess Georgina's striking beauty, but her simple, classic features made her undeniably attractive. There was a lovely symmetry to her oval-shaped green eyes, slender nose, and rosy pink lips.

"Why don't you go lie down on the couch and let me make you some breakfast? Or lunch. I promise it'll make you feel better." Hillary slid off her stool and began searching the refrigerator for fixings. "How does eggs and toast sound? Maybe some turkey bacon on the side?"

"It sounds amazing, thank you." Sloane crept over to the couch, sinking her tired body into the fluffy cushions. "Though I can't promise I'll be able to keep it down."

She'd frequently thought about what a wonderful mother Hillary would make when the time came, and here was another demonstration of her friend's innate maternal instinct. No one she'd met, not even women who already had multiple kids, had a more obvious instinct for nurturing other people than Hillary. Well, perhaps with the exception of Sloane's sister, Amy. She had been born to parent.

Sloane remembered like it was yesterday when Amy had given birth to the first of her three children—Carter, the angelic baby boy who'd captured everyone's heart in an instant. Sloane had watched her sister, beaming from her hospital bed, as she'd gazed down at this teeny tiny cantankerous blob of love. And she'd known in that moment that Amy's greatest purpose in life had come to be.

It'd been the same story when she'd had Ella and then Jane. The two girls—same age distance as Amy and Sloane—that Amy had said she'd always dreamed of. Sloane had commented that Amy was going to have her hands full with three. She'd said it was finally going to humanize her, bring her back down to earth with all the other moms who struggled with just one or two. But it hadn't. Amy had gone about her days in the same fashion as always, making it look far easier than it was.

Sloane's best guess was that Hillary and Greg had been trying for about two or three years. Greg was much more open about it than Hillary was, occasionally sharing details with Sloane and Eddie that Hillary had not. It was Greg who'd confided in them that he wanted to try fertility treatments. And that Hillary wasn't sure. It was also Greg who'd told them that he'd always envisioned a house bustling with children, but now—given that they were already in their mid-thirties—he was hoping for two, maybe three, tops. Hillary, in turn, barely spoke of their troubles in trying to conceive.

She was phenomenal with Madeleine, though. Sometimes when Hillary was over and Sloane would excuse herself to answer the phone, she'd come back and find Hillary and Madeleine spread out on the living room floor with sheets of white paper, creating a vibrant mural. Or Hillary helping Madeleine craft homemade valentines for her classmates. Sloane had also noticed that Hillary spoke to Madeleine as if she were an adult. It was probably the family counselor in her, but—whether Madeleine realized it or not—it had gone a long way in endearing Hillary to her right from the start.

"Here you go." Hillary came into the room with another mug, swapping it with the one in Sloane's hands. "Drink this instead."

Sloane took a whiff of the pungent liquid. "This smells putrid. What is it?"

"Green tea mixed with a little hangover potion." She walked back toward the kitchen. "Trust me. You'll thank me in about twenty minutes."

"If I didn't know better, I'd think you were a closet alcoholic," Sloane called after her.

"Nope. But I have listened to enough sixteen-year-old drunks to pick up some nifty tips."

"I guess that's one benefit of your job."

A few minutes later, Hillary appeared again, this time proffering a cheese omelet, buttered rye toast, and two links of pork sausage. "And, voilà! But I think we're out of turkey bacon. Georgina must have eaten the last few strips. I'll put it on the grocery list."

"Georgina is up?" Sloane arched an eyebrow.

"Did I hear my name?" Georgina sashayed into the room in a pair of cropped black Lycra pants and a white sports bra, her toned limbs gleaming with perspiration. "That porch is outstanding for practicing yoga. My downward-facing dog has never been better."

"Am I the only one who can't hold my liquor?"

"It appears that way, doll." Georgina kissed Sloane on the forehead. "Ooh, you're clammy."

"Thanks," Sloane griped, swatting at Georgina's hand as she tried to pilfer a piece of toast.

"Grouchy, aren't we?" She dropped her body onto the sofa.

"Would you be careful? I'm just a little queasy."

"*Sorry.* It's not like you quit smoking. Try that on for size. I was a raging, lurching lunatic the first few hours after I gave it up. And it hasn't gotten much better."

"Well, I'm glad you did it. Finally."

Georgina ignored her. "So, what's on the schedule for today?"

"I'd like to go into town and mill around, maybe head to the beach later this afternoon when it's not as humid," Hillary offered.

"Sounds good to me." Georgina leaned back on the arm of the couch, stretching her legs in the air. "We should totally hit King Neptune's after dinner."

"What's King Neptune's?" Hillary curled herself into a rocking chair facing them.

"I keep forgetting you've never been here! We are *definitely* going now." Georgina lowered her legs until she was sitting upright and leaned forward, as if she was about to divulge a deliciously juicy secret. "King Neptune's is only the coolest pub around. Or at least it was the last time Sloane and I were here. They have killer food, drinks, live music, and an unbelievable view of the lake. There are three bars on three different levels and a rooftop deck." She smirked. "Plus, I may have gotten wind that there's a hot band playing tonight."

"I don't know." Sloane was alert now. Georgina had managed to leave out one important fact about King Neptune's. It was where she and Luke had met for the first time. It was also his preferred hangout. Of course that was over a decade ago. Not that she hadn't considered running into him as she drove up here. What it would be like. How it would make her feel. What she would say. What he would say. What she would be wearing. What he would be wearing. She knew it was ridiculous to muse about such things, but she couldn't seem to help herself.

"Don't you want to see Luke?"

"It hadn't even occurred to me, to be quite honest." She avoided eye contact with Georgina so that she wouldn't read the truth on her face.

"Right. And I'm a teetotaler."

"That's a laugh," Sloane quipped. "Excuse me if I don't spend my spare time obsessing over my exes."

"Whatever, if you're too scared to bump into him, I understand."

"Scared? Why would I be scared? I just told you he's the very last thing from my mind."

"Great."

"Great, what?" Sloane braced herself for the response.

"Then it's decided." Georgina grinned mischievously. "King Neptune's, here we come!"

It was exactly as Sloane had preserved it in her mind. All wood paneling and hunter green trim with stone columns and walls of windows presiding over the glasslike serenity of Lake George, glistening under the mansions' flickering lanterns lining its shore. Georgina snatched Sloane's hand, guiding her through the congested space filled with raucous twenty-somethings packed tighter than sardines in a can.

"Jesus Christ, you practically pulled my arm out of the socket," Sloane sputtered breathlessly once they'd finally reached the bar. "And you completely left Hillary behind."

"Every man or woman for herself." Georgina motioned to the bartender. "Two shots of tequila. And make it the good stuff."

"THREE SHOTS." Sloane tried to project her voice, though she feared she was the only one who could hear herself amid the hubbub. "Would you stop intentionally leaving her out?"

"Thought I'd lost you there for a minute." Hillary appeared no worse for the wear. "I think someone pinched my butt."

"An excellent way to kick off the night!" Georgina accepted their drinks from the bartender and raised her index finger to signal for another. "For you." She handed the first shot glass to Hillary and the other to Sloane, just as hers arrived. "Cheers, ladies!"

"What do we owe you"—Hillary squinted to decipher the scribbled lettering on the bartender's name tag—"Demon?" She widened her eyes. "Well, isn't that an interesting name."

"They're on the guy in the blue shirt at the end of the bar." Demon shrugged. "Says he knows you."

Sloane whipped her head around and was quickly comforted by a familiar, but not too familiar, face. The man waved and started walking toward them.

"Sloane Allen. As I live and breathe." He encompassed her in a bear hug, lifting her feet clear of the beer-soaked floor. "Wait a minute. Is that? Shit! Georgina!"

"Cooper Collins, you nasty devil. Get over here." Georgina kissed him directly on the lips, somewhat to his surprise but to his obvious delight. "Sorry, doll. That's how we do it overseas."

"I'm not complaining." He laughed.

"I'm Hillary. Sloane's friend." She offered him an outstretched hand, but he pulled her into an unexpected embrace instead.

"Well, you know what they say. Any friend of Sloane's is a friend of mine."

"Cooper and I have known each other forever. My aunt is friends with his mother from way back when. But it's been . . . God, how long has it been?"

"Since the summer you broke my boy's heart."

"Yeah, right." Sloane's throat swelled. She could feel the first shot of tequila warming her insides and infiltrating her thoughts by way of a heady buzz. "I'd hardly say that."

"That's because you didn't stick around long enough to pick up the pieces."

"Refills all around?" Georgina interjected, a subtle favor Sloane acknowledged with a smile, and then signaled to the bartender for another round.

"You must have had a great time together. I've only heard bits and pieces." Hillary accepted another drink as Georgina passed them around and quickly lifted the shot glass to her lips. Her torso shuddered from the bitterness.

"Those were the days." Cooper nodded.

"I know. Don't you wish, sometimes, that we could go back?" As Sloane looked down, her gaze stilled on the bejeweled navy sandals Eddie had bought her for her birthday, a wave of guilt submerged her. "Not for real. I mean, just for a week or something."

"Oh, to be young and free again," Georgina mused. "Cooper, do you still hang out at Frog Hill?"

Frog Hill Farm, perched on a fifty-acre cliff jutting from one side of the Adirondack Mountains, was the ironic moniker for Luke's parents' enormous estate, where he'd been raised by multiple nannies while his mother and father—Edwina and Arthur Fuller—gallivanted across the globe making boatloads of money and spending even more. Sloane and Georgina had passed countless sun-soaked days and booze-sodden nights that summer skinny-dipping in the Fullers' Olympic-sized infinity swimming pool, pilfering posh wines from their well-stocked cellar, and smoking anytime they could escape from the staff of fifteen that was catering to their every whim.

Cooper was Luke's oldest and closest friend, as well as one of nineteen grandchildren of the late Marjorie Markman, the wealthiest woman in the Lake George area. Luke was the best man at Cooper's over-the-top wedding to the woman he was, by the looks of his bare ring finger, no longer married to. Sloane didn't find that altogether surprising, since she knew Lucy, as a waitress on his father's yacht, had not met with the approval of Cooper's grandmother— the woman who controlled the purse strings and could on a whim cut everyone off from the excessive fiscal freedom they'd become so accustomed to.

Frog Hill Farm was also where Sloane had slept with Luke for the first time. In one of the six guest bedrooms on the second floor. It'd been the first time she'd had sex with someone who wasn't Eddie. And the last. To this day she'd never forgotten how different it had felt to sleep with another man. How he'd made her feel like the woman she'd so desperately wanted to be. Especially when he gazed into her eyes afterward, stroking her cheek with the back of his hand. Then he had kissed her softly on the lips, again and again, before going to fetch her a tall glass of cold water from the upstairs kitchen. Because of course there were three separate indoor kitchens at Frog Hill.

Luke. She hadn't been able to stop thinking about him lately, especially now that they were revisiting the sites of that summer she'd spent with him. What if she hadn't called things off at the end of the summer? What if she hadn't run home and into Eddie's waiting and forgiving arms? What would her life be like now?

But her daydreaming about what might have been always ground to a halt right there. Sloane hadn't been able to contemplate beyond that point. After all, no Eddie meant no Madeleine, and that was not something she cared to think about.

"Hang there? I practically live there." He snorted. "The Fullers still own the Frog. But they're only there for Thanksgiving and Christmas and even then Edwina can't wait to get back to their place in St. Bart's."

"So the house just sits empty?" Georgina's blue eyes twinkled.

"Not exactly." He gestured at someone across the room. "Luke's there when he's in town. And I've been crashing there ever since the divorce. Had to give our place to Lucy."

"I'm sorry to hear that." Sloane followed Cooper's stare. Until she saw him. Coming toward them. And quickly realized there was no place to run. No place to hide.

"Dude." Cooper shook Luke's hand and patted him on the back in the way men did. "Glad you could make it. Haven't seen you in these parts lately."

"Well, when Georgina called . . ."

"Hi, Luke! Sorry, just have to run to the restroom. Won't be a minute." Hastily, Georgina turned and made her way through the throng, leaving Sloane rendered speechless and Hillary appropriately confused.

"Sloane, you're just as gorgeous as I remember." Luke leaned in and placed a gentle kiss close to her left ear.

"I . . . um . . . ," she found herself stammering as a bead of sweat trickled down to the small of her back.

"It's *really* great to see you."

"Yeah . . ." She nodded, praying the right words—*any* words—would make their way from her brain to her mouth.

"I think what she's trying to say is that it's great to see you too," Hillary cut in.

"Well, good. Because I'm here for the rest of the summer." His penetrating brown eyes locked with Sloane's. "And I hope to see a lot more of you."

chapter 8

Sloane spent the entirety of the car ride home brooding in the backseat—she was seemingly incapable of doing anything more than staring silently out the window with her arms folded across her chest. As soon as Hillary pulled into the driveway, before she could even come to a full stop, Sloane flung the car door open and dashed toward the house. She made it to the bathroom just in time to spew the regurgitated remains of her dinner into the toilet, heaving repeatedly until there was nothing left, including her dignity.

"Are you okay in there?" Hillary knocked softly on the door, and the tranquil tenor of her voice came as a soothing balm to Sloane's utter humiliation. "I have your toothbrush and toothpaste. Some mouthwash too. Can I come in?"

"Sure," Sloane managed, steadying herself on the sink until the room finally stopped gyrating.

"Oh, sweetie." Hillary approached her cautiously and then led

Sloane to the couch in the great room, propping her against a stack of pillows and covering her with a gray and purple crocheted blanket. "Let me get you a glass of water."

"No more drinks," Sloane groaned. She'd imbibed more alcohol in the past two days than she had in the two years prior.

Sloane had never been a big boozer, nor had Eddie. Even now, it was nearly impossible to get him to open a bottle of wine for a special occasion, much less to linger over a glass at home. Sure, he'd partake on the infrequent occasion that they were at a friend's house or when a couple of the guys came over to watch football—another rarity. A beer here. A vodka there. But only to be social.

"Don't worry. This time it's just going to be water."

"So, where is she?" Sloane could hear the coolness in her tone.

"Who?"

"Who else?"

"I think she went upstairs to take a shower. She said she'd be down in a bit." Hillary continued bustling around to make sure Sloane was comfortable on the couch.

"I can't believe she did this to me."

"Did what?"

"Called Luke!" Her hands clenched into fists involuntarily and her jaw tightened.

"Were you unhappy to see him?"

"What's that supposed to mean?" Sloane snapped, and immediately regretted it. "Sorry, you're not the one I'm irritated with. I didn't mean to jump down your throat."

"It's okay." Hillary handed Sloane a glass of chilled water before placing a moist washcloth on her forehead and sitting down next to her. "I guess I'm not sure why you're upset with Georgina. For calling him."

"Because she did it without telling me."

"Maybe she wanted to surprise you. Don't you think that could have been it?"

"I have no doubt about that. But I'm pretty sure she knew it would be an unwelcome surprise."

"So you didn't want to see him?" Hillary curled her legs underneath her and bit into a sourdough pretzel she'd found in the pantry.

"I didn't say that."

"So you did?"

"I don't know." Sloane ran her fingers through her crusty hair. "I suppose I just wanted the option of deciding for myself."

"That's fair."

"I mean, it's not a huge deal. It's just so . . ."

"So what?"

"So Georgina." Sloane sighed. "It's like it gives her a rush. Meddling around in my life like this."

"Maybe it does."

"So she gets off on seeing me squirm? That's nice. She's supposed to be my best friend."

As soon as the words left her mouth, Sloane realized their significance and searched Hillary's face for any perceptible reaction. But her demeanor was completely neutral. Sometimes it was hard to separate Hillary the friend from Hillary the family counselor. Was she analyzing Sloane's every word? Her every expression? Was she judging her for being sent into a tailspin over running into an exboyfriend? Hillary had had a front-row seat to witness the train wreck of her long overdue reunion with Luke, when, apparently, not only had the cat gotten her tongue, but he'd run off with it. What if she'd observed a significant look or emotion? What if she'd seen Luke's eyes meet Sloane's and noticed the unspoken dialogue they had exchanged? Would she say something to Greg? Would Greg say something to Eddie? Did Sloane even care? It wasn't like she'd done anything wrong by running into Luke.

There was also the considerably more likely scenario that Sloane was reading the situation as if it were an epic love story when in reality it was nothing more than a cheap paperback relegated to the sales bin at the supermarket.

"Sloane, Georgina is who she is. She's not going to change. Most people don't."

"So I'm just supposed to accept that?"

"That's up to you. You have thus far." Hillary tilted her head to one side. "You can't expect people to change their colors and act the way you want them to act when you've accepted them for who they are for this long."

"Yeah." Sloane thought about this for a moment. What Hillary was saying did make a lot of sense, but wasn't it always easier to find the exit when you weren't the one lost in the intricately woven maze to begin with? "I guess I'll have to take your word for it."

"Is it safe to come in?" Georgina materialized in the doorway in a midthigh white cotton nightie with "I Was at Kate and William's Wedding and All I Got Was This Lousy T-shirt" emblazoned on it in hot pink.

"Enter at your own risk," Hillary cautioned her.

"Please don't be mad at me." Georgina swung her damp, deep

red braid over her shoulder and knelt at Sloane's feet, resting her arms on her friend's knees and adopting a pouty face. "I knew you wanted to see him, but I also knew you'd say no if I suggested it."

"Aha!" Sloane raised her index finger. "That's exactly it. You knew I'd say no. Perhaps that should have told you something?"

"That I should call him and invite him myself?"

"Um, no. Try again."

"That I should have been an obedient, boring girl, and respected your wishes."

"So you do know the difference between right and wrong? Remarkable." Sloane cracked a smile for the first time since they'd arrived home. "Anyway, how'd you even have his number?"

"He gave it to me a couple of years ago." Georgina stood up, walked across the room, and dropped into a wide and inviting armchair dressed in a dark blue linen slipcover, like its neighboring twin.

"A couple of years ago when?" Sloane came to immediate attention.

"When I saw him in Paris." Georgina chipped at her raspberry-colored toenail polish absentmindedly. "I could really use a pedicure. Can we put that on the schedule for tomorrow?"

"I'm sorry, Paris? I don't believe you ever mentioned it to me." Sloane clenched her teeth, trying to remain cool, or at least to appear to.

"No?" Georgina asked innocently.

Sloane couldn't tell whether Georgina was really so naive as to think that this particular nugget of information wasn't worthy of sharing with her. Or whether Georgina knew precisely what she was doing. Years ago, during their college days, Sloane would have been able to strip away Georgina's pretense. To cut right through to the root of her intentions. She'd had regular experience with Georgina's wily ways. But now, with over a decade having passed since they'd spent more than a week here or there together, Sloane was rusty at deciphering her behavior. And Georgina had likely honed her skills.

"No. I'm fairly certain I would have remembered that."

"Right. Huh. Must have slipped my mind."

"Okay. And?"

"And what?" Georgina remained cagey.

"I don't know. What did you do together? More importantly, how did it even come about in the first place?"

"You know, it was a funny thing. I was passing through. Hugh and I had just had one of our really wicked fights, so I left. Hopped on the Chunnel and in less than two hours there I was in gay Paris!" She flung her legs over the arm of her chair. "I checked into the Hotel Mon Cheri and ran smack into Luke in the lobby."

"What was he doing there?"

"His family had just acquired the property."

"I didn't know they were international now."

"Mon Cheri was their first foray into Europe. He said they were looking into Dubai. That's where he was headed next."

"I'm shocked you didn't offer to go with him."

"I'd be lying if I said I didn't think about it. Hugh was being a real wanker. And Dubai was one place I'd never been. Still haven't."

"I'm sure you'll get there." Sloane rolled her eyes. She had to admit to being somewhat relieved that Georgina and Luke's chance meeting had been just that.

"Maybe you'll come with me." Georgina shot her a friendly grin.

"And then what happened with Luke?" Sloane disregarded her attempt to redirect the course of the conversation.

"And then we had dinner. He invited me to join him and some of his colleagues at the restaurant in the hotel."

"That's nice." Or not.

"It was lovely actually. Those boys and I had tons to talk about." Georgina reflected on the memory with a smile.

"I bet you did." Sloane could picture the whole affair. Georgina looking effortlessly spectacular. A table of men ogling her, throwing their heads back in adoring laughter each time she opened her mouth to speak in her irresistible, albeit phony, British accent. And Luke. What had he been doing? He'd been one of the few men Sloane had ever known who hadn't been instantly captivated by Georgina. One of the many things she'd appreciated about him.

"So, does it all make sense now?"

"I guess," Sloane grumbled. She couldn't help but wonder if there was more to the story. Because there was always more to every story when it came to Georgina. Though this did sound relatively innocuous.

"And you're not mad at me?" Georgina offered Sloane another grin, this time cheeky.

"You're off the hook."

"Splendid, because I've got one more little surprise."

"Oh, yeah? What's that?"

"I've invited Luke to join us for dinner tomorrow night."

chapter 9

Hillary lay alone on the back deck, gazing at the constellations, her bare legs peeking out from beneath a large handwoven throw she'd poached from one of the chairs in the great room. Save for the chorus of crickets chirping their nightly symphony, she relished the peace and quiet. Unpredictably, given their soothing surroundings, it had been hard to come by until now.

Sloane had gone to bed angry at Georgina. Again.

Georgina had gone to bed—or at least up to her room—having been told by Sloane to "grow up" on the heels of their third spat of the day. It seemed to be their rhythm. No sooner had they squabbled than they'd act like nothing had ever happened, cackling like schoolgirls who'd inhaled their first hit of marijuana.

Hillary had been left to her own devices, and despite the late hour, she wasn't complaining. If these two weren't a psychological case study, she wasn't sure who was.

Of course Hillary had noticed Sloane's emotional reaction to

Luke. Even before they'd seen him in person. It was obvious that there was still something between them. Something that ran deeper than a trivial flirtation. She knew it. Georgina knew it. And if Sloane was being honest with herself, she had to know it as well.

She'd wanted to tell Sloane that it was natural. Who wouldn't get a little nervous when faced with an ex-boyfriend, especially when seeing him had come as a complete shock? Not to mention that what Sloane and Luke had shared seemed to transcend a casual summer fling. Plus, there was no denying the fact that he was hot. Gorgeous, actually, with his dusty blond hair, a five-o'clock shadow along his chiseled chin, and a pair of piercing brown eyes. Yet if she hadn't known the history between them, Hillary wouldn't have figured Luke for Sloane's type. He reminded her of Josh Lucas's character in the movie *Sweet Home Alabama*—sensual and enigmatic. Sure, Eddie was adorable and the sweetest man you'd ever meet. He worshipped Sloane and she him. But after Hillary had seen Luke in the flesh, Eddie's devotion to Sloane had taken on a puppy dog quality in her mind. Furthermore, temptation was a persuasive beast.

How many times had she witnessed it happen to the parents of the kids she counseled? There'd been Lily Noble, whose mother had run off with her personal trainer to an ashram in Nepal. Such a sad stereotype come to life. Also Cash Griffin's father, who'd pursued a road less traveled when he'd decided to shack up with his business partner, Bob. But perhaps the most memorable case of infidelity Hillary could recall was that of Rachel johnson's parents. Unfortunately, Rachel's father hadn't been able to keep his johnson in his pants. He'd slept with three of the teachers at the school, in addition to the principal and the girls' tennis coach—who Hillary had been certain was a lesbian. She'd been almost insulted that Mr. Johnson hadn't made a pass at her. In the end, it turned out that Rachel's mother had also been making the rounds around town. The butcher. The baker. If only there'd been a candlestick maker, she'd probably have lit his fire too.

Hillary dismissed the thought and yawned, guzzling a mouthful of fresh lake air. She knew that Sloane wasn't like any of those other women she'd come across through her work. She and Eddie were unconditionally devoted to each other. In fact, until Sloane had invited her to Lake George, Hillary never would have guessed she'd so willingly have left Eddie behind. It had almost seemed like she was trying to get away from him. As she stretched her arms above her head, she thought about how late it was getting and realized that if she had any intention of keeping up with Georgina for the next few weeks, at least six to eight hours of beauty sleep was nonnegotiable.

Just as she was about to head upstairs to bed, her phone vibrated with an incoming call from Greg.

"Hey, honey." She smiled in anticipation of hearing the soothing hum of his voice.

"Hey. How's it going?" It surprised her to hear how tired he sounded, possibly even stressed.

"It's going well, aside from these two ladies fighting like cats and dogs. How are you? You sound exhausted."

"You could say that." He exhaled loudly into the receiver.

"Is everything okay?" It was rare to even consider that Greg might be tense about something. He was always so even-keeled; an eternal optimist, he called himself. A glass half-full kind of guy.

"Uh, yeah. Everything's fine. Of course everything is fine." He yawned. "I just haven't been sleeping well."

"Must be not having me beside you." Hillary laughed quietly, if somewhat uneasily.

"Must be." The edge in his voice softened. "I do miss you a lot. Are you taking your vitamins?"

"What vitamins?"

"Your *prenatal* vitamins."

"Oh, yes, absolutely. Sorry, brain-freeze moment."

"It's important. They're important. All of the websites say that the folic acid, iron, and calcium they provide are integral in the process of trying to conceive."

"I know, honey. You've mentioned as much. About a zillion times. Are you sure everything is okay?"

"Yeah, sorry. I probably just need a good night's rest. I love you."

"I love you too. And I can't wait to see you."

"I can't wait to see you too. Let's both get some sleep, then, shall we?"

"Good night, honey."

"Good night, my love."

Once they'd hung up, and Hillary—as she often did—had thanked her lucky stars for the gift of a husband like Greg, she crept into the dark house, feeling her way through the faintly lit great room and up the stairs. As she walked down the hall, she could hear the hushed murmur of Georgina's voice wafting from her bedroom. She paused just outside to make sure everything was okay.

"I told you not to call me." Georgina's tone was urgent. "I understand, but this is the way it has to be."

Silence.

"No, I'm not coming home now. . . . No . . . I don't know, for God's sake," Georgina lamented. "Please just leave me alone."

Hillary couldn't decipher whom she was speaking to or exactly what they were speaking about, but Georgina sounded flustered and distressed. Two words, Hillary surmised, that were not commonly used to describe her. She slunk away from the scene, inadvertently stubbing her toe on the edge of the rug. "Shit!"

"Who's there?" Georgina's door flung open and Hillary froze.

"It's just me." Hillary turned around, catching Georgina's tear-stained face in the soft light. "Sorry, I was on my way to bed. Is everything okay?"

"Everything's fine." Georgina was instantly defensive. "Why wouldn't it be?"

"No reason." Hillary shrugged. "Good night."

Georgina ducked her head and disappeared into the shadows without saying a word.

chapter 10

Sloane looped a section of obstinate brown hair around her brush and tugged firmly, blasting it with warm air. Damn humidity. At home, it took her exactly eighteen minutes to get ready. Four to dress herself. Six to wring her damp tresses into submission. And eight to dab on what little makeup she bothered to apply on a regular basis. But something about the oppressive daytime heat mingled with the breeze off the lake at night had forced her typically manageable mane to revolt. Come morning she'd look as if she'd stuck her finger in an electrical socket.

"Shit, shit, shit!" she growled, yanking harder this time, desperate to obliterate the creases that had molded themselves into position before she'd had the chance to outsmart them, especially the ones front and center framing her face.

"What in the bloody hell is going on in there?" Georgina called out over the tedious purr of the blow-dryer.

"Nothing. I'm fine," Sloane replied, before realizing she'd wound the cord around a bottle of her aunt's Chanel No. 5, which was about to plummet to an untimely and fragrant demise on the master bathroom's elegantly appointed limestone tiles. "For Christ's sake."

"Would you open up?" Georgina rapped persistently on the bathroom door.

"Go away."

"You know I can pick the lock, Sloane, so let's not beat around the bush." Sloane imagined Georgina standing in the hallway with her arms crossed, wearing a smug expression.

"What do you want?" She cracked the door and poked her head through.

"Ooooh, that does not look good, my friend." She pointed at Sloane's overgrown, and now crimped, bangs.

"Really? I hadn't noticed."

"You slay me." Georgina twisted her porcelain doll face into a scowl. "I'd hardly say this is the time to hold a grudge."

"Oh, yeah? And why is that?"

This ought to be rich, Sloane thought, in part regretting she'd asked. Of course Georgina would have an excuse for why she'd blindsided Sloane at King Neptune's and—after Sloane had been visibly annoyed about that—had then extended an invitation for Luke to join them for dinner at the house. Sure, she'd probably argue that she'd thought it was what Sloane would have wanted. Or perhaps she'd take it a step further, as she had so many times in college, and insist that even though Sloane didn't *think* she wanted to see Luke twice in two days, Georgina actually knew what was best for Sloane. Perverted rationalizations if you existed in the real world, but Georgina had always inhabited her own warped worldview.

Last night Sloane had dreamed about him. And even when she'd awakened at three in the morning, peevish that a full bladder had interrupted her delicious reverie, she'd willed herself to drift back into the same guilty fantasy. The one where she'd never married Eddie. The one where there was no house in Brookline. No mounting bills to agonize over. No daily dinners to cook. No surfaces to be scrubbed and polished. No Madeleine.

In her dream, they were very obviously together. Oh, how they were together. His nimble hands had explored every inch of her eager body, while his lips pressed against hers, neither of them willing or able to control the impassioned squall that was gusting around them. She'd woken again later that morning feeling refreshed, satisfied even. Until she'd opened her eyes to her own reality. Was that alternate life what she really wanted? It had certainly felt that way in the dark and deceptive depths of her slumber. But no Madeleine? That was a deal breaker. There was no way she would trade in the life she'd built with her husband and daughter, even if things felt difficult at home at the moment.

Of course, it was all so ridiculous to contemplate. She'd never have known Madeleine in the first place if she'd chosen to pursue a different path. Not to marry Eddie after all those years of dating. So, instead of dwelling on what the dream might have meant, Sloane simply resolved to put her unhappiness at home out of her mind for a couple of days. Compartmentalization was her new motto. Plus, it allowed her to fantasize while she was away on vacation. And every girl deserved to dream, right?

"Because you need me to help you." Georgina pushed the door in. "Oh, it's even worse than I thought."

"I do not need your help, thank you very much." *And no apology necessary.*

"I beg to differ. Now, give me that."

Sloane grudgingly handed her the hairbrush and blow-dryer.

"If you're lucky, I'll do your makeup too."

"Okay." Sloane submitted to her friend's skilled ministrations.

"One rule."

"What?"

"You can't look until I'm done."

"Fine."

Sloane had long maintained that Georgina should have gone to beauty school. It was remarkable how, with no formal training, she could widen Sloane's eyes into alertness, paint her cheeks with an attractive blush that looked perfectly natural, and color her lips until her pout appeared as plump as Jennifer Lopez's rear end. And she did want to look her best for Luke, whether it was the right instinct or not. Georgina knew it. But, still, the words didn't have to be spoken between them. That was the thing about old friends.

Fifteen minutes later, Georgina took a few steps back, examining her handiwork.

"Done?" Sloane fidgeted anxiously.

"Just a dash more here." Georgina smeared something shimmery on her eyelids.

"What is that stuff?"

"Highlighter. It was in your makeup bag."

"Huh, what do you know?" She took the compact and examined it. "Must have been a free sample or something."

"And now, a final swipe of mascara."

"Didn't you put some on already?"

"Yes, I did. But that was midnight black. You have to let it dry and then seal it with a top coat of clear, and . . . voilà!" Georgina trilled victoriously. "You are stunning. Absolutely stunning." She spun Sloane's chair to face the mirror.

"Wow." She stared at her reflection, hardly recognizing her own vigilant brown eyes and contoured cheekbones. "Really, really amazing. I'd almost forgotten how good you are at this."

"Is that a compliment?" Georgina placed her hand on her chest in mock surprise.

"Don't let it go to your head." Sloane grinned irreverently.

"How could I?" Georgina's expression was solemn.

"What do you mean?"

"Nothing." She shrugged.

"Well, it's obviously not nothing."

"It's not a big deal—it's just you haven't exactly welcomed me with open arms here this week." Georgina looked down. "It's okay. I'm not upset or anything. You just seem really grouchy. And it feels like it's directed at me."

Sloane wasn't sure what to say. The last thing she wanted or needed at the moment was to get into it with Georgina half an hour from when Luke was scheduled to arrive. And she still hadn't selected an appropriate outfit—something straddling a line between sex kitten and schoolmarm—which would be another whole process in and of itself. "Maybe it's early PMS."

"I know you, Sloane. *Something* is on your mind."

"Maybe it's because I'm worried about Maddie. You know, what with her being at sleepaway camp for the first time ever." She tried not to let the edge creep into her voice. Sleepaway camp, after all, was not something that factored into Georgina's childless—and typically *childish*—manner of thinking.

"If that's really all it is . . ."

"I think so. I'm not trying to make you uncomfortable. It's good that you're here." Sloane tried to inject a dose of sincerity into her voice.

"Well, I'm glad I could help." Georgina smiled genuinely. "Luke won't know what hit him."

"You think so?" Sloane let her guard down, if only for an instant, reminding herself that Georgina could be intoxicating—in both the best and worst possible ways.

"I *know* so." Georgina clasped Sloane's hand. "Now let's go pick out something fabulous for you to wear."

"Thank you."

"For what?"

"For being you when I needed it most."

"Oh, sweetie." Georgina's eyes watered, and for a brief moment she gazed blankly at the wall, as if her mind had completely left the room and gone somewhere else. "Believe me, I'm the one who should be thanking you." She exhaled. "This trip couldn't have come at a better time."

By eight o'clock on the nose the house sat eerily silent. Georgina was upstairs weeding through the piles of clothing that were still littering her bedroom floor. Hillary was setting the table for four—the first dinner party of their vacation, if you could call it that. And

Sloane was pacing back and forth in the kitchen, hoping one of them would have the sense to answer the door for her when the bell finally chimed.

Luke was never on time. It was something she'd forgotten about him, until this evening. But now there was a rush of other unremembered details about the only other man she'd ever known intimately. Like the way he used to brush her bangs off her face using his thumbs only. Or how he would trace the outline of her lips with his index finger, so gradually that this one elusive gesture seemed to ignite every pleasure-transporting synapse from her head to her toes and all the parts in between.

Sloane's mind was racing from the past to the present and back again, stampeding over the many people, places, and milestones in its trail. Eddie had called again that afternoon. They'd spoken briefly. About nothing of significance. The weather. His golf game that morning. How she was enjoying her getaway. "It's been nice," she'd replied, eyeing a long pink sundress in her closet as they spoke and wondering if it was too much for a casual dinner at home. He hadn't pressed any further. Sloane was thankful for that. And, simultaneously, disappointed—if it was possible to be relieved and annoyed by the very same thing. Sure, part of her wanted Eddie to put his foot down. To say, "Enough is enough. Come home to your husband." But another part of her—the much, much brasher part—wanted to pretend he didn't exist, as she had that summer with Luke. Out of sight, out of mind. Or in Georgina's prophetic words, "What happens in Lake George . . ."

She shook her head, as if to physically exterminate the thought from her mind. They were just having a shared meal. With other people. And whether things were perfect with Eddie or not, he was her husband. For better or for worse.

"Got the place mats, plates, glasses, silverware, and . . . what am I forgetting?" Hillary walked into the room, dressed in a knee-length jean skirt and pale pink sweater set, with the cardigan knotted over her shoulders.

"Napkins?"

"Good thinking."

"There are more in the drawer with the aluminum foil and plastic wrap."

"Thanks." Hillary knelt down to retrieve them. "Should I open a bottle of white?"

"Yes!" Sloane replied a little too enthusiastically. *Wine.* Why hadn't she thought of that sooner? Nothing like a little liquid courage to help her navigate the tempestuous seas of breaking bread with an ex. And not just any ex. Luke had meant so much more to her than a summer fling. Their relationship had been all-consuming, albeit brief, but she had always felt that there had been something significant between them. "Actually, I'll get it. There are napkin rings up there." Sloane motioned to a cabinet above the stove top, while snagging a bottle of Chardonnay from the refrigerator, along with an elaborate cheese and vegetable platter that Hillary had picked up at the supermarket earlier in the day. "This looks amazing!"

"Doesn't it? The guy let me customize everything." Hillary came back into the room, gratefully accepting a full glass of wine from Sloane. "I'm telling you, if not for Greg, I might never go home. This place is paradise."

"You say that now. But wait until the frigid temps rush in,"

Sloane advised. "Trust me, the ice-choked lake is far better for figure skating than skinny-dipping."

"Well, I do like hot cocoa. . . ." Hillary smiled just as the doorbell rang. "Do you want to do the honors?"

"Um." She hesitated. Where was Georgina when you needed her? Oh, right. "Sure. I guess so."

In reality Sloane wanted to decline. To ask Hillary to greet their guest instead so that she could sit in the kitchen sipping her wine as if the whole thing were so terribly casual. But she had to be careful about raising red flags around her friend, even if she was being overly cautious, and even if Hillary would say she understood—whether she actually did or not. Sloane certainly didn't want it to seem like she was interested in Luke. Or that she cared too much about what he thought of her. Or how she looked. And why was vanity always the bottom line? She hadn't spent the day tanning or allowing a wrinkle-shrinking mask to set on her skin for twenty minutes because she planned to wow him with her intellect.

"Hey, you." Luke stood in the opened doorway with a sexy grin, proffering a small white cardboard box with an unmistakable gold sun-shaped sticker sealing it.

"Hey." Sloane grasped the knob like her life depended on it.

"Can I come in?" he smirked, his dark brown eyes twinkling in just the endearing way she recalled.

"Oh, yeah, of course." She was stammering again. "I was, um, seeing if it had gotten any colder. This weather has been crazy, huh?"

"Not really." He laughed. "In my thirty-plus years, this is pretty much how it's been. Eighties by day, fifties by night." Luke handed Sloane the box. "For you."

"You didn't."

"I did." He followed her into the kitchen.

"You did what?" Hillary had opened the oven to check on her lasagna.

"Brought our girl her favorite fudge."

"*Our* girl? We thought she was *your* girl." Georgina appeared as if out of nowhere, winking at Sloane, and prancing over to Luke. "Come here, you handsome devil." She kissed him on the cheek, a little too close to the mouth for Sloane's taste.

"Once upon a time." A sober expression crept across his face, but in a flash it was gone.

"What's everyone drinking?" Georgina asked, looking directly at Sloane's and Hillary's glasses of wine. "Anyone care to join me for something a little stronger?"

"No more tequila for me," Hillary interjected. "Luke, we met at the bar the other night." She extended her hand toward him.

"The pleasure was all mine, I'm sure." He grinned and shook her hand, which reminded Sloane of another thing about Luke. He knew his effect on women.

"I'm sure." Hillary blushed and then straightened her back. "I'll just go put the bread in."

"I'll have a shot," Luke called over his shoulder to where Georgina was crouched on the ground, already taking stock of the near-empty bottle.

"Looks like we've made quite a dent here, ladies. We'll have to chip in and buy Aunt Annabel some more Señor Patrón to keep her cozy at night."

"I don't think that'll be necessary." Sloane nodded as Georgina poured a shot for her as well. "Did you forget she's selling the place?"

"Really?" Luke seemed surprised to hear it—and was she imagining the hint of disappointment she heard in his voice?

"Yeah." Was she supposed to have told him? To have called him out of the blue with the breaking news? Not that she'd had his number, though clearly Georgina could have shared it. That is, if Sloane had been able to reach her. "Sad, huh?"

She could already feel the first glass of wine numbing her rough edges and caressing her nerves. Why had she made such a fuss? Luke was just a guy. A human being. She didn't need to impress him. Not anymore.

"For sure." He nodded. "The end of an era."

"Well, let's not get all sappy!" Georgina held up her shot glass to make a toast. "It may be the end of an era. But the night is still young."

chapter 11

"This lasagna is absolutely outstanding." Luke commended Hillary's culinary prowess for the third time in twenty minutes, and Sloane feared that next he too might start musing about the weather.

Georgina had been right about one thing. The night was still young. Unfortunately, it hadn't been aging gracefully.

As Hillary had gathered the fixings for dinner, Sloane had pretended to help, in an effort to avoid being stuck alone with Luke. Of course this had meant leaving him in the other room with Georgina, but—for once—she'd been grateful for her friend's uncanny ability to entertain anyone, anywhere, at any time. Many years ago, Sloane's mother had commented that Georgina could amuse a monkey in a molehill. And while it hadn't seemed a particularly clever analogy back then, her point had been spot-on nonetheless.

Sloane couldn't understand her sudden instinct to avoid him.

Hadn't she been hemming and hawing for hours on end about the types of things they might talk about? Or what information about her own life she'd choose to share with him. If any. It wasn't like the old days, where she and Georgina had been able to congregate in one of their dorm rooms, passing a box of stale Honey Nut Cheerios and a forty of Bud Light back and forth, while they hatched a game plan. Oh, how she'd wanted to do that. Georgina would have been on board. But that would have been juvenile, not to mention entirely inappropriate.

Still, she couldn't help but recall the way Georgina could be counted on to stretch her reedy legs down the length of her futon, while Sloane had been forced to crumple her body into a ball so she could sit at Georgina's feet, dutifully developing a list of all the things Georgina wanted Sloane to strategically drop into conversation with any given guy she was lusting after at the moment. Georgina always had her reasons for why she needed to convince him she was something she wasn't. And, after a while, Sloane learned not to question them.

The funny thing was, Sloane couldn't actually think of anything so fabulous about herself that it was worth asking anyone to mention it in conversation. What was Georgina supposed to tout? Sloane's married! Sloane's a mom! Sloane's a former teacher! Sloane goes to the gym! Sloane hasn't found one gray hair on her head yet! Sloane makes lasagna too, but it sucks in comparison to Hillary's!

Hillary. She'd probably noticed by now that Sloane was acting out of character. You didn't have to be a family counselor to pick up on that. But if she had, she hadn't said a word about it. All evening she'd simply provided Sloane the menial tasks she'd asked for and kept their chatter light, while Georgina's boisterous laughter had soared from room to room and the contents of the bottle of Patrón had dwindled into oblivion.

"Thank you. I'm so glad you like it." Hillary smiled, taking a small sip of wine.

"It's not often I get a home-cooked meal." Luke wiped a splash of tomato sauce off his chin. "What with being on the road so much."

"Oh?" Hillary handed him a warm loaf of bread and nudged the butter plate in his direction.

"I travel a lot for work. I don't know if Sloane mentioned it, but my family is in the hotel business. So I'm typically out of town two or three times a month."

"Wow, that must be hard."

"Sometimes. But I also realize how fortunate I am to see so much of the world."

"Isn't it the best?" Georgina cut in, slurring her words. "I mean who wants to be tied down, right?" She slammed her glass on the table to make her point.

"Whoa there. I think someone's had enough to drink." Hillary soaked up the puddle of tequila Georgina had sloshed onto the table with a white cloth napkin.

"Sorry, *Mom*!" Georgina flared her nostrils and then she stuck her tongue out at Hillary. "Someone has to say it, right?"

"Say what?" Hillary raised an eyebrow.

"That marriage is bullshit. Kids are bullshit. The whole fucking nuclear family, we're-the-fucking-Brady-Brunch thing, is total . . ." She lost her train of thought.

"Bullshit?" Luke asked, grinning at Sloane.

"Yes! Bullshit!" She pointed at him, as if he'd miraculously read her mind. "He knows exactly what I'm talking about. So does she." Georgina turned her focus to Hillary. "Well, kind of. She's got the ball and chain. Just not the snotty little ball and chainlets."

"That's enough, Georgina. You're drunk," Sloane reprimanded.

"Drunk?" Her hand flew to her mouth. "The horror. The shame. You know it's okay to pull the stick out of your ass sometimes, right, Sloanie?"

"Georgina." Sloane shot her a stern look.

"What? Hey, Lukie . . ." She hiccuped. "Is it okay if I call you that?"

"Why not?" He nodded, as if he had a choice.

"Excellent! Now, what was I saying? Oh, right. Don't you remember when Sloane was actually *fun*?"

"She still seems fun to me." Sloane's heart clenched. It was certainly polite of him to say, but she'd given him absolutely no reason to believe it. Especially since she didn't necessarily believe it herself. Hadn't she been fun at one time? Or had she been gripping Georgina's coattails with such sycophantic zeal that it had rubbed off on her? In any case, fun by association. Did that count?

"Well, you're wrong. She's not. She's a big party pooper." Georgina made an exaggerated expression of boredom.

"Why don't we go upstairs and put you to bed?" Sloane suggested.

"But the night is still yooooouuuunnnggg." Then Georgina actually howled, getting up out of her seat and promptly stumbling to the ground.

"I can throw her over my shoulder if you want," Luke offered to Sloane and Hillary.

"No, that's quite unnecessary." Sloane shook her head. "She's not your responsibility."

"See. Party pooper." Georgina got to her feet, using both the table and Luke's leg as leverage.

"You all right there?" He steadied her.

"Let's go before they start playing Scrabble." She stage-whispered the words, fastening her hand to Luke's thigh. "Believe me, I'm a lot more interesting than a double word score." Georgina snorted.

"I said that's *enough*." Sloane jumped up, linking her arm with Georgina's. "I'm so sorry." She looked at Luke. Really looked at him for the first time all night.

"You have nothing to apologize for." He gave her a steady look in return that she couldn't decipher.

"I'll be back as soon as I can." She started dragging Georgina toward the stairs, assuming most of the burden of her body weight.

"Are you sure you don't need help?" Hillary called after them.

"Nope. We'll be fine. . . ." Sloane sighed, muttering under her breath, "At least I think we will."

By the time Sloane had stripped Georgina down to her pink lace thong underwear, raked her hair off her face with the teeth of a large plastic clip she'd found on the floor, and practically wrestled her into the bathroom in the way one does a defiant toddler, Luke had gone. And Sloane's heart had dropped in a free fall as she forced herself to face facts.

What had she been expecting? Should he have waited around, shooting the shit with Hillary—the one person in their trio he didn't know or have anything in common with—until she'd been done corralling the untamed beast that was Georgina? Yes, if she was honest with herself, she supposed that was what she had been expecting. Or at least hoping for. As she'd tussled to ready Georgina for bed, Sloane had been chanting silently to herself that in just a few short minutes she'd be back downstairs. With Luke. Her Luke.

Her Luke who wasn't even hers. But had he ever been? Sometimes it was dangerously easy to romanticize the past. In her memory perhaps she painted a canvas with bright primary colors, one where the vibrant blues and yellows didn't fraternize into a muddy green. The muddy green that was real life. Full of real people. People who weren't set to a soundtrack of one-hit-wonder eighties songs that, with the apex of a desperate refrain, could unleash a treasure trove of preserved memories.

"He waited for a while, if it's any consolation." Hillary looked up from her newspaper. "And he asked me to give you his number." She handed Sloane a slip of paper with Luke's familiar, albeit barely legible, handwriting scribbled on it.

"Oh." Sloane couldn't manage anything more than that one word. Maybe it was somewhat mollifying that he hadn't run out the door at the first chance he'd received. That he wanted her to know how to reach him. But it didn't matter. He was gone. What was the difference if it'd been a minute or an hour since he'd left?

"He seems like a really nice guy. He insisted on helping me clean up everything." Hillary got out of her chair and moved toward the couch to sit next to Sloane. "I know tonight wasn't how you'd pictured it."

"It was fine. I'm just sorry that Georgina ruined everything. She was the one who invited him here in the first place, and then look how she behaved." Sloane set her magazine on the coffee table, crossed her arms, and scowled. She hadn't been able to read a word of it anyway. Her mind was spinning far too fast and furiously for that.

"Luke was right. You don't have to apologize."

"She's my friend. I'm the one who brought her here."

"Maybe so, but she's not your child, Sloane. You have to stop feeling responsible for her actions. She's a grown adult."

"It's hard to think of her that way."

"I'm sure." Hillary nodded astutely.

"And what she said to you."

"What?"

"About kids."

"Oh, that." Hillary waved her hand. "I can take it."

"It's just so wrong. She doesn't realize that she can't just divulge whatever comes to her mind." Sloane sighed. "She needs one of those bleeping machines. You know. When people curse live on air."

"Totally!" Hillary laughed, extending a bag of pretzel rods toward Sloane, who gratefully accepted the snack.

"Except hers would sound like this: bleep, bleep, bleep, bleep, bleep bleeeeeeeeeeeeeeeeep!" Sloane snorted involuntarily.

"You're probably right." Hillary smirked.

"She doesn't make you mad?" Sloane gathered her hair into a ponytail and then let go, allowing it to fan across her shoulders.

"Not really." Hillary cocked her head to one side, but she didn't say anything further.

"How is that possible? She's *so* infuriating." Sloane clenched her fists to emphasize her position.

"Honestly, I feel sorry for her."

"Sorry for Georgina? Really?" This intrigued Sloane. No one had ever felt anything but envy or adulation when it came to Georgina.

Through the years, how many times had Sloane watched necks crane for the chance at a glimpse of Georgina walking by? How many times had she overheard girls hissing to each other in hushed tones about how they would give anything to look like her? To stride a city block in her size nine black leather motorcycle boots. If only for a day.

One might have presumed it would have been tough being Georgina's best friend. The Bonnie to her Clyde. The Ginger to her Fred. The Laverne to her Shirley. But it had never mattered to her. Sloane had been wholly content to play second fiddle, to bask in the light of Georgina's aura and, by virtue of this, be towed along for the wild ride.

"Sure you don't?"

"Definitely not right now!"

"I see that." Hillary cleared her throat. "Sloane, Georgina is text-book."

"What do you mean?"

"I mean she's the case study you read about. When you're in my line of work." Hillary paused, as if she was searching for a simplistic explanation. "She's racked with insecurity, for starters."

"Insecurity?" Sloane sniffed in disbelief and then bit off the tip of a pretzel rod. "I'd hardly say Georgina is insecure. Have you met her?"

"Trust me on this one. It's all an act. A production for other people's sake. You don't behave the way Georgina does unless you're vulnerable in some significant way."

"Another word I wouldn't use to describe her." But Sloane thought about what Hillary was saying. She knew that the parents at Hillary's school swore by her assessments and advice, not to mention the ones who traveled hours from Rhode Island, Maine, Connecticut, and even New York City to seek out her therapy on a freelance basis. The same ones who sat in her office, amid her walls of honors and degrees, and begged for her to "fix" their wayward children or troubled teenagers. And if that didn't work, to please medicate them. Thank you very much. "'Selfish' would be one. 'Unpredictable' would be another. Oh, and let's throw in 'disappointing' for good measure. Shall we?"

"Hey." Georgina's greeting was almost imperceptible, until Sloane caught sight of her, standing in the doorway, her face blanched a whitish gray, and her typically lithe body drooping languidly against the wall.

Sloane didn't say anything. She just stared at her. Maybe she should have felt sorry for her. Maybe her outburst at dinner had been a cry for help. Sloane laughed bitterly underneath her breath. Or maybe Georgina had duped Hillary too, entwined her in her complex web of manipulation.

"I'm going to bed." Sloane stood up and brushed past her oldest friend.

"Good night," Georgina rasped as Sloane stalked up the stairs.

Sloane didn't bother to reply. She didn't have the energy to deal with Georgina tonight. All she wanted to do was bury herself under the covers.

And allow herself to dream.

chapter 12

This summer would mark three years of trying. Greg had pointed it out to Hillary before she'd left for Lake George. Not in an accusatory way, as husbands so often did, placing the blame safely in the wife's lap for fear that someone, anyone, might think them less virile. Fortunately Greg wasn't that guy.

Nonetheless, month after month she'd watched the disenchantment register on his face. Heard the optimistic lilt in his voice sag. And observed the way his shoulders no longer stood at attention, but rather wilted into resigned acceptance as he went about his day. It wasn't easy being a failure every thirty days. Not to mention all the money they might as well have thrown in the trash, along with the negative pregnancy tests.

So much had changed between them since that fateful day a few years ago when he'd approached her on an ordinary Sunday morning after they'd both devoured a stack of buttermilk pancakes and their respective sections of the *Boston Globe*—Arts and Lifestyle for her, Business and Sports for him. Before she had recognized the serious air about him, he'd taken her hand and led her from their modest but cozy kitchen out onto the screened-in porch Greg's father had built for them as one of his projects since his partial retirement.

She could still bring to mind in crystal clear detail the look on his face as they'd swayed back and forth on the white wicker two-seat swing—a thin veil of forced calm, so transparent it barely obscured the exhilaration effervescing beneath his skin. He'd locked his fingers with hers, while they'd gazed out the wall of windows, absorbing the maudlin sky and the mud puddles that had overtaken their lawn.

"Let's have a baby," he'd blurted, before she'd had a chance to wonder what he was thinking, as she so often did. Both a curse of her chosen profession and an inherent female instinct. "I'm ready to be a dad."

At first Hillary had said nothing in return. She'd just smiled meaningfully and positioned herself closer to him, nuzzling her head into the crook of his arm.

Greg hadn't actually bothered to ask whether she wanted a child too or if she was ready to be a mother. His failure to question her did not happen because he was selfish or oblivious to her needs, but because he assumed it went without saying. After all, they had talked about it many times. They'd even cooed in unison as strangers strolled by them on the street with newborns in designer carriages.

Hillary had braved those baby superstores only twice and each occasion had been equally terrifying—once to honor her cousin Lena's first pregnancy and then again when her colleague Rachel had been about to burst with twin girls while her husband, Andrew, was serving their country in Afghanistan.

All Hillary could think as she perused the store aisles was, how was it possible that seven pounds of sugar and spice and everything nice could require all that stuff? Pumps and pads. Pillows and potties. Blankets and Boppies. There were complete bottle "systems" to promote easier sucking and ward off that pesky gas. It was all so foreign to Hillary. And daunting. Was an entire *system* really compulsory to feed someone who could subsist safely on breast milk alone? She wasn't sure. But, still, she'd turned each corner to a fresh aisle bursting with "necessary" gear—specifically tailored to bath time, play-time, sleep time . . . Whatever time you had, they had just the thing to make new motherhood appear as flawless and straightforward as surely it wasn't.

Of course when Greg had originally proposed a leap into parent-hood, he'd never thought about all the crap they'd inevitably amass in their quaint ranch house, the rooms of which were already erupt-ing with their own crap. He'd also failed to consider how long it could take for her to become belly-full and barefoot. Those weren't the sorts of details men considered.

So, naturally, after a year had passed, Greg had started to be-come anxious. "Do you think there's something wrong?" He'd asked her the same question three months in a row. All three times, she'd cupped his cheeks in the palms of her hands, kissed him tenderly on the lips, and replied, "In good time." And he'd believed her.

Until another year had gone by. That was when Greg's anxiety had quickly turned to action and he'd started researching. She'd heard him into the wee hours of the night tapping away at the computer keyboard in the guest bedroom across from theirs, which they'd turned into a shared office. Greg had started calling it "the baby's room" right around the time he'd declared himself ready for fatherhood.

And what a father he would be. There was no denying it. Hillary knew he'd be the one to bound to the changing table at the smell of a poopy diaper, to jump out from under the warm covers at two o'clock in the morning to quiet their newborn's wails, and—later— in the years to come, it would be Greg coaching Little League and soccer. He would teach their child to ride a bike. To ice-skate and ski. Hillary had yet to define her role outside of the generic idea of mom, with its many intrinsic implications.

"I read about something called Clomid," he'd said one Saturday morning over breakfast. "It's this pill you can take to help you ovulate or produce more eggs or something." She could tell that he was taking her temperature on the suggestion. "Maybe we should try it?"

"Maybe." Hillary knew exactly what Clomid was. A few of her friends had hopped on that hormonal roller coaster, so desperate to be knocked up that they'd been oblivious to their erratic mood swings, which had everyone around them tiptoeing on eggshells.

"I mean, I don't think we need anything as drastic as intrauterine insemination or in vitro fertilization. Yet."

"Definitely not," she'd agreed. Meanwhile it hadn't escaped her notice that he'd really done his homework.

"So?" He'd watched her expectantly, nodding his head with fitful exuberance. An exuberance that she wanted to bottle up and submerge herself in, so—if only for a moment—she could feel the same way he did.

"Let's give it a few more months and then we'll regroup. Okay?" She'd watched his smile wilt like a wildflower beneath the blazing sun. And then she'd touched his cheek softly. "I promise."

Greg had nodded silently in agreement. Because he loved her more than he loved himself or their unborn child. He'd told her the first part the day he'd proposed. At the time it had seemed like a strange thing to say. But Greg had never had a way with words. Fortunately, it didn't stop him from expressing himself.

At thirty-two, they'd met at an educational conference in Arizona for teachers, professors, principals, family counselors, and other industry leaders. They'd spotted each other across a crowded room. Quite literally. It was hard to say whether it had been love at first sight, but—regardless—there had been an undeniable magnetic force that had drawn them together. That and their seat assignments had been next to each other.

They'd gotten to talking immediately and the conversation had parlayed itself into a romantic dinner for two. As luck would have it, they'd both hailed from the Boston area and were on the same flight home. Twelve dates and two months later, he'd crouched down on bended knee, proffering a simple solitaire diamond set on a slender rose gold band, and said, "Hillary. I've been waiting all my life for someone I love more than I love myself. And now I've found her. Will you do me the unbelievable honor of becoming my wife?"

Three weeks later, Hillary had been at Greg's side in an unadorned white sheath dress, delivering her vows in front of a justice of the peace. She'd felt like the luckiest woman in the world to have found a man so unconditionally devoted, not to mention adorable, with his irresistible dimples and kind blue eyes.

"Oh, hey." Georgina crept onto the back deck, her breathtaking silhouette in the darkness rousing Hillary from her musings.

"Wow, you scared the shit out of me."

"Sorry about that." Georgina giggled.

"You think it's funny?" Hillary was sitting on the precipice of the balcony, her legs dangling over the edge. She patted the place beside her for Georgina.

"No, no. It's just I don't think I've ever heard you curse."

"Ah, well, I try not to. I suppose until someone scares the *shit* out of me!"

"Fair enough." Georgina lowered herself down next to Hillary. "She hates me."

"Who does?"

"You know who. Sloane."

"I'm sure she doesn't hate you."

"Fine, then she's pissed as hell at me." Georgina hugged her knees to her chest and tugged her nightshirt over them.

"Can you blame her?" The wind off the lake had grown stronger, compelling Hillary to secure the blanket she'd draped over her shoulders.

"I guess not." Georgina shook her head. "I'm just so sick of always being the bad guy in our relationship."

"I hear you." Hillary thought about how very different she and Georgina appeared on the surface, in practically every tangible way. It was one of the first things Sloane had told her when Georgina had invited herself along to Lake George. But now she wasn't so sure.

"Yeah, right," Georgina scoffed. "When was the last time you humiliated yourself in front of everyone, while managing to alienate the only person who really cares about you?"

"I can't say it's been recently. Or ever, for that matter." Hillary hesitated. "You really think she's the only person who cares about you?"

"The list is short. Trust me." Georgina leaned back on her elbows, casting her red hair out into the gusty breeze. "In case you haven't heard, my parents weren't exactly June and Ward Cleaver."

"That makes two of us."

"Really?" Hillary saw Georgina visibly perk up. "I'd kind of assumed you were raised by saints or nuns or something like that."

"Hardly."

"Very interesting." Georgina turned toward her, crossing her legs Indian-style. "So, what were they like?"

"My mom and dad?"

"Yeah. I mean, how did they fuck you up?"

"Well, I don't know if they fucked me up, as you put it." She laughed lightly. "Contrary to popular belief, it's not really fair to blame *everything* on your parents."

"I guess I subscribe to popular belief."

"My father was a big-time lawyer. A prosecutor. You know, the guy you see on television battling it out for this major corporation or that high-profile billionaire."

"So he defended the bad guys."

"Oh, no, my dad didn't defend anyone. He prosecuted. It was in his blood." Hillary hadn't thought about her father—really thought about him—in a long time. "Anyway, he worked crazy hours. Left before I woke up in the morning and didn't come home until well after I'd gone to sleep. And on the weekends, if he wasn't back at the office, then he was playing golf or tennis with his country club buddies."

"He didn't pay any attention to you at all?"

"Only when my report card came. If it was all As, I got fifty dollars. If not, I got nothing. Even if there was only one A minus." Hillary sniffed. "You know the funny thing?"

"What?"

"I didn't even want his fifty bucks. I wanted him to take me out for ice cream. Or come to one of the father-daughter dances at my school. All that fifty bucks bought me was bitterness."

"What about your mom? Where was she all that time?"

"My mom." Hillary exhaled. "She was there. . . ."

"And?" Georgina was as captive an audience as Hillary had ever seen her.

"And she was there. But not really."

"What does that mean?"

"Today they'd probably diagnose it as severe depression. Maybe borderline personality disorder. God knows she had an intense fear of abandonment."

"But your father stayed with her?"

"Oh, sure. Anything to keep up appearances. That was all that truly mattered to him." Hillary cleared her throat. "He said she wasn't like that until I came along."

"Jeez."

"Yeah, so while he was off pursuing his career and every assistant attorney or paralegal in a short skirt, my mother was dipping further and further into a black hole. Some days she'd sit on the couch for eight hours straight, staring at the television in a comatose state.

I'd come back from school and the Home Shopping Network would be blaring. My dirty cereal bowl from that morning would still be sitting on the table in the same exact place I left it. Every so often, I'd find all of the stove burners turned to high and I'd thank my lucky stars that the whole house hadn't burned down in my absence."

"Where are they now?"

"Living in the same house, about forty minutes from ours. She's medicated. But too much damage has been done between us for there to be any kind of real relationship now."

"Do you see them often?"

"Twice a year. Christmas and Easter. Can you believe they want grandkids? My dad actually had the gall to bring it up last time we got together."

"Speaking of that." Georgina fidgeted with the sleeve of her nightshirt. "I'm really sorry about what I said tonight. You know, about the ball and chainlets."

"It's okay."

"No, it's not."

"You were being honest."

"I was being a bitch."

"It happens to the best of us." Hillary smiled, pushing herself to her feet. "I'm beat. You?"

"Eh." Georgina smiled back. "I think I'm going to sit out here for a little while longer. It's a beautiful night." She looked out over the water. "I'll see you in the morning?"

"Yes, you will."

"Sweet dreams." Georgina offered her a gentle smile.

"You too, Georgina." Hillary let herself into the house quietly and ascended the stairs to her bedroom, where there was a note on her pillow from Sloane saying that Greg had called, but that he was going to sleep soon, so not to bother phoning him until tomorrow.

Next she walked into the bathroom, opened the medicine cabinet, and reached inside to retrieve the familiar blue packet. Hillary popped one out with her thumb and placed it on her tongue. Her birth control pill.

Then she filled her collapsible plastic travel cup with water, took a large gulp, as she did every evening, and swallowed the pill along with her pride.

chapter 13

Sloane cracked one eye and then the other, blinded by a blade of sunshine streaking through the curtains. She'd fallen asleep in her clothing from the night before, and she had cursed under her breath at Georgina as she'd drifted in and out of consciousness.

Predictably, she'd awakened no less furious with her best friend. More to the point, she had started thinking of her as her *supposed* best friend. Because a real best friend didn't get wasted, cause a scene, insult everyone within earshot, all the while flirting with *her* supposed best friend's former love interest. Unless of course your best friend was Georgina.

But before Sloane could really muster up the wrath that was thrashing against her chest, she reached her hand into the cubby of her nightstand, urgently searching for the crumpled piece of paper she'd placed there before surrendering to the comforting embrace of slumber. The piece of paper with Luke's telephone number scribbled on it. The one he'd given Hillary to pass along to her in the wake of Georgina's Patrón-inspired, Academy Award–worthy exhibition.

Sloane had quite intentionally decided not to leave it out, concerned that she might spill a glass of water on it or that, God forbid, it could disappear amid the frenzy of her tossing and turning, never to resurface again. And then what? Would she dare ask Georgina how to reach Luke? Fat chance. She'd sooner slather her body with honey and lock herself in a room full of bees.

Still, despite her best intentions, the paper wasn't there. With a sudden surge of energy Sloane threw back her covers and scrambled out of bed to search, crouching down on all fours to clear out the nightstand and check under every piece of furniture, just as the landline's offensively shrill ring intruded on her mission.

Sloane hurled herself toward the receiver. What if it was Luke? What if he'd telepathically realized what she was doing? She'd be damned if she let Georgina get to him first. "Hello?" she answered, attempting to sound demure.

"Hey." One word was all she needed to identify that it wasn't Luke on the other end of the line. "Sloane?"

"Yes?" She knelt on the carpet again, still frantically in pursuit of the scrap of paper.

"It's me. Eddie." He cleared his throat when she failed to respond. "Your husband."

"Oh, hey." Reluctantly, she stopped what she was doing and sat motionless on the ground, exasperated by the unwelcome interruption. "Sorry. It didn't sound like you at first."

"It's okay." She'd deflated his enthusiasm. As usual.

"What's up?" Even she could hear the clipped tone to her voice, but she couldn't help it. She felt sorry for Eddie, always calling at the most inopportune times. Or was it that, in her mind, there was never a good time for them to talk?

"Nothing." He sighed. "I mean, a lot of stuff. Work is really busy."

"That's good." Sloane tried to come across as encouraging in an effort to placate him. And as a means of getting him off the phone faster. It seemed like whenever Eddie called, even though he had nothing in particular to say, he was desperate to keep her engaged for as long as possible. As if each time he let her go, he worried that he was that much closer to losing her forever.

"I guess." There was silence. "How are you?"

"Good, good. Everything is really good."

"Good."

"Well, now that it's been established that we're both good"—Sloane laughed awkwardly—"if there's nothing specific . . ." She spotted a sliver of something white out of the corner of her eye, wedged between her nightstand and the wall, and lunged for it, irrationally fearing it might take flight in the stagnant air surrounding her.

"I spoke to Maddie this morning."

"Who?" She unfolded the crinkled slip of paper and exhaled as soon as she saw those seven sacred digits scrawled in Luke's familiarly messy handwriting.

"Maddie. Our daughter." There was an appropriate tinge of irritation lacing Eddie's reply. "Are you listening to me at all?"

"I'm so sorry." Sloane smiled to herself despite her husband's obvious irritation, silently thankful that he wasn't present to see her face. "I, um, thought I heard someone calling me from the kitchen."

"She's doing really well at camp. She sounds so mature."

"She really does. We chatted for a while yesterday." Sloane balled her hand into a fist, securing the scrap of paper that suddenly felt like a fifty-pound weight dragging her arm to the floor. "I miss her."

"I do too." His voice cracked. "I miss both of you."

"I know." Sloane lay down on the bed and closed her eyes, trying to transport herself back to the reverie she'd been prematurely roused from.

She'd dreamed about Luke again. Only this time he'd been living in her reality. In her house in Brookline. Her house and Eddie's house. Yet there'd been no Eddie in sight. Maddie, however, had been very much there, dancing around the room like the exuberant nine-year-old she was. They'd been a family. The three of them. It was the first time she'd ever thought about that. Did she truly expect to pluck one man out of the picture and insert the other one in his place as if she were exchanging a dead battery? Was that really what she wanted? In the harsh light of day, she didn't think so. But what then?

It wasn't as if she were prepared to have an illicit affair. Those were strictly reserved for characters in romance novels or guests on Jerry Springer's seedy talk show. Occasionally a drunk and damaged reality TV star. No one that Sloane would ever associate with.

"Hello? Sloane? Are you still there?" Eddie's beckoning drew her back to reality.

"Yeah, I'm here. Sorry, I'm a little distracted."

"I can tell." He paused. "Is everything okay?" There was that temperature taking again.

"It's fine. I'm fine. I was just going to head to the beach, so . . ."

"Right, of course. I'll talk to you later?"

"Sure." Sloane crossed the room to retrieve her laptop from on top of the dresser and walked toward the window, curling herself into the padded seat underneath it and lifting the screen of her computer to sign in.

Her password, as with everything else she needed one for, was "Maddie." Eddie had told her not to pick something so obvious, but the truth was that if it wasn't something so obvious, she'd never remember it herself. She'd made that mistake once before when she'd concocted an elaborate combination including part of her Social Security number, Eddie's birthday, and their wedding anniversary. As a result she'd spent three days convincing a series of bank tellers and, ultimately, the branch manager that she was who she said she was. And that, yes, she really had completely forgotten the password she'd set up only weeks earlier.

"Great. I'll call you tonight." He waited. Probably for her to say something. "I love you, Sloane."

"I love you too," she murmured, forcing each syllable from her mouth, questioning their veracity, before hanging up.

Sloane stepped out of the shower and wrapped her towel around her damp body, tucking one edge into the top to secure it. She reached for her hairbrush and slicked her soggy tresses into a ponytail before coiling it into a plaited bun. After drying off, she slathered an ample amount of sunscreen on her arms, legs, neck, and face and the parts of her back she could reach, and then slipped into a simple black one-piece bathing suit.

After hanging up with Eddie, she'd found herself surfing the Web on her laptop . . . and Googling divorce and infidelity. The statistics had been alarming. One website she'd found boasted that in forty-one percent of marriages, one or both of the spouses admitted to cheating. Fifty-seven percent of men had been unfaithful in a relationship. And fifty-four percent of women had done the same. But perhaps the most disturbing and telling data came courtesy of the seventy-four and sixty-eight percent of men and women respectively who said they would certainly step out on their significant other if, and only if, they were guaranteed not to get caught with their pants around their ankles. Classy.

Sloane mulled over those shocking figures as she packed her bag for the beach, including the latest chick lit novel she was reading, a stack of magazines in the event that she needed a break from her book, an extra tube of sunscreen, a fresh towel, a hat, a cover-up, and finally her iPod with headphones, so she could lose herself in the 1980s somewhere between "Forever Young" and "In Your Eyes."

If her hasty online research was to be believed, roughly three-quarters of people in committed unions would do the nasty, or at the very least *something* nasty, with a friend, colleague, stranger, or even an ex-boyfriend—bottom line, someone who was most definitely *not* their partner—as long as said dalliance remained safely under the radar. In other words, fifteen to twenty percent more men and women would flush their marriage vows and promise rings down the toilet as long as they could get away with it.

Was that what really mattered when it came right down to it? Did philanderers actually sit around debating whether to stray based on the likelihood of getting caught? One might argue that any relationship worth its weight in household appliances wouldn't be subject to such conjecture. And what about the people who might want to cheat, but decided not to solely from fear of being discovered? After all, how many times had Sloane heard the phrase "emotionally unfaithful"?

She'd never really bought into the concept of being wronged by someone who hadn't actually done anything wrong. At least not anything physical. Would it hold up as evidence in a court of law to say your husband had flirted excessively with his secretary or your wife had brushed up against the mailman one too many times? It seemed unlikely. In her mind, those people were still innocent of any wrongdoing.

That was until she'd witnessed her friend Stacy's marriage unravel. Stacy was a housewife with too much time and money on her hands. Her husband, Scott—a self-made multimillionaire who traveled the globe by way of his entrepreneurial pursuits—had never once, to her knowledge, so much as kissed another woman since they'd married. To her knowledge. He had, however, been carrying on numerous online "conversations" with eccentric and well-endowed women, in the manner of a sleazy politician. There had been photos involved, in addition to descriptive and crude e-mails, which Stacy had forwarded to Sloane, insisting that they were far too uncivilized for her to read.

"Should I leave him?" Stacy had probed, most likely praying Sloane would say no. Because then what? Stacy had no marketable skills to speak of. Or money that she'd either earned or saved. They had no kids for her to hold over his head. Not even a dog or a cat.

Sloane had told her to talk to Scott. To see if he was willing to "get help," as in serious marriage counseling or possibly a sex thera-pist to address his needs. And why they weren't being met by his wife. Then they'd gotten off the phone and Sloane had crawled into bed with Eddie and spooned her body around his, quietly thanking God that she had a solid man who would sooner cut his own penis off than let another woman see it.

Stacy hadn't listened to Sloane's advice, not that it necessarily would have helped. And three months later, Scott had left her, unaware that she'd uncovered his salacious e-mails in the first place. These days, Stacy could be found, in uniform, wandering around Sephora offering customers her tips for disguising angry pimples and perfecting their eyeliner application. When she'd been named employee of the month a year ago, Stacy had called Sloane, hysterically crying. She'd finally realized that Scott wasn't coming back.

Of course, when her husband's emotional infidelity had hap-pened to Stacy, Sloane had been indignant on her behalf. She'd said Stacy would be better off without him, even though she wasn't sure she meant it. And Stacy certainly hadn't proved it to be true.

But, now, it felt like she was in the same place. Scott's place. She hadn't sunk to his level and she had no intentions of doing so. Still, wasn't it at least worrisome that she'd dreamed of ripping Luke's clothes off? It was certainly not on the level of exchanging racy pic-tures, but it also wasn't something she'd feel comfortable confiding to her husband. Especially since, if she was being completely honest, she'd given a good deal of thought to Luke's body in the light of day as well. Not that she'd actually *do* anything.

Sloane eradicated the thought of her attraction to Luke from her mind. Eddie loved her. He cared for her. He would crawl to the end of the earth for her. On broken glass. And then there was Madeleine. Her sweet Maddie with her brown eyes that sparkled like a cake full of birthday candles when she saw her daddy. Was Sloane prepared to blow them all out in one fell swoop in order to satisfy her own selfish daydreams?

She slung her beach bag over her shoulder and moved toward the door. But something stopped her in her tracks before she reached the hallway. She went back to the bed and sat staring at the telephone before lifting the receiver and dialing the number on the white piece of paper.

For a split second, she thought about hanging up, but he answered after one ring. "Hey, pretty girl." Damn caller ID.

"Hey," she whispered, already aware that she'd dipped her toe across an invisible line that she'd meant to remain safely behind. "I'm so sorry about last night."

"You don't ever need to be sorry." Even his voice attracted her to him. Sloane pictured him lying in bed shirtless, and a shiver skulked slowly and ominously up her spine. "I want to see you." Luke had never been one to mince words.

"I want to see you too." Her heart throbbed to the beat of her disgrace.

"How about lunch tomorrow?"

"Okay. Where?"

"Where else? Frog Hill Farm."

"Okay." Sloane flinched at her own willingness. There would be no more crossed lines. None.

"Twelve o'clock."

"I'll see you then."

"And, Sloane?"

"Yeah?"

"Maybe you should leave your friends home this time." He laughed.

"You got it." Sloane hung up the phone and let out the smallest shriek of excitement. Part of her wanted to run and tell Georgina and Hillary of her new plans with Luke. But another part of her thought better of it. She'd fill them in, just not quite yet.

chapter 14

It was one of those beautiful days evocative of cherished summer memories of childhood. Bare toes wriggling in the sand, bodies slick with sunscreen, and sticky hands and faces lacquered with the remains of rainbow-colored ice pops fresh from the Good Humor truck.

Hadn't every summer day felt that picture-perfect when you were a kid? There was no recognition of the unbearable humidity or the rainstorms that erupted at four o'clock on the dot each afternoon. Or the way it felt to have your shirt plastered to your back with perspiration, while the skin on your nose peeled until it was raw and then tightened into a crusty scab.

Sure, Sloane had vague memories of sunburns so painful that her parents had been forced to bathe her in a tub full of tepid milk. There had also been scraped knees shredded by the blacktop at the playground and outbreaks of invisible lice that called for a dousing with some putrid-smelling shampoo in order to decimate the little fuckers. Still, life had been good. Lice or no lice.

That was how Sloane felt today, as she set out for the beach alone to procure some of the well-deserved rest and relaxation she'd intended for the trip in the first place. With the sun suspended in the blazing sky, casting a haze of warmth over God's creatures, or at least the ones vacationing in Lake George, she closed her eyes and sucked in a breath of fragrant air.

When she'd finally made it downstairs to the kitchen, following a few necessary moments of meditation after her brief phone call with Luke, Georgina and Hillary had been nowhere in sight. She hadn't bothered to look far for Georgina—well aware of the fact that she had nothing nice to say to her. She had, however, checked Hillary's room and the back porch, bellowing her name throughout the house. It wasn't until she'd walked outside to find her car missing that she'd realized they were both gone, apparently together. Sloane had tried not to let it irritate her that they'd taken her car, the only one they had for the three of them, without leaving so much as a note or firing off an e-mail or a text, anything to say, "Hey, we decided to leave you stranded at home. Hope you don't mind!" She also tried not to let it bug her that they were off somewhere together. The two most unlikely people in the world to enjoy each other's company, but apparently they were tolerating it.

Instead, she decided to ride one of the old bikes in the garage the half mile to Rogers Memorial Park, home of the closest public beach in Bolton Landing, which also boasted tennis and basketball courts, docks, picnic tables, grills, and a pavilion for refuge when it rained. In the summer months, the park hosted free movies and concerts, in addition to modest fireworks displays on the Fourth of July and Labor Day.

As she rode, Sloane thought back to the first time she'd been there. With Amy. They'd stuffed their backpacks with sandwiches and sodas, biked the distance in bikini tops and the skimpiest of jean shorts, and spent the day tanning themselves with a bottle of baby oil and a roll of tinfoil Amy had lifted from their aunt's pantry. They'd been approached by a group of older boys, one of whom had gone to second base with Amy later that night at a bonfire he'd invited them to. His friend had tried to hook up with Sloane, but he'd had one fierce red pimple on the tip of his nose, which she'd been unable to look past. When they'd arrived home just after ten o'clock, Amy and Sloane had been positive they were going to be in hot water with their aunt. But Annabel had been fazed by neither their late arrival nor the fact that they'd been gone for over twelve hours. She'd simply pulled a carton of milk from the refrigerator and a box of stale glazed doughnut holes from the cabinet and invited them to sit down and regale her with the details of their adventure. Because everything was an adventure when it came to their aunt Annabel. Even an average trip to an average beach.

But, to Sloane, Rogers Memorial Park was more than just an average beach. The last time she'd been there, it'd been with Luke. Of course, she hadn't done much of anything without him by her side after they'd met on her second day in Lake George that summer. There'd been another towering bonfire and a boisterous group gathered around it. She and Luke had taken their time walking hand in hand to the far end of the beach, stopping a few times to kiss under the haunting glow of the moon. Eventually they'd found a small cove and, sheltered by a jetty, had made love on a dank towel, unaware that anything existed beyond the passion burning between them. A week later, Sloane's cheeks had still felt raw from the brush of his stubble. Not to mention that she'd found sand in her nooks and crannies every morning in the shower. As the memory besieged her, Sloane could still feel how swollen her lips had seemed from his tender kisses.

Now, over a decade later, she was back at the same beach with the same man on her mind, despite the stark reality that everything had changed. Sloane pulled her bike into a spot, pretended to lock it around a post, and lifted her beach bag out of the small pink basket on the front. She'd been tempted to honk the horn a couple of times on the ride over, but had refrained for fear of being heckled by a pack of teenagers who appeared far cooler than she did in their beat-up red Mustang convertible, wielding brown paper bags that surely did not contain lemonade or iced tea.

She lifted her sunglasses on top of her head and scouted out a somewhat peaceful clearing in the sand amid the shrieking infants and their visibly fatigued parents.

She shook her towel onto the sand, leveling the wrinkles, so she could stretch her whole body down the length of it. Then she lifted her cover-up over her head and scrunched it into a ball to use as a pillow. She smoothed on an extra layer of SPF 30 and, just as she was about to place her headphones over her ears, she heard someone calling her name. Before Sloane could reply, she turned toward the voice to find Hillary coming toward her, waving both arms in the air.

"You made it!" Hillary stopped at the side of Sloane's towel to catch her breath. Even for someone in great shape, running in the sand was no easy task.

"I did." Sloane looked up, positioning her hand above her fore-head like a saluting soldier in order to block the sun. "No thanks to you two." She tried to inject a joking tone to her voice, even though she kind of meant it.

"Didn't you get my note?"

"Nope."

"Oh, that's strange, because I left it right next to the coffeepot. I said to myself, 'If I know Sloane, there's only one thing she won't leave the house without.' I figured it was a sure bet."

"Normally you'd have been right!" She laughed, relieved at the reminder that Hillary was a good egg. "I totally forgot my coffee this morning. I must have been distracted." She chose not to mention what that distraction had been. Or more precisely, who.

"We thought you might want to sleep in after . . ."

"After the events of last night?" Sloane was pretty sure there'd been no *we* about it. Georgina's mind didn't work that way.

"Right." Seemingly unconsciously, Hillary traced a line in the sand with her toe. "Anyway, I wanted to let you know that we'd decided to head to the beach and to give me a call when you woke up so I could come get you. How'd you get here? Please say you didn't walk. I'd feel awful."

"No, no. I grabbed one of the bikes in the garage. I think it's actually meant for a five-year-old girl." They laughed together over the image it conjured.

"Well, we're just over there." She pointed off into the distance, where Sloane could make out only a sliver of Georgina's red hair. "Come join us."

"I'm not sure. . . ." Sloane had been looking forward to a few hours of peace and quiet, something she would not be able to achieve in the presence of Georgina. "No offense or anything."

"For what it's worth, I think she's sorry." Hillary smiled genuinely and Sloane could tell she was taking her temperature on the situation. Just like Eddie.

"Georgina doesn't do sorry," Sloane scoffed.

"Maybe she does now. I mean, it has been a while."

"A while since what?" Sloane tilted her head to one side, ever the cynic when it came to Georgina's capacity for change.

"Since you've spent any real time with her." Hillary's tone was soft, but even-keeled. She was the kind of person who gave people the benefit of the doubt, saw the best when there was no best to be seen. And that included Georgina.

"That's the funny thing. It's so hard to spend real time with someone when they act the way she does." Sloane shrugged. Was she being too harsh?

"Well, at least keep me company. I barely know the girl and she never shuts up."

"That means she likes you." Sloane smiled now.

"Oh yeah?"

"Yup, if she didn't, she wouldn't bother."

"Lucky me." Hillary extended her hand to help Sloane to her feet. "Come on. I think she may have finally nodded off anyway."

"Fine. Under one condition, okay?"

"What's that?"

"You sit in between us. And hold me back from strangling her with my bare hands."

"That, my friend, I can do."

———

Just about an hour later, Sloane opened her eyes to find Hillary sitting next to her perusing a copy of *Good Housekeeping* and Georgina on the other side of her still fast asleep.

"Look who's alive!"

"Hey," Sloane croaked, stretching her arms above her head and rotating her neck in a circular motion to relieve the kinks. "How long was I out for?"

"Maybe forty-five minutes or so. It must be contagious." Hillary motioned to Georgina.

"Wow, she's still asleep? I guess being an enormous asshole can make a girl tired."

"You didn't hear her phone ringing in the middle of the night?"

"No, I must have been in a coma last night. There were two missed calls from Eddie when I woke up."

"I think it was around three or four in the morning. And it rang six times in a row. She must have heard, but she didn't answer it."

"That's Georgina for you."

"Is it? I almost went into her room to throw her cell out the window."

"Bummer you didn't. I'd have liked to see that."

"Do you think everything is okay with her? It's not the first time her phone has been ringing nonstop at night like that."

"I wouldn't give it a second thought." Sloane noticed Hillary's grave expression. "Seriously, this is Georgina we're talking about. It could be some guy she met at a bar in Paris. Or a friend who doesn't realize she's not in London. It's par for the course with her."

"Okay, whatever you say. You've known her a lot longer than I have." Hillary didn't appear to be convinced, but she dropped the subject regardless. "What would you think about renting a few of those tomorrow?" She pointed into the distance at two Jet Skis speeding across the lake.

"*You* want to drive a Sea-Doo?" Sloane knew she sounded dubious, but she couldn't help it. Hillary had never expressed an interest in anything even remotely athletic or thrill seeking before.

"Or ride on the back, whatever. I've never done it and it looks fun!"

"It definitely is." Sloane hesitated. "The thing is, I kind of set up a lunch for tomorrow."

"Oh, cool. Where are we going?"

"It's not exactly a *we* thing."

"That's fine." Hillary pulled a bottle of water out of her beach bag. "Want one? I brought extra."

"Sure, thanks." Sloane accepted it gratefully. As midday approached and the clouds began to scurry off, the heat from the sun's penetrating rays was growing more potent and her throat was parched. "It's Luke."

"Where?" Hillary looked around.

"No, not here. It's Luke, as in he's my lunch date tomorrow." She caught herself. "I mean, not *date*, but you know . . ."

"Okay. So maybe Jet Skiing another day?"

"Sounds like a plan." Sloane nodded, feeling relieved. Hillary wasn't going to pry. Or even gently press her for further details. And it wasn't a manipulative tactic on her part. It was just who she was. There to listen if you needed her, but not one to derive any pleasure out of beating the nitty-gritty details out of you in the way Georgina most definitely would have.

Quite honestly, she couldn't decide which approach would have been better for her in this situation. There was something very adult about being given the chance to remain reticent. And accepting it. But there was also something seductively indulgent about being badgered to divulge every last morsel of information and how you felt about it.

For example, if she'd revealed her lunch plans to Georgina, the litany of questions would have been launched immediately and continued rapid-fire style until either Georgina's insatiable curiosity had been quelled or Sloane had been drained dry of material. *When had she spoken to him? What had he said? How had he said it? Did he bring up lunch? Or did she? Where were they dining? At what time? What would she eat? What would she drink? What would she wear? Did she want Georgina to do her hair and makeup? What time would she be back? Was she excited? Nervous?* And so on and so on.

Never once would she ask if Sloane was feeling reluctant or, even less likely, guilty. Those two emotions were not on Georgina's radar and it occurred to Sloane, shockingly so, that—in this instance—she might be acting more like Georgina than herself.

"Excellent." Hillary smiled. "Should we start gathering our things and head back to the house for a bit? It's hot out here. And I'm getting hungry."

"Me too." Sloane gestured toward Georgina. "Care to wake the beast?"

"I'm up," Georgina rasped, rolling onto her back and then sitting up. "The beast, that is."

"Can you blame me?" Sloane couldn't even look at her.

"No, I can't." She massaged her temples. "I think I'm still hung-over."

"Not surprising." If it was sympathy she coveted, she could shove it you-know-where.

"I'm sorry," Georgina murmured.

"What was that? I don't think I heard you." It couldn't have possibly been an apology. Because as far as Sloane could tell, hell had yet to freeze over. The fat lady had yet to rock and roll.

"I said I'm sorry. Really, Sloane, I'm truly sorry." Georgina looked directly at her, maintaining eye contact and everything. "I was drunk and acted inappropriately. I didn't mean what I said."

"Do you actually remember what you said?"

"Some of it. The rest is a bit hazy." And then came the pièce de résistance. "Thank you for helping me upstairs and with everything else."

Sloane was almost speechless. "You're welcome."

"So can we all agree to move forward now?" Hillary interjected hopefully.

"I'm in if she is." Georgina piled her hair into a haphazard knot on the top of her head.

"Fine," Sloane relented. "Let's go home."

"Actually, I have a better idea. . . ." Georgina winked, jumped to her feet, and kissed Sloane forcefully on the cheek before racing off. "Last one to the car is a rotten egg!"

So much for Georgina's hangover, Sloane thought as her toes curled over the edge of the cliff and she stared down at the lake below. Far below them. She tried to estimate how deep the drop actually was before realizing that her calculations were only making her more anxious and slightly dizzy. Georgina had driven them directly to Dead Man's Cove without offering a clue as to where they were headed. She'd sworn on her good looks—vintage Georgina—that it would be both fun and exhilarating, which had sounded like just the antidote they all needed. "Trust me," she'd said. And—God knows why—they had. As it turned out, Georgina's definition of fun and exhilarating had remained unchanged for the last fifteen years, and Sloane's had not.

They'd been standing there—side by side—for ten minutes. First Georgina had tried to coax her gently. She'd asked things like, "Don't you remember how carefree it felt?" and "How many times have you done this before without a worry in the world?" In other words, without any consideration for the stark reality that she might crack her skull, or break her neck, or belly flop so badly that she'd be lucky to crack a rib at best. Not to mention that back then—"back in the good old days," as Georgina had referred to them—there'd been no Maddie to consider. Sloane was a mother now. And, in her mind, one of the main responsibilities that came with that title was not taking unnecessary or frivolous risks just for the sake of a fleeting thrill. Something Georgina could not comprehend.

"I can't." Sloane looked at Georgina, who was raring to go. And then back at Hillary, who'd already adamantly declared she was out. That it looked awfully dangerous.

"You can." Georgina nodded. "I'll go first as long as you promise to follow." She'd resorted to pushing, still gently, but pushing nonetheless. Georgina tilted her head down toward the water.

"No! Wait. . . ." Sloane closed her eyes and tried to silence her fear. "Wait a minute. I need a minute."

"You don't have to do it." Sloane felt Hillary's reassuring hand on her shoulder. "You have nothing to prove to us or yourself."

"I know." Sloane nodded. It was only the fifth time she'd said it. The thing was, part of her wanted to do it. A nagging part of her. She wanted Georgina to give her that nudge. And perhaps she did want to prove something to herself. And to Georgina. Was there anything so wrong with that? At the same time, her whole body was shaking like Shakira's hips.

"Sloanie. Take a deep breath. This is an adventure. A leap of faith. Literally. I've seen you do it many times before and you *can* do it again."

"Shit." She smiled at Georgina. "Okay. I think I'm ready."

"Take my hand." Georgina extended her arm. "We'll go on the count of three."

"I'm sorry, but I can't watch." This was Hillary. "I'll meet you at the bottom with warm towels."

"Let's do this." Sloane took Georgina's hand in hers. "You count."

"Okay. We go on three."

"Just get on with it."

"One . . . two . . . three!"

Without thinking, Sloane tightened her clasp on Georgina's hand and jumped, shrieking all the way down, until she felt the curl of her toes release as they broke through the cool, glassy tranquillity of the lake.

"That was amazing!" she called to Georgina once they'd come to the surface.

"I told you you could do it!" Sloane observed the pride in Georgina's eyes. Maybe she was being too hard on her. Maybe she'd failed to appreciate that these were the types of things Georgina excelled at. The escapades. The opportunities to push yourself to do something you wouldn't normally do, at least not at this stage in your adult life.

"Fuck, this water is cold."

"But it feels damn good, doesn't it?"

"It does." They both made their way to shore and onto the beach, where Hillary was racing toward them. Towels in hand.

"You guys are crazy!" She wrapped one towel around Sloane's shoulders and then another around Georgina's. "I can't believe you did that. I'm impressed!"

"Ahhhhhh." Sloane released a long sigh of relief. Relief that she'd taken the plunge. Relief that she'd survived it—physically and emotionally. But—most of all—that she had her friends by her side, the risk taker and the caretaker.

Now more than ever, she needed a dose of both.

chapter 15

Sloane sensed another presence in the room before Georgina spoke up and asked, "You're not really going to wear *that*, are you?" She'd placed her hands on the curves of her hips and arched a perfectly plucked strawberry blond eyebrow judgmentally.

"Why not? What's wrong with it?" Sloane glanced down at her outfit—a worn-in, somewhat-on-the-short-side jean skirt to complement the black tunic embroidered with white stitching she'd pilfered from Georgina's floor. "I found the top in your bedroom."

"Really?" She appeared legitimately surprised. "Well, you can have it, because it's ugly. And you look like a cross between Mother Teresa and Miley Cyrus."

"That's one I've never heard before." Sloane giggled.

"Don't get excited. It wasn't a compliment." Georgina sighed, as if dressing Sloane was as exasperating as wrestling a three-year-old out of his pajamas for the first day of preschool. "Take it all off and we'll start from scratch."

Sloane did as Georgina said, admittedly grateful—once again—for her friend's proficiency when it came to all things fashion and beauty. Areas that were not Sloane's expertise and most certainly not Hillary's. In fact, if Sloane had bothered to consult Hillary, she'd likely be walking out the door in a mishmash of Vineyard Vines and Lacoste, with a color-coordinated sweater set to match her monogrammed ankle socks.

It wasn't that Sloane had absolved Georgina for her atrocious behavior over dinner. Far from it. She had, however, given a lot of thought as to whether it was worth holding a grudge. And, if so, how long she could realistically do that while they were inhabiting the same house. Part of her longed to lay it all out on the table. Get it off her chest and tell Georgina how she'd felt when she didn't hear from her after Amy died. What then, though? Could she expect Georgina to see the error of her ways and apologize? Two days ago, Sloane would have said absolutely not. But then yesterday it was the oddest thing when Georgina had said she was sorry—granted, her remorse had been reserved strictly for her abhorrent behavior with Luke. She wasn't exactly expressing regret for anything else she'd done. Namely, the way she'd abandoned their friendship when Amy had been losing her battle with ovarian cancer. The fact that she'd been categorically missing in action before, while, and after Amy had succumbed to her illness. Or that not only had Amy's name yet to escape her lips in the near week they'd been in Lake George, but she hadn't so much as sent a condolence note to Sloane or her family either. And it wasn't like Amy died yesterday.

"That's Georgina for you," Sloane's mother had reminded her on countless occasions when Sloane's griping had grown repetitive.

"She's always been this way and she always will be. You just have to let it go."

Let it go. But hadn't that been what she'd been doing for the last fifteen years? Forgiving. Forgetting. And then forging forward with a relationship in which she wasn't sure she really knew her partner in crime anymore. She certainly hadn't expected an apology to be forthcoming from Georgina as soon as she arrived at Lake George, but a part of her had expected that they would have had it out by this point and cleared the air between them. Instead it continued to linger and color things between them so that their vacation still hadn't really gotten off on the right foot. Nor had it been the relaxing, stress-free getaway she'd imagined when her aunt had first suggested the house and before Georgina had decided to barge in on their plans.

Why did Georgina get one free pass after another? No one else was allowed to blurt out whatever came to mind at any given moment. And then be called charming. Above all, no one else could get away with treating her best friend like complete crap and then assuming she could join her on vacation. *That* was Georgina for you.

And Sloane was finally beginning to realize, after a decade and a half of being on the receiving end of Georgina's often selfish and imprudent behavior, that she didn't have to be a glutton for punishment anymore. That, in spite of everything, if the mouse continued to chase after the cheese, it would eventually get snapped by the trap. She was the mouse.

Then there were times like this—and, yes, they'd become fewer and farther between—when Georgina would refresh Sloane's memory as to why she'd fallen for her in the first place. Because, in many ways, that's what it felt like with Georgina. She wasn't someone you became friends with gradually. She was a heady force of exhilaration that, once you were vulnerable to it, you weren't sure if you'd ever be able to live without. Georgina was someone you fell in love with, even if it wasn't in the traditional romantic sense of the word.

The question was, did Georgina ever fall in love back?

If not, Sloane had been the one and only friend who'd come close.

"Now what?" Sloane stood practically naked in a tan T-shirt bra and matching neutral-colored underwear. Her hair was still damp from the shower and dribbling beads of cold water down her back. "I don't have that much time and I haven't even blow-dried my hair or done my makeup yet."

"You know I'm going to do that stuff." Georgina shooed away Sloane's concerns. "And I said take it *all* off."

"I did."

"The rest of it too, please."

"What? Are you trying to get in my pants?"

"You should be so lucky." Georgina smirked and then left the room, only to return moments later with a pair of white lacy thong underwear, a leopard-print push-up bra, and a gauzy turquoise dress. "Here. Put these on. You'll be girl next door on the outside with a little sex kitten underneath. It'll give you a boost of confidence. Trust me." Georgina cocked her head to one side, and it struck Sloane that sometimes Georgina still looked as innocent and young as she had on the day they'd met.

"I'm not wearing your underwear!"

"As if you've never done it before."

"That was different."

"Why? Was I cleaner in college?"

"Possibly."

"Oh, stop. Have I ever failed you before?" Georgina wagged her index finger. "Eh, eh, on second thought, don't answer that."

"Fine, but I'm going to look like a prostitute in this bra."

"That's the idea."

"To look like I should be standing on the corner of Forty-second Street?"

"First of all, hookers don't stand on the corner of Forty-second Street anymore."

"How do you even know that?"

"I don't." She shrugged. "I just think it's kind of obvious at this point, don't you?"

"G., I'm pretty sure hookers aren't trying to be discreet." Sloane slid her arms through the bra straps and Georgina fastened it for her. Then she slipped on the underwear and dress, which fell just above her knees.

"All women *try* to be discreet at first. Then they resort to hiking their skirts as high as they can go."

"You're disgusting."

Georgina disregarded her. "Now, let's get a look at you."

"I actually love this dress." Sloane twirled in a circle. "It's so not you, though."

"It's yours."

"You're giving it to me?"

"No, I mean it's yours. I stole it from you in college. Sorry. Haven't worn it since. You're right, it is so un-me. I have no idea what possessed me to pack it."

"I knew it looked familiar!" Sloane shook her head and laughed. "Do you think it's too dressy? I don't want to look like I tried too hard. You know?"

Sloane bowed her head, ashamed to admit to herself that she actually *was* trying too hard. And furthermore she knew Georgina didn't care, which was precisely why she could speak freely. Well, at least in part. After all, it was one thing for Georgina to realize that she wanted to look good for an ex-boyfriend and quite another for her to think that there were problems in Sloane's marriage to Eddie. As much as Sloane could admit to herself that things weren't perfect at home, she found in this moment that she really wasn't ready to admit it out loud. It seemed like that would make it too real, and she needed time to work out what she was really feeling toward her husband.

"I do know. Hold on a minute." Georgina skipped out of the room and returned again in a flash. "Wear these." She set a pair of casual but delicate beaded leather sandals at Sloane's feet.

"Ooh, gorgeous! Are these mine too?"

"Very funny. And no, they are not. I'll have you know I purchased them at a very posh shop in London. Well, Hugh purchased them for me, but whatever." Georgina's expression changed for a minute and then, just like that, the unfamiliar look that had crossed her face disappeared. "Anyway, I've never even worn them. So enjoy."

"Are you sure you don't mind?"

"Of course I'm sure."

"Thank you."

"It's the least I can do." Georgina smiled genuinely. "Now let's go spruce up the rest of you."

Twenty minutes later, with Georgina by her side, Sloane stood at the front door, her long brown hair cascading down her back in loose, beachy waves and subtly applied makeup highlighting her best features.

"I'll see you later." Sloane waved to Hillary, who was curled up on the couch in the great room reading the newspaper.

"See you later!" Hillary said, peeking out from above the travel section of *USA Today*.

"You look really beautiful, Sloane." Georgina fidgeted with a stack of what looked to be a dozen or so gold bangle bracelets dangling around her waifish wrist.

"Thanks to you."

"I had an easy subject." Unexpectedly, Georgina pulled Sloane into a hug. And then held her at arm's length, speaking softly so Hillary couldn't hear. "He's going to fall in love all over again."

Once she'd reached her destination, Sloane stopped in front of the menacing iron gates wound in climbing ivy and rolled down her window to press the call button.

"Welcome to Frog Hill Farm. How may I assist you?" A clear and competent female voice reverberated through the intercom, catching Sloane off guard.

"Oh, um, hi. This is Sloane Davis. For Luke Fuller." She cleared her throat. "We're scheduled to have lu—" Before she could finish her sentence, there was a loud buzzing sound and then the gates opened very gradually, giving way to a long, snaking driveway lined with trees, which led up a sharp incline to the main house.

Sloane zigzagged her way to the top, too anxious to really take note of the surroundings she remembered so fondly. The two guest chalets to the right, the six tennis courts to the left, and a nine-hole golf course off in the distance registered as a mere blip on her radar. Under other circumstances, she would have been imagining what it was like to have fifty undisturbed acres at one's disposal. It was a grueling problem to have.

She parked in the vast roundabout by the front door, which would have been plenty big enough for a game of tag football, if not for the elaborate center island in the shape of an F, for Fuller, featuring vibrant sprays of flowers. The landscaping at Frog Hill Farm could give the Luxembourg Gardens in Paris a run for their money. After getting out of her car, and upon closer examination, Sloane was able to identify African violets, alstroemeria, and aster. Calla lilies, carnations, and chrysanthemum. Daisies, dahlias, and delphinium. Not to mention hydrangea, peonies, roses, snapdragons, sunflowers, tulips, and all manner of tropical varieties that Luke's mother had probably had flown in from some of the most far-reaching estates around the world. Or at least her landscaper had. Nothing but the best for the Fullers. Even though they barely lived there. It was remarkable to Sloane, given that she was now raising a family of her own, that she'd never appreciated quite how much money the Fullers had or quite how irresponsibly they squandered it. The cost of their plantings alone could probably put Madeleine through college and graduate school.

Throwing back her shoulders and standing tall, Sloane walked up the front steps to the hulking white mansion and took a deep breath. Quickly and hopefully discreetly, she felt under one arm to make sure she hadn't perspired through her dress, and then she ran the fingers of her other hand through the waves in her hair one last time. Before she could even ring the bell to announce her presence for the second time, the door opened and an attractive blond woman, who by Sloane's hasty estimation didn't look to be a day over twenty-five, stood before her with her lips pursed into a thin line.

"Welcome to Frog Hill Farm." Sloane recognized her voice from the intercom. "Please come in."

"Thank you." Sloane smiled politely as she entered the grand foyer with its dark wood floors, polished antique furnishings, and stuffed deer heads mounted on the walls. There were knickknacks on every table. Knickknacks that, together, were quite possibly worth more than Sloane and Eddie's home in Brookline.

"I'm Serena. Luke's assistant." She extended her arm after introducing herself.

"I'm Sloane. Luke's . . ." She paused. "Friend. Old friend."

"I know who you are."

"Oh, right. Of course." So she'd been briefed. The question was, how much did she know about their history? "Wow, that's some handshake you have."

"Luke said it's very important in business."

"Did he, now?" Sloane smiled.

"Yes." Serena did not smile back. She just nodded definitively, as if anything Luke said was gospel. "Please follow me."

"Okay." Sloane trailed Serena through a wing of the house she was certain she'd never entered before and, finally, out onto the terrace, which was suspended on a cliff protruding from one side of the Adirondack Mountains and hovering over Lake George. To say the views were breathtaking would have been tantamount to calling the Grand Canyon a crevice.

On the far end of the terrace, there was a table set for two, undoubtedly with some of the Fullers' finest linens, china, and stemware. Serena led Sloane toward it and pulled out one of the chairs for her.

"Luke will be right with you. He's just finishing up a conference call." Serena quickly turned back in the direction of the house.

"You don't have to cover for him. He's really primping himself in front of the bathroom mirror, right?" Sloane laughed a little too boisterously.

"I assure you he's on a call. With Asia. I'll send Paulo out to take your drink order."

"Thank you." Sloane put on her best sober expression. Clearly, Serena took her job seriously. She was like one of those guards at Buckingham Palace in front of whom you could literally dance a naked jig with tassels on your exposed nipples and he still wouldn't crack even the teeniest, tiniest grin.

She wondered how many women Serena had walked through the exact same motions. Was it a weekly gig? Did some of them eat in the dining room? Or, God forbid, perched on barstools at the kitchen counter, if he ruthlessly decided he didn't like them after the first glass of wine? Was she any friendlier to the ones who returned for a second or third date? Did any of them come back? It was no secret that Luke's reputation wasn't exactly synonymous with the phrase "committed relationship."

Sloane thought about where she fit in the slew of women that Luke must have invited here over the years. Was he longing to catch up with an old friend, or was he perhaps looking for something more? She had to send off the right signals to make sure Luke didn't get the wrong impression from her. She needed him to view her as somewhere between undesirable and unattainable, she decided, until she felt his strong hands on her shoulders and his supple lips caress her cheek. "Hey, you." The warmth of his breath sent an electric shiver down her spine. "I'm really glad you could make it."

chapter 16

"May I present your first course?" A clean-cut young gentleman appeared at the side of their table balancing two small white bowls with metal covers—the kind you'd expect from room service at a swanky hotel.

"Yes, thank you, George." Luke nodded without disengaging his intense eye contact with Sloane.

"Excellent. We have a lovely chilled gazpacho with sliced grapes and almonds." He set the delicate porcelain tureens in front of them and lifted both tops at the same time in expert fashion. "Fresh ground pepper for the lady?" George wielded a large wooden mill over Sloane's soup.

"No, thank you. I'm fine." Sloane swiped her napkin off the table and laid it in her lap, as she noticed Luke had already done.

She'd been to Frog Hill Farm countless times the summer they met, but, given that they were in college at the time and Mr. and Mrs. Fuller were still in residence, at least in part, there'd been no

formal dinners complete with butler and waitstaff. In fact, when
Paulo had disappeared to fetch their drinks, she'd had no expectation that yet another person would arrive with a basket of bread and
that then a third person would be the one to deliver their food. It
seemed a little excessive, quite honestly, especially since Luke had no
reason to impress her. Sloane was keenly aware of just how much
money the Fuller family had. Well, maybe not *just* how much, but she
knew there was a whole lot of it. Enough to keep the next ten or so
generations in butlers and waiters.

"Sir?"

"Two twists. No more." George leaned over, following Luke's or-
ders to a T, and then made himself scarce.

Sloane couldn't help but speculate silently to herself whether
the whole lot of them—Serena, Paulo, George, the assembly of
nameless faces she'd spotted merely passing through the first floor
of the house—were off somewhere gossiping about who this new
girl was and what had brought her to Frog Hill.

Did they think Luke was a nice guy? Were they happy acting as
his faithful employees? Or did they bad-mouth him behind his back
and glower acrimoniously as soon as he left the room? More important, how did Luke treat them? If there was one thing Sloane's mother
had done right, it was to ingrain in her children the Golden Rule of
reciprocity.

Unlike so many other things her mother had taught her, specifically the religious lessons, the concept of doing unto others as you'd
have done to you had stuck with Sloane. To this day, she was fastid-
ious about being appreciative of those who worked for her in any
capacity, tipping them generously. And she never took out her frus-

trations on, for example, the woman behind the cash register at the supermarket, or Bob, the crossing guard at Madeleine's school. The latter, unfortunately, was a special kind of challenge, since Bob was not only slow but also grouchy and often downright rude. There'd been more than one occasion when Sloane had been forced to simultaneously bite her tongue and shoot Madeleine a warning glare to do the same.

"Two twists? I see someone's gotten particular in his old age," Sloane teased. "Let me know if there's a granule of pepper too many and we can swap."

"Can you blame a guy for knowing what he likes?" He waited for Sloane to take the first spoonful. "Go on. Let me know what you think."

"Didn't he say this was gazpacho?" Sloane looked down at the thick white liquid in her bowl.

"Yes. Why? Is there something wrong? I'm sorry, I should have asked your preferences before you came for lunch." Luke gazed out over the lake. "It's just that it's been quite some time. . . ."

"No, no. It's totally fine. Only, forgive me if I'm wrong, but isn't gazpacho supposed to be red?"

"You're right. Sort of. This is white gazpacho. Think of them like cousins. They share similar ingredients, except rather than tomatoes, this variety has bread, ice, almonds, and grapes."

"So you're a chef now too, huh?"

"Hardly. But I do know my way around the kitchen." His lips curled into a puckish grin. "Among other rooms."

"I remember." Sloane felt a blush slink up the back of her neck and warm her face.

"So, tell me how you are, Sloane." She delighted in the simple pleasure of hearing him say her name. The way it rolled off his tongue like he was whispering it to her in bed.

"I'm good. Really good."

"That's it?" He raised an eyebrow. "Fifteen years later and all you've got for me is 'good'?"

"Okay, well, I guess I'm married."

"You guess you're married?" he cut in, bantering playfully, the way they once had.

"You know what I mean." She cocked her head to one side and smiled. "Definitely married. To Eddie. And we have a nine-year-old daughter named Madeleine."

No visible reaction. Had Georgina told him that when they'd met in Paris? She kicked herself now for not even grilling Georgina on whether Luke had asked about her.

"And do you work?"

"Not anymore. I used to be a teacher."

"Admirable profession." He thought about this. "What makes you happy, Sloane?"

"What do you mean?" Had he not just heard her say she was a wife and mother? Did he think professional fulfillment was the only way to achieve true happiness? Or could he detect that something wasn't right in her life? She couldn't quite put it past him. To somehow have an instinctive understanding that she didn't feel whole. He'd always been able to read between her lines. To decipher the backstory behind the plot of her life.

"I mean what do you do for fun?"

"I don't know." She shook her head, realizing that it probably sounded entirely pathetic to him. The man who spent his days, weeks, and months globe-trotting from one continent to the next.

The thing was, no one had ever asked her that before. What was she supposed to say? Her definition of "fun" these days was when Eddie took Madeleine somewhere for the day so she could wake up late, eat brunch in front of the television in her pajamas, go for a manicure, and then sink her sleep-deprived body into a hot bath before being thrust back into the grind of everyday life. The variety with no servants on hand to attend to your every whim.

"Well, I think we need to fix that." Luke motioned to George to come remove their dirty dishes and utensils.

"Was everything to your liking, madame?"

"Oh, yes, thank you. Beyond delicious." George cleared her bowl and Sloane turned back to Luke. "I'll have to get the recipe from you." He didn't say anything. He just sat quietly, staring at her with a bemused expression.

"Your lobster salads will be out shortly. I'll send Paulo to refresh your drinks."

"Thank you so much." Sloane wondered if it would be gauche to slip George a twenty-dollar bill on the way out, quickly deciding that it definitely would be. Not to mention that he'd probably laugh at her. By Sloane's estimation George wasn't palming anything smaller than hundos.

"As I was saying . . ." She could feel Luke's eyes on her, watching as her gaze followed the path of a great blue heron landing on its stiltlike legs by the edge of the swimming pool. "Earth to Sloane."

"Sorry. They're just so beautiful. I've always loved their long necks and yellow bills."

"They have a six-foot wingspan."

"Really?"

"Would I lie to you?"

"I don't know. It's been a long time. Would you?" She looked at him, sitting across from her. Close enough to touch. But yet so far.

"Come out on my boat tomorrow with me."

"I can't." It was her gut response, though her heart was already lobbying against her refusal.

"Why not?"

"Because I'm here to spend time with my friends." *And because being around you is dangerous.*

"Bring them."

"Are you sure?"

"Am I sure?" He hesitated for only a brief moment. "If it means you'll have some fun, Sloane, then yes. I'm absolutely sure."

Sloane hadn't lingered long after lunch with Luke, promising to see him tomorrow for their boat ride. She'd returned home to an empty house, finding no indication of where Hillary and Georgina had gone or how long it would be until they got back. They couldn't have gotten too far, she had rationalized, given that Sloane had taken their only car. But then two hours had passed with no word until her cell phone had started to trill from within her purse. Assuming it was them, and therefore not bothering to consult caller ID, Sloane had answered to the sound of Eddie's petulant voice on the other end of the line. She'd felt her muscles immediately clench in response as she spoke into the phone.

"Where have you been? I've been trying to reach you all day." If he'd been annoyed, that would have been easier to digest. As it stood, his whining had served only to grate her nerves like fingernails dragging slowly across a chalkboard.

"Sorry, my ringer was off." Sloane had remembered switching it to vibrate right before Luke had walked out onto the terrace—the smallest voice in the back of her head telling her not to in the event, as unlikely as it was, that Madeleine might somehow need her. And the irreversible guilt that would result from being unreachable to her only child.

She'd consulted the clock and noticed it was already five, which meant it was happy hour. Instead of reaching for a bottle of wine, as she normally would have done, she'd grabbed the Absolut instead. "Is it something important?" There'd been a tangible coldness in her tone. He'd detected it too.

"No." How was it possible that one word, one syllable, could carry such a weighty burden?

Their conversation had continued in that manner for another few minutes. They'd touched on the weather. Again. Eddie had tried to parlay it into a lively conversation about what he should pack for the week after next, when they would *finally* be together again. But Sloane hadn't been in the mood to play along, so he'd swiftly, albeit reluctantly, dropped it, turning their idle chatter to the one thing he knew Sloane was always willing to talk about. Madeleine. Finally, and it couldn't have come soon enough for Sloane, they'd exchanged pleasant good-byes—sounding more like two strangers who'd shared an airplane flight than a husband and wife.

And then Sloane had refilled her glass, indulging in a bout of self-pity as she badgered herself with all the questions that had been plaguing her for the better part of the last year.

What if she'd chosen the wrong path in life? What if Eddie wasn't the right one for her? What if she'd come too far to turn things around? What would happen to Madeleine if she asked for a divorce? What would happen to her? What if Eddie was the one for her and she was just falling prey to temptation? Could one run forever? What if the grass was always greener until you found yourself barefoot in a mud puddle?

At that moment Georgina and Hillary burst in the front hall, laughing raucously, their noses and shoulders tinged cherry red from what appeared to be too much sun. Sloane bristled. Best of friends now, were they? They were prattling on at warp speed, so engaged with each other that neither of them even noticed Sloane sitting at the kitchen counter nursing a drink by herself until she cleared her throat.

"Oh, hey!" Hillary smiled. Her face was glowing and her blond hair was slicked back into a tight bun. She looked healthy. Radiant even. It was likely Georgina's aura rubbing off on her.

"Hey." Sloane swigged the shot of vodka in front of her and poured herself another.

"You didn't tell me this one was a wild woman." Georgina approached Hillary, wrapping an arm around her waist and drawing her close.

"I guess I didn't know." Sloane realized she sounded peeved, but couldn't help it.

"Oh, yes. First, we hitchhiked to Million Dollar Beach."

"You know that's not safe anymore, Georgina. You two should really have been more careful!"

"It was actually my idea," Hillary took credit, and Sloane watched Georgina light up, as if she'd found another worthy minion.

"Well, it's still dangerous," Sloane grumbled.

"You're right." Hillary nodded. "It was an old couple in a fancy Mercedes, so I thought I'd throw caution to the wind. They actually pulled over for us. The thumb was for effect."

"Seriously, Sloane. We could have easily taken them," Georgina insisted, biting into a ripe peach.

"Oh, really? What if they'd had a gun?"

"How much have you had to drink?" Georgina danced over to the cabinet, retrieved a box of table water crackers, and set them in front of Sloane. "Here, eat some of these."

"What are you, the drunk police now? That's rich." She tore into the sleeve of crackers and ate an entire cracker in one bite. "Happy now?" The excess crumbs tumbled out of her mouth.

"What has you so grumpy? Didn't lunch go well?"

"Lunch was fabulous. Perfect, actually." She was instantly defensive. Wouldn't Georgina just love it if things had gone awry with Luke? If the reason that Sloane was drinking alone in such a wallowing manner was due to the harsh reality that Luke had no use for her anymore? Not because Georgina wanted Luke for herself, but because it had always been difficult for her to stomach Sloane receiving more attention from any guy—hot or not. And seeing as it barely ever happened, you'd think she could throw her a bone every once in a while.

"Well, that's good. I think."

"It is good. Very good." Sloane downed more of the vodka.

"Easy there." This was Hillary.

"I'm just trying to get loooooosey-gooooosey. What's so wrong with that?" Sloane thought her words sounded a little slurred and the suspicion was confirmed when she saw Georgina and Hillary share a knowing look. "Ooh, Mom and Dad, are you going to punish me? Send me to my room without supper. No, no, dock my screen time. Or, wait, you're more like two mommies." She chortled. "That's what I should have done. Become a lesbian. Sooooo much less complicated."

"I don't think you just become a lesbian." Hillary laughed. "And I'm not sure if it's any less complicated."

"Yeah, yeah, yeah." Sloane pointed her finger in the air as if she was about to say something revolutionary. "You know what, Georgina? You're right. You're abso-fuckin-lutely right."

Instead of gloating, Georgina wore an expression of confusion. "Don't get me wrong, as I've been waiting almost twenty years for you to say that, but about what?"

"About marriage. What else?" Sloane nodded her head as if the statement were self-explanatory.

"Oh, sure. Of course. Refresh my memory."

"That it's bullshit. Marriage is Fucking. Bull. Shit." She slammed her glass on the counter, spilling most of the alcohol. "Oops."

"You don't mean that." Hillary wiped up the liquid with a paper towel. "Maybe it's best we take you up to bed."

"But I'm not tired!" Sloane protested. "The night is still young! Right, Georgina?"

"Right." Sloane saw Georgina wink at Hillary and thought about how lovely it would be to have such long, elegant eyelashes. "How about a little disco nap to give you a second wind?" Georgina helped

Sloane off the barstool, supporting her. "I'll wake you in a couple of hours. Okay?"

"Okay. Bye, Hill! See you later. Ooh, maybe we'll hitchhike into town tonight."

"That sounds like a fabulous plan," Georgina agreed, dragging Sloane up the stairs, one step at a time.

"G.?"

"Yeah?"

Sloane stopped. "I've really missed you."

"I've really missed you too, Sloane." Georgina kissed her clammy forehead and smoothed a few strands of hair out of her eyes. "You have no idea how much I've missed you."

chapter 17

Hillary coiled herself into a wooden Adirondack chair beside the small glass table on the back deck with a mug of steaming coffee in one hand and half of a toasted English muffin with butter and raspberry jam in the other. She set down her cup and spread the newspaper out in front of her before securing the sash around her robe so it wouldn't flap open in the morning breeze.

Inhaling deep breaths of the air eddying off the lake, she closed her eyes, and let every taut muscle in her body gradually slacken. Fifteen minutes after taking Sloane upstairs the previous night, Georgina had resurfaced to let Hillary know that she was going to remain in bed next to Sloane for a little while to make sure she was okay and didn't get sick. In truth Hillary had been looking forward to dinner out, but aloud she'd said she understood given the circumstances. Instead, she had decided to grill a piece of swordfish, toss a salad, pour herself an ample glass of red wine, and set a place for one out on the deck, where she now sat eating breakfast.

She'd needed time to think. To figure out exactly what she was going to say to Greg, if anything, when he arrived at the house the week after next. She couldn't very well avoid getting pregnant forever. Not without an explanation. But she also couldn't tell him that she'd been on the birth control pill throughout the entire three years they'd been trying to conceive. That every month when Greg's heart had plummeted to the floor in a shock wave of frustration and failure, she'd been lying directly to his distraught face. Going so far as to pretend that her own sense of defeat exceeded his and, further, apologizing for letting him down.

If she looked back at how she had gotten herself into this predicament, she had to admit that deceit had come alarmingly easy to her, which was both a surprise and a grave disappointment. She was the good girl, always had been. The one who'd scored straight As through high school and college. The one who'd never played hooky. Not even once. Perhaps she'd been a prude and sometimes judgmental, but also kind and honest. Always honest.

Of course Greg wasn't even the sort of husband with whom you had to resort to dishonesty. She knew plenty of wives who went to great lengths to hide credit card statements and receipts for yet another bag, pair of shoes, or piece of jewelry they didn't need—at least not by their spouse's estimation. She'd even heard of some women who refused to tell their significant others about the tens of thousands of dollars they sank into Botox injections, glycolic peels, and dermabrasion treatments. So what if they couldn't crinkle their foreheads with concern or if their eyebrows were frozen into a permanent state of curiosity? As long as they could hide the evidence, there was no chance of getting in trouble with their man.

For her part, Hillary had never concealed a purchase or service of any kind, though she wasn't exactly the type to splurge on over-priced shoes—red soles or not, if she could walk comfortably in them, she was perfectly content. Nor had she considered doing anything to her face beyond having the space above her lip waxed. She didn't own a Gucci or Louis Vuitton purse or wear any jewelry outside of her simple rose gold wedding band and the chip of a diamond solitaire engagement ring Greg had presented proudly on bended knee in front of an IHOP in Tampa, Florida. He'd wanted to fly her to Paris, he'd said, but it'd turned out that airfare to the Sunshine State was substantially less expensive than to the City of Light.

Still, when it came to one of the most important milestones in their life, Hillary had, without much thought past desperation, betrayed the trust of the person she loved most in the entire world. A man who had sat at her grandmother's deathbed, pressing cold compresses onto her forehead. How could Hillary look at herself every day in the mirror knowing exactly what she was doing?

She was a monster. And the worst kind of monster at that. The kind who appeared to be pure and innocent on the outside but, beneath the angelic facade, carried a corrosive secret that could severely impact the lives of those she held closest. She knew what the ramifications could be if he ever found out. Or if she summoned the nerve to come clean. Above all, she knew how damaging her actions were. If she kept this up, they would lose something irreplaceable between them.

Yet, despite knowing this for some time now, she still hadn't been able to tell him. What if he left her? What if he walked out the door, so repulsed by her duplicity that he couldn't stand to inhabit the same space for another second? Would it have all been worth it? She couldn't bear the thought of losing him. Above all, she loved her husband. And she wanted to be honest with him. She just didn't know if she was ready to bear his children.

And to think that Sloane might be in a different predicament altogether. Hillary had seen the way she'd gazed at Luke adoringly over dinner. The way her eyes widened every time someone muttered his name. Not to mention the way she'd looked yesterday before heading out to meet him for lunch. In all the years they'd known each other, Hillary had never seen her make such an obvious effort with her appearance.

The worst part of all was that she'd judged her. She could admit it now. Not aloud, but silently. Hillary had actually patted herself on the back for never having been tempted, as Sloane clearly was, by another man. What a joke. When was the last time she'd heard about a couple divorcing over a shared meal with an ex-boyfriend? Then why was Hillary so quick to throw stones? Did she want Sloane to make a misstep? Perhaps to fall guilty of a greater indiscretion than she was making? It had never been Hillary's style to profit from her friends' transgressions. She was beginning to wonder if she knew who she was anymore.

"Hey there." Georgina's appearance out on the deck inadvertently intruded on Hillary's brooding, but she was ready to welcome the distraction from her morose thoughts. "It's chilly out here." Georgina tugged at the edge of her black silk chemise, constructed of barely enough material to cover her rear end.

"It's early yet. The weatherman said it would be a blistering ninety by noon."

"Yikes. Maybe not a beach day, then." She slouched into the chair next to Hillary and then curled her body into a ball and hugged her knees to her chest.

"Any word from Sloane?" Hillary nudged her plate with the other half of the English muffin toward Georgina, who scrunched her nose and shook her head.

"Not even a stir."

"How long were you in bed with her last night?"

"Until about three." Georgina poached Hillary's coffee mug and helped herself to a sip without asking. Hillary wasn't sure when they'd gotten to that place, but apparently they had.

"That was nice of you."

"Least I could do, don't you think?"

"I guess." Hillary tilted her head back to face the sun, which was just exposing itself from behind a dense blanket of clouds. "So, what do you make of the marriage stuff?"

"What?" Georgina laughed derisively. "Her 'marriage is bullshit' diatribe?"

"Yeah, why?"

"Nothing. I make absolutely nothing of it."

"Really?" Hillary was caught off guard by Georgina's flagrant disregard for Sloane's outburst. After all, hadn't Sloane declared that the very institution she'd shaped her life around had suddenly become complete crap?

"Really. Sloane's all talk. She's madly in love with Eddie. God knows why."

"You don't like Eddie?"

"Oh, no, I adore Eddie. He's just massively boring."

"Huh." Hillary considered this. "I've never thought of him that way."

"Anyway, it doesn't matter what I think. Eddie and Sloane are the golden couple. They always have been."

"And what about Luke?"

"Ah, yes. Luke." Georgina took a deep breath and then exhaled. "I suppose he's the eternal question mark."

"Are you guys talking about me?" Sloane slid open the screen door and walked outside, hovering over them with her arms folded across her chest and the hint of a scowl contorting her ashen face.

"Whoa, nice eyes." Georgina squinted to get a better look. "I'd slap some cucumbers on those babies."

"What's wrong with them?"

"They're just a little puffy." Hillary pulled out a nearby chair and patted the seat so Sloane would join them. "How are you feeling?"

"I've been better." Hillary couldn't help but notice that, in addition to Sloane's swollen eyes, her overall skin tone was the palest shade of green and when she caught sight of the remains of the English muffin on the table, she looked as if she might lose her lunch. From the day before. "Don't try to change the subject. I heard my name and Luke's mentioned in the same sentence."

"Someone woke up on the wrong side of the bed." Georgina took another sip of Hillary's coffee, which she'd apparently commandeered as her own.

"Forgive me, but I believe I drank an entire bottle of vodka."

"If you'd had an entire bottle of vodka, you'd be dead." Georgina rolled her eyes.

"Excuse me."

"Georgina stayed in your room with you almost all night to make sure you were okay." Hillary thought Sloane should know, even though she didn't seem to be in a grateful sort of mood.

"Thank you." She acknowledged the considerate gesture verbally, but there was no sign of gratitude in her expression. Not even the slightest smile. "So?"

"So what?" Georgina dropped her long, tanned legs to the ground and sat up straight.

"So what were you saying about me?"

"It was really nothing." Hillary diverted her attention to the gentle waves lapping up on the shore of the lake.

"Well, that's not true because I heard both my name and Luke's with my own two ears."

"You got a little chatty in your drunken stupor last night. That's all." Georgina cackled a little too loudly. "God knows it's happened to the best of us."

"What did I say?" Hillary saw her expression morph into one of palpable concern. Was she hiding something? Trying to rack her brain to recall what she'd spilled aside from the vodka?

"Nothing important," Hillary cut in. There was no reason to douse her open wound with salt.

"Georgina?"

"Hillary's right. It really was insignificant."

"Then if it was so trivial, just tell me, for God's sake!" There was a note of desperation in her voice.

"Fine." Georgina shrugged. "You said you agreed with me that marriage is bullshit."

"Oh." Sloane sat quietly, noticeably confused. And, most likely, trying to piece together the puzzle of the previous night. Unfortunately, thanks to her excessive drinking, a few of those pieces clearly had gone missing from her memory and were unlikely to resurface.

"I suppose you also don't remember insisting that you wanted to go out by way of hitchhiking into town?"

"Not really." Sloane pressed her fingertips to her temples, massaging them in a circular motion. Hillary could tell she was hurting, physically and emotionally. This getaway had definitely brought out a very different side of Sloane.

But wasn't that always the case the first time you traveled with a friend you'd never done more than share a lingering dinner or spend an afternoon with? People's true colors could easily be dulled for a few hours, but not when you were staying in the same house with them for three weeks. In truth, Hillary had expected to grow even closer to Sloane during the time they spent together at her aunt's lake house, but given the secrets each woman seemed to be concealing, it felt as if there was an insurmountable distance growing between them.

"Well, I wouldn't worry about it. Certainly neither of us took it seriously," Hillary hastened to reassure her. "We know you're crazy about Eddie and vice versa."

"Right. Yeah." Sloane nodded, clearly distracted. "Of course I am. Eddie is the best." Her smile was forced.

"Well, now that that's settled, what do you girls want to do today?" Georgina twisted her body to one side and then the other. "One more cup of coffee and I'll be raring to go."

"I forgot to mention, Luke invited us out on his boat." Sloane stretched her arms above her head. "Well, maybe 'forgot' isn't the right word. More like, I was too wasted to remember."

"That sounds amazing." Hillary welcomed the chance to get to know Luke better. So far, he just seemed like a reasonably nice, entitled rich guy, with a killer body and a movie star mug. Not that there was anything wrong with those attributes. But she was pretty sure she knew Sloane at least well enough to infer that there was much more to him than that. Otherwise Sloane wouldn't still be hooked after so much time had passed since they had dated.

"Are you sure he wants all of us?" Georgina asked dubiously.

"That's what he said."

"Well, then I'm in." Georgina clapped her hands together.

"Me too," Hillary agreed.

"Cool. I'm going to shower. See if I can wash the remnants of last night away." Sloane stood up and started heading into the house.

"Cucumbers on the eyes!" Georgina called after her, just as her cell rang from inside.

"Do you need to get that?" Hillary questioned. Her suspicion that something was up with Georgina had only intensified over the last few days.

"Nah. If it's important, they'll call back." Which is exactly what they did. Two times in rapid succession. And each time, Georgina pretended as if she didn't hear it, while Hillary feigned reading her newspaper until she couldn't take it anymore.

"If you're not going to get it, I am."

"No!" Georgina protested with a jerk of her body, and then collected herself. "It's probably just a wrong number." Her phone rang again and she shot up out of her chair and ran into the house.

Once Georgina was out of sight, Hillary crept toward the door, overhearing only a snippet of what Georgina was saying before returning to her seat. There was someone whom she wanted to stop bothering her and he wasn't taking the hint. That was for sure. Hillary wondered if she was in some kind of trouble. Could she have broken up with someone who refused to accept that things were truly over? Now that they'd become more friendly, she wondered whether Georgina might be willing to let her help with whatever it was that was so urgent.

"I was right." Georgina walked back onto the porch, attempting a smile.

"About what?" Hillary could see the strain on her face.

"It was the wrong number."

chapter 18

For Sloane, there had been three major defining moments in her life. The kind of moments that shape who you are—for better or for worse. Either the ones that evoke unadulterated joy . . . or the ones that blindside you with a searing sucker punch, flattening you to the ground like a flapjack.

The most recent of these defining moments was the day her sister had called with her terminal diagnosis. Before that, there was the instant she'd laid eyes on Madeleine nine years ago. And earliest of all was the first time she'd kissed Luke. *Really* kissed him.

She hadn't expected to feel the prodigious swell of emotions with Maddie. Sure, all of her mommy friends had vowed that there was nothing like cradling your newborn baby in your arms. Nothing like finally getting to meet the tiny human being who'd been growing inside you for forty long weeks and booting your stomach with a passion that seemed highly unrealistic for a five-pound fetus. They'd told her to anticipate that she'd be laughing boisterously one minute and weeping excessively the next over nothing more than a fabric softener commercial. That the fact that her midsection would still be bloated and her cankles would remain in full force weeks later, and she wouldn't sleep for the next, say, five to ten years, wouldn't matter at all. Because every hushed breath Maddie took would be reason enough to throw a ticker tape parade. And nothing else—absolutely nothing else—would seem remotely important. How could it, by comparison?

Sloane had nodded more vigorously than she'd felt like doing each time one of her friends had imparted such hard-earned wisdom. Regardless, until she'd experienced it for herself, she'd had no point of reference. But sure enough, as soon as she'd held her own baby in her arms, the feelings had been just as strong and overwhelming as everyone had predicted.

It was similar, just at the opposite end of the emotional spectrum, when Amy had phoned her on that sunny Saturday afternoon. She'd never forget how perfect a day it had been. Madeleine had woken up extra late, at nine thirty, allowing Sloane and Eddie to sleep in. They'd gone to breakfast at the diner, savoring thick cuts of French toast made from challah bread and drenched in warm maple syrup. Then they'd driven over to Eddie's parents' house, where Madeleine and Eddie had splashed around in the pool, while Sloane had reclined on a lounge chair, flipping through the latest copy of *Vogue* and touching up her hot pink pedicure. She'd felt so lucky.

They'd gotten home around five, all three of them blissfully exhausted and famished. Eddie had pulled three steaks out of the refrigerator, seasoning them in preparation for the grill, and Madeleine, ever his dutiful sous chef, had been chomping at the bit to shuck four ears of corn—one for each of them and a spare in case anyone wanted seconds. Sloane had been preparing to toss a big salad and mix a pitcher of iced tea with fresh mint when the phone had rung. She'd seen Amy's number on their caller ID and had picked up immediately, raring to tell her how impressed she'd been with Maddie's backstroke. Maddie had been struggling with it at camp, and just two weekends earlier, Amy—who'd always been a remarkably strong swimmer, unlike Sloane—had worked fastidiously with her on perfecting it.

"You're amazing!" she'd answered without saying hello. There was no need for introductions between the two of them.

"Oh yeah? Why's that?" Amy had sounded different. Weaker.

"Madeleine's backstroke is so much better. Can I hire you?" Sloane had laughed uncomfortably, sensing straightaway that something was off.

She'd already known about the lump the doctor had found on Amy's uterus during a routine pelvic exam. She'd also been aware of the stomach pain Amy had been withstanding in addition to her loss of appetite and the fact that she was suddenly running to the bathroom constantly. But when Amy had told her all that, she'd also made it very clear that the doctor had said, "Most lumps are not cancer." And, further, her doctor had gone on to advise her that even if it did turn out to be malignant, since Amy was young and healthy, she would be an excellent candidate for a minimally invasive laparoscopic procedure to remove the tumor. Although that initial diagnosis had felt surmountable, Sloane had quickly come to despise the words "procedure" and "tumor." After what Amy had endured,

Sloane now recognized the dire significance behind them. The dire significance she'd initially managed to rebuff.

"While I'd love the job, I don't think I'll be up for it given the circumstances." There'd been a quiver in Amy's voice, and without warning, hot bulbous tears had started rolling down Sloane's cheeks. Even before her sister had broken the terrible news. "Please don't cry."

She'd held her breath through the rest of their conversation. Or at least it had felt that way. She listened to everything Amy had said. How the cancer had spread. How there was nothing they could do. How she planned to enjoy every minute of the time she had left. Two months at most. A mere sixty days to jam half a lifetime of experiences into. Half a lifetime of "I love you's."

Although Sloane had never before experienced pain like the untimely loss of her sister, it was concern for her brother-in-law and their three kids that still kept her up at three in the morning. Their faces haunted Sloane's sleepless nights. Amy had been everything to those kids. The one who always woke them up with a wide smile and always put them to bed as well, pecking them on their tender little noses. She was the proud mom on the sidelines at all of Carter's soccer games, cheering louder than anyone else. She was the only person whom Ella would even look at when she was sick. Carter, Ella, and baby Jane would have one major defining moment in their lives: the day they lost their mother.

She'd thought about Luke after Amy had died. About their first kiss. Not because she'd wanted to be with him or because she'd expected him to even remember Amy. They'd met only once. But because she'd wanted to transport herself back to a very specific space in time when she'd been unconditionally happy. A sensation she was certain she'd never be able to capture again. A sensation that had expired along with Amy.

And now here she was, over a year later, hopeful that—what? Luke would be able to revive her? To bring her back to life?

"That was fast." Hillary walked into the kitchen, where Sloane had been lost in solitary contemplation for the past few minutes, and set a small monogrammed beach bag on the counter.

"Greg says I can be showered, dressed, and out of the house in six minutes!" She laughed. "Not quite, but you know I'm no fuss."

"Yes, I do. I wish I could look as good as you do with so little fuss." Sloane picked at her blueberry muffin.

"That's sweet. But you look especially pretty."

"Thanks." Sloane had applied the sheerest coat of makeup and pulled her hair into a slick chignon, throwing a gauzy cover-up over her favorite and most flattering purple bikini. "It took a while for my eyes to de-puff."

"And it looks like you've got your appetite back."

"Marginally." She was still somewhat queasy from her drinking binge the night before. "I figured I should eat a little something before jumping on a boat."

"Good idea. Hope you don't get seasick."

"Nah, I have a stomach of steel. What about you? I didn't even think to ask, sorry."

"Same as you. But I brought some ginger pills just in case."

Sloane grinned.

"What?"

"Of course you did! You always think of everything. Especially since you didn't even know we'd be going out on a boat."

"I try." Hillary riffled through her tote. "I also have about ten kinds of sunscreen in the event anyone needs some."

"I have no doubt. And this is precisely why you're going to make a great mom."

"You think?" Hillary stopped what she was doing and turned to Sloane.

"I don't think. I know." Sloane smiled. "You were made for the job."

Three hours later, Sloane was perched flat on her stomach on the back deck of Luke's boat, detoxing in the scorching sun. As she and Hillary and Georgina had walked the length of the dock, speculating about which boat was the *Edwina*, named for Luke's mother, Hillary had first pointed to a forty-foot Formula and squealed, "Oooooh! I hope it's that one."

Then Georgina had signaled to a Cobalt of the same size, with a sparkling blue stripe bursting down both sides, and shrieked, "No, *that* one! It looks faster."

Sloane, knowing better, had smirked, motioning toward what could only be referred to as a hulking yacht, and said, "I'm going to hazard a guess that that's our ride, ladies." And right she had been.

With no less than a dozen in staff on hand to anticipate their needs, the *Edwina* stood taller and larger than most mansions on land. Of course she'd have expected nothing less from the Fullers, who always had to have the biggest and best of everything.

They'd been greeted and assisted aboard by Luke's assistant, Serena, who'd been equally frosty as when Sloane had first met her at Frog Hill Farm. She'd dressed in a white skirt suit with navy trim.

Georgina had commented that she hoped it was tear away, in the manner of male stripper pants, and that Serena had an itsy-bitsy string bikini on underneath. Sloane and Hillary had giggled. Serena had not. And, since that time, Sloane had noticed that Serena was going out of her way to avoid Georgina when at all possible. She was either intimidated by her, offended by her, or ferociously jealous of her. Or all of the above. Naturally, that was par for the course when it came to Georgina and other women. Sloane almost felt sorry for Serena. She would have, if only she'd been a bit nicer when they first met.

"What are you doing back here all by yourself?" Hillary crawled up onto the raised deck beside her, and Sloane rolled onto her back, tipping her wide-brimmed straw hat to shield her face from the sun.

No more wrinkles, thank you. Her dermatologist had already informed her of the irreversible damage she'd done in her teens and twenties. It seemed so unfair. If she'd known back then what she knew now, she would have worn sunscreen every day and taken more care to avoid direct, prolonged exposure. At least she thought she would have. Her seventeen-year-old self might not have seen the writing on the wall, even if someone had spelled it out for her in boldface. After all, teenage girls had far more important things to concern themselves with than crow's-feet. Such as teenage boys.

"Just relaxing." Sloane gave her a big smile before closing her eyes. If she was being honest, Georgina and Hillary and Luke had been engaged in such a boisterous conversation that she hadn't felt they would miss her if she rested for a while in another spot. Was she peeved that her friends were monopolizing her ex-boyfriend on an excursion she had invited them on? It was true they had commandeered Luke's attention for close to an hour. Still, she needed to grow up before they accused her of a case of jealousy more appropriate for a teenager than a married, middle-aged mom.

"I hear you." Hillary lay down carefully, parallel to Sloane, and exhaled. "I can't get over this boat. And what a gorgeous day. Really perfect, Sloane. Thanks for making it happen."

"You have Luke to thank."

Sloane knew Hillary would detect her curt tone, but she found she couldn't help it. She wasn't even irritated at Hillary. It was just that she'd imagined the day going differently. She'd imagined it being her and Luke. She wasn't sure why, what with Hillary, Georgina, and the twelve silent but present employees roaming around and materializing to refresh your drink, towel, or whatever when you least expected them to. She'd barely seen Luke, save for their hug and chaste peck on the lips when he'd welcomed them. They'd locked eyes twice, but that was it.

"Oh, believe me, I already did." Hillary sat up and took a healthy swill of chilled sparkling water. "I like him. He's a charmer, huh?"

"You could say that." Sloane's lips pursed into thin line.

"Is everything okay?" Hillary's expression was one of sincere concern.

"Fine." Sloane sat up too. "Have you seen the way Georgina's been throwing herself at him?" She rolled her eyes.

"I hadn't noticed." Hillary set her glass down. "Is it bothering you?"

"Me? Why would it bother me?" She was instantly defensive.

"I don't know, because he was your boyfriend." Hillary smiled. "It would be completely natural, by the way."

"I just think it's tacky, that's all. And she's obviously doing it to get under my skin."

"You think?"

"You don't?"

"Actually, no." Hillary shrugged. "I'd say it's got way less to do with you and more to do with her unquenchable demand for attention. I think it's just who she is. As I've told you before, Georgina is a textbook case."

"Kind of ironic, since I don't think she's ever actually opened a textbook!" Sloane laughed. "You know what? I'm about ready to head home. It's only getting hotter out here."

"You do know there's thousands of square feet of indoor space on here? And it's air-conditioned."

"Yeah. Still, I'm ready to go." She'd had quite enough of stewing at Georgina, whether her obvious flirting with Luke was calculated or not.

"Sure, let's head up and grab Georgina." Hillary stood up and held out a hand.

"If we can tear her away."

Thirty minutes later, after the boat had turned back toward shore and docked and after another virtuous hug and kiss from Luke, they were packed up and prepared to return to a less luxurious lifestyle.

"Bye, dolls!" Georgina flung herself on Luke in an enveloping hug and then waved to the crew, tendering a gratuitous flash of her barely covered rear end for the umpteenth time.

"Thank you so very much again for your graciousness." Hillary shook Luke's hand. "It was a real treat."

"It was my pleasure." Luke smiled magnanimously and then ducked back inside while Carlos, the captain's assistant, helped Georgina and then Hillary off the *Edwina*.

Just as Sloane was about to offer Carlos her hand to do the same, Serena came up behind her.

"Excuse me, Sloane?" She tapped her arm forcefully with one pointed, bony finger.

"Yeah?" Sloane turned around.

"Luke asked me to give this to you." She held out a small white envelope.

"Oh, thank you." Sloane took it from her, tucked it into her bag unread, and followed her friends to shore.

chapter 19

Sloane put off reading the note until they'd arrived back at her aunt's house, so she could retreat to the shelter of her bedroom for complete privacy. She even locked the door for fear that Georgina might burst in unannounced. Or that Hillary would come knocking. She needed solitude. Silence. Time to disown the immature petulance that had been plaguing her all day.

What was wrong with her? She'd never been this readily provoked. Quite the opposite. Sloane had always prided herself on her level temperament. When Maddie was a toddler, she'd been alarmed at how so many of the mothers on the playground would harangue their two- and three-year-olds for sullying their brand-new sneakers with mud or, God forbid, getting their hands dirty in the sandbox. Little did said mothers know that the minute they bowed their perfectly coiffed heads to tap out texts on their iPhones, Junior was not only cupping the sand, but also partaking in a gritty snack.

It wasn't that Sloane never got annoyed with Maddie. She knew she wasn't a perfect mother by any margin. There were those days when they were racing out of the house to make it to school on time and she snapped at her for dawdling. Or nights when Maddie was being exasperatingly obstinate about going to sleep and Sloane would be forced to use her firm voice. She was human, after all. But, still, she much preferred to go with the flow as her parenting strategy. Easy breezy. Sloane was always the first to jump in and help out a friend at the eleventh hour without expectation of a quid pro quo—whether it was assisting with the car pool or dropping off a heat-and-eat dinner when the friend or the kids were under the weather. It was how she'd been raised. Do unto others . . . and do it without complaining.

But this time at the lake—and noticing how easily Georgina and Hillary got on her nerves—had shown her that ever since Amy died, things had been different. Her inherent generosity had been dwindling. Somehow the chip on her shoulder against the world at large had hollowed into a cavernous chunk. The dynamic with Georgina certainly wasn't helping, especially since she was the only person who'd been able to really get under Sloane's skin in the first place. But how had she lost such an inherent part of herself? Sloane wondered whether her sister would even recognize the hardened person she had become since her death.

To add insult to injury, her inscrutable feelings for Luke weren't going anywhere either. If anything, she was feeling more drawn to him each time she saw him. All she knew was that she felt like she owed it to herself to sort out her feelings about Luke and Eddie in order to come out whole on the other side. And she wasn't exactly sure how to accomplish that.

As she sat on her bed, propped against a stack of downy white pillows, gripping Luke's note, she couldn't decide whether she was ready to open it. What if it said he never wanted to see her again? He had been distant on the boat. Somehow in all of this he had come to represent the possibility that she could overcome the tumult she currently felt immersed in. Would she be able to endure the sudden descent back to reality if he made himself scarce? On the other hand, if she didn't read it, she'd never know. The suspense held more promise than the probable result, as it so often did.

Sloane unsealed the envelope with her finger, nicking it on the fine edge of the front flap. "Shit." She extinguished the speck of blood with her tongue, then pulled out the ecru-tinted card made of thick, expensive-looking stock and emblazoned with Luke's bold-faced navy blue monogram. "LHF." Luke Henry Fuller. It immediately took her back to how many times over the course of that long-ago summer she had considered the moniker "Sloane Fuller." And she was mortified by how quickly it rolled off her tongue once more.

S,

Please meet me tomorrow at sunset. At our place. Come alone.

—L

She held the note close to her heart, closed her eyes, and released the quietest yelp of delight she could manage. The last thing she wanted was for either Hillary or Georgina to overhear her and inquire what had prompted her giddy exclamation. Then she placed the card in the drawer of her nightstand and returned downstairs to her friends.

Anyone familiar with the Fuller family and their waterfront property knew that if you were coming from the main house, there were various paths leading to the beach, even a few winding staircases. After all, the home was set atop the highest occupied bluff within twenty miles. However, Sloane would hazard a guess that most people didn't know there was a back way to sneak down there—at least she hoped it was still there.

As Sloane drove her car into the parking lot of a small, infrequently visited local beach about a mile away from the entrance to Frog Hill the following day, she checked her reflection in the mirror. She'd decided to go au naturel for this, their fourth meeting since she'd arrived in Lake George, though it felt like she'd barely seen or spoken to Luke in any significant way, save for their brief lunch. More to the point, she didn't have much of a choice, given that she hadn't told Georgina or Hillary where she was going.

Of course they'd asked as she'd prepared to leave the house. She hadn't mentioned any solo plans before receiving Luke's note. But she'd just said that she was meeting up with an old friend of her aunt's who had called the night before, and, fortunately, neither of them had asked to come. Actually, Sloane had been surprised that Georgina hadn't badgered her at all. If she hadn't been so pleased, she might have been suspicious.

At various points during the past twenty-four hours, she'd considered not showing up. Or at least she'd told herself she was considering it. For one thing, did Luke think she had nothing better to do than jump at the chance to see him? Further, wasn't it sort of presumptuous of him to assume she was readily available? It was the point of the matter.

Then she'd asked herself why she was playing hard to get when she wasn't even available to be gotten, and that had been all the justification she'd needed to convince herself to meet him. That coupled with the knowledge that Luke didn't like games. Funny, since his penchant for passing notes might have come off that way to anyone else. To someone who wasn't as intimate with the mechanics of his mind. But not Sloane. She was well aware that if Luke wanted something, he asked for it. And if he felt something, he expressed it. Hard to get wasn't part of his repertoire, nor was it a device he engaged in with others.

Sloane pushed her car door shut and snuck through a barely visible clearing behind a menacing barrier of rocks meant to deter interlopers from doing exactly what she was doing. She slipped off her sandals, holding them in one hand and the bottom of her billowing white maxi dress in the other, and walked about a quarter of a mile down the beach to their spot—a secluded enclave that was roughly another quarter of a mile from Frog Hill Farm, even though all of it was the Fullers' property.

Luke wasn't there yet, but there was already a picnic basket and a blanket, which Sloane sat down on, burying her bare feet in the sand in front of her. She couldn't help but wonder if Serena had set it up. Such a romantic scene. Had she been vexed while doing so? For some strange reason the thought of it gave Sloane a rise of satisfaction. There weren't many men who would pick her over the Serenas of the world these days, with their silky blond hair, chiseled physiques, and eager, unlined faces. For a moment, she wondered whether Serena was aware that Sloane was married. Probably. From what she'd observed, Serena's wealth of knowledge was vast.

Sloane closed her eyes and let the breeze off the lake pirouette around her like a prima ballerina.

"Hello, beautiful." Sloane opened her eyes to find Luke standing in front of her in a pair of threadbare khakis, rolled at the ankles, and a wrinkled white linen shirt. What? There was no one to iron his clothing?

"Hey." She moved over to make room for him on the blanket.

"I'm glad you came." He kissed her gently on the cheek.

"Did you have any doubt?"

"Truth?"

"Always."

"Then no." He gave her a soft smile.

"Thanks!" Sloane laughed. "I guess I'm just that easy." Luke was quiet. "Is everything okay? You seemed a little distant on the boat yesterday."

"It's Teddy." Luke hung his head.

"Oh." Sloane couldn't find the right words. She knew if it was Teddy, it likely wasn't anything good.

"I'd just learned that he left rehab." He exhaled and the entire upper half of his body hunched over, as if the burden of his brother were weighing on him both literally and figuratively.

"Again?"

"This would be the tenth time he's done it." He looked up at her with bloodshot eyes.

"He's been in rehab ten times?"

"Thirteen. But only three have been successful." He shook his head. "Well, not entirely successful, obviously, but at least he stayed to finish the program."

"Wow, I'm really sorry to hear that."

Teddy was Luke's younger brother by a year. He too was rakishly handsome. Too smart for his own good. And a genuinely good guy—when he wasn't drinking excessively and snorting too much cocaine. On those occasions he was not nice. At all.

Unfortunately, Sloane had been on the receiving end of one of his drunken diatribes that summer in college. He'd called her "one of Luke's whores," which had ignited a fistfight between the brothers, culminating in a broken nose for Teddy and a severely bruised hand for Luke. Apparently it hadn't been the first time it had happened. The only difference was, Sloane had stuck around, where the other girls had not. She'd sat with Luke all night, tending to his wounds, both external and internal. He'd said she was the first woman who'd ever seen him cry.

The next day, they'd driven Teddy to a rehab facility in Connecticut. He'd checked himself out a week later. And, for three weeks, no one had been able to find him. Until one Sunday morning when he'd ambled through the front door of Frog Hill saturated with liquor and as high as the Empire State Building. Luke had wanted to kick him to the curb, but Sloane had convinced him to let Teddy stay. Then she'd taken it one step further and drawn him a bath and put him to bed, leaving a glass of water on his nightstand. Luke had said he would never forget what she'd done for Teddy and for him.

"Not as sorry as I am," Luke exhaled.

"What are you going to do?"

"Nothing."

"Nothing?"

"What can I do, Sloane? At some point . . ."

"I know." She rubbed his back with her hand. It felt natural. Maybe too natural. But she'd have done the same for any friend, right?

"He's beyond help at this point. I've had him living here, where I can keep an eye on him. I've had him in practically every top rehab center in the country. And how does he repay me? By getting sloshed and hitting on the director of psychology."

"Sounds like Teddy."

"That's exactly right, Sloane. It does. You know why?"

"Why?" she humored him.

"Because that's who he is. And he's never going to change. I could send him to rehab thirteen more times and it wouldn't make a damn difference."

"I can help you if you want. Whatever you need."

"You are amazing." He turned to her now. "I'm just so scared I'm going to get a call one day and . . ." Luke's voice cracked.

"And what?"

"And it'll be over. He'll have driven himself off a cliff or taken one too many pills."

"You can't focus on that." She thought about Amy. About how someone who barely ever drank alcohol and had never so much as smoked a joint—someone who had an adoring husband and three perfect children—could be taken so suddenly and ruthlessly, while

Teddy's life, which he'd essentially handed over on a silver platter, could be preserved.

"How can I not?" The despair was evident on Luke's face as he looked at her.

"Maybe you're right. Sometimes I wish I'd seen it coming with Amy. Then I would have had the luxury of knowing I was going to lose her, so I could have been a better sister."

"Amy died? I had no idea." He pulled her close to his side and kissed her on the forehead. "I'm so sorry. What—"

"Ovarian cancer." She cut in before he could finish asking the question. It was always people's next question. In the beginning Sloane had resented this. What did it matter *how* she'd died when the fact remained that she was gone?

"Shit. I wish I'd known."

"There was nothing you could have done."

"I could have been there for you." He reached out to grasp her hand.

"I kind of have a family for that now." And yet she tightened her grasp of his hand imperceptibly.

"Right. Eddie. And Madeleine." She was impressed he remembered her name.

"Yup."

"And where is your daughter while you're here?"

"She's away at summer camp right now."

"And your husband?"

"Home. He has to work." She intentionally left out the fact that he was coming in a week's time.

"You must miss him."

"I guess." She remained quiet, even though Luke was giving her a look that invited her to say more.

"That doesn't sound auspicious."

"Let's just say I'm trying to figure some things out."

"If you need a listening ear." He offered a feisty grin.

"I'm not sure you're the right person to talk to about this particular subject."

"Why's that?"

"Oh, I don't know. Let's see. . . . Because we used to sleep together?" Sloane grinned at him in return.

"You make it sound so cheap." He smirked back.

"You? Cheap? Never."

"Speaking of which . . ." Luke lifted the lid of the picnic basket and pulled out a bottle of chilled champagne and two glasses. "Some Dom Pérignon for the lady?"

"You'd better not be trying to seduce me." Her words didn't hit with much impact considering the tight grip he had on her hand and how close they were sitting.

"Trust me, if I was trying to seduce you, you'd know."

"I'm pretty sure I've been there."

"Well, then." He handed her a flute of champagne and held up his glass. "Shall we have a toast? To old friends." He clinked her glass.

"To old friends." She smiled contentedly.

As they sat together in heavenly silence, for one delicious moment in time, Sloane desired nothing else.

chapter 20

It had taken all of Georgina's willpower not to expose Sloane's plans for the day and catch her red-handed in keeping secrets, if only to demonstrate that—even now—Sloane couldn't manage to pull one over on her. If for no other reason than to make Sloane admit that Georgina still knew her as well as she ever had, despite the distance between them these days. When you'd been as close as they had for as long as they had, one bad year didn't nullify the friendship.

More than that, though, Georgina had played along because she suspected there was a reason for Sloane's dishonesty and a decent explanation for why she seemed abnormally cranky and, also, unnaturally drawn to Luke. She'd overheard Hillary spout a couple of offhand comments about how normal it was to harbor certain feelings for a former flame and that it was nothing to feel ashamed of or self-critical about. Georgina could not have agreed more—if she had thought that was the case with Sloane and Luke.

But she knew better. She knew Sloane. Whether Sloane cared to admit it or not.

But rather than try to cajole her into a heart-to-heart, she held her tongue, because she was well aware that she was on a tightrope and one misstep would have her free-falling into the despair Sloane felt over losing Amy. Or, more to the point, the way Georgina had failed her during such a tragic time in her life.

If only Sloane had had any idea what Georgina had been going through over the last year. Of course Georgina was to blame for keeping it all from her—how could she expect her to understand or extend any forgiveness for something that appeared, at least on the surface, like such a clear transgression? A small part of Georgina had wanted to confide every sordid detail to her best friend, to finally relieve herself of the multi-ton Mack Truck that had been pressed against her chest, stifling her so she couldn't breathe. Still, the larger part knew Sloane would be too quick to judge. Because what Georgina had done this time was clearly wrong. So horrific she'd outdone even herself. And Sloane would be the first one in line to point that out and attempt to educate her about right and wrong.

Even though she'd successfully kept it under wraps for the past year and a half, Georgina wasn't sure how much longer it would be until Sloane wondered whether something was up. Hillary was already suspicious. There was no doubt about that. She'd heard the calls early in the morning and into the wee hours of the night. Georgina also suspected she'd caught snippets of conversations, which meant she had to know that someone was in hot pursuit of Georgina; she just didn't know who and why. And she'd yet to have the balls to ask, which was for the best.

The last thing Georgina had ever expected was to experience any sort of genuine feelings toward Hillary. More like she'd *desperately* wanted to hate her. For one, usurping Sloane was a major no-no. No matter that she'd probably been a better friend to Sloane in the last few years than Georgina had been in a long time. But it wasn't only that. Hillary, if you looked beyond her preppy female-equivalent-of-Dan-Quayle wardrobe and her schoolmarmlike posture, had proved herself to be a surprisingly warm companion. She was easy to talk to. And she'd had some moments of unexpected levity and irresponsibility. Sloane would never have hitchhiked to the beach, at least not sober. She probably wouldn't have been drinking nearly as much either if it weren't for Hillary's indulgent behavior. In some strange way, Hillary had become the perfect buffer between Sloane and Georgina, allowing them to battle but not brawl and to make up hours later no worse for the wear.

Georgina had thought about unburdening herself to Hillary. She was a family counselor after all, which meant she must have seen some real crazies through the years. Plus, she didn't harbor any preconceived notions about Georgina in the way that Sloane did. Whereas Sloane would say something acrimonious, like "This is so typical of you, Georgina," or "When will you ever get your act together," Hillary wouldn't be laden with the same spite, which might make Georgina's recklessness that much more palatable.

Except she couldn't bring herself to say the words aloud. The words they'd exchanged—as well as the images that flashed across her mind—were haunting her to the point of permanent insomnia. A stronger person would have confessed her transgressions to her best friend and tried to find a way to move forward from there. But Georgina knew she was a terrible person. A sad excuse for a human being.

Still, what was done was done. There was no going back—literally or figuratively. Now if she could just get them to stop calling. First it had just been him and then he'd gotten her on board. Typical. Everyone against Georgina.

She'd like to have been able to say she didn't deserve it, but that was about as far from the truth as Sloane's visit to her "aunt's friend's house" the night before.

It was time to put an end to the wallowing for now. Georgina swung her legs off the side of the bed, slipped her feet into a cozy old pair of sheepskin slippers, and walked into the bathroom. She turned on the tap, waited until the water was ice-cold, and splashed two palmfuls on her face. Then she gazed at her reflection in the mirror. She'd been doing that a lot lately. Just looking at herself. Studying the darkening sunspots around her hairline. The deepening creases that fanned from the corners of her eyes and furrowed across her forehead. The sparse growth of new hair in places she'd never noticed it before, like on the top corners of her lips. She'd even found two lonely whiskers on her chin a few months ago and had immediately rifled through her cabinet for a pair of tweezers to pluck them into oblivion.

But it wasn't just the aesthetics that she was probing; she was looking for something more. Who was she beneath the physical specimen that she presented to the world? Did she have anything more to offer anyone beyond a beautiful distraction as she strode down the street? Where would she find herself when her youthful beauty faded? Somehow it felt like the years had caught up to her too quickly—she was starting to look her age, and yet had managed to accumulate no wisdom or success to show for the past decade. Was she destined to leave no impact on those around her? Simply slipping away like the bubbles in an uncorked bottle of champagne?

She ran a comb through her long, silky red hair, taking care to shake the burdensome thoughts from her mind, and afforded herself another quick glimpse in the mirror before heading downstairs to have a long overdue powwow with Sloane. And to conquer another inscrutable day in Lake George. The best way to forget, Georgina knew, was to shine the spotlight on someone else.

"You're up bright and early." Sloane earmarked the page of her magazine and set it down on the kitchen island next to her coffee. "Can you believe this mug I found?" It read, "What Happens in Lake George . . ."

"See, I told you." Georgina kissed Sloane on the top of her head. "Good morning, my little minx."

"What's that supposed to mean?" Sloane was immediately defensive.

Rule number one, Georgina thought but didn't say. *The lady doth protest too much, methinks. Hamlet* was one of the only Shakespearean plays she'd actually taken the time to read. That Will really was ahead of his time.

"You know, like siren, temptress . . ."

"I don't need the definition." Sloane rolled her eyes. "I want to know what *you* meant by it. Honestly, if either one of us is a minx . . ."

"Okay, let me rephrase. I meant to ask—how was your time with Luke?"

"What time with Luke?"

"Yesterday. When you left Hillary and me here, remember?" Georgina poured herself a large glass of fresh-squeezed orange juice.

"I told you I was going to my aunt's friend's house." Sloane fidgeted in her seat. "Would you leave some of that for Hillary?"

"Relax, there's a whole other pitcher. And stop evading. I know you too well for that to work."

"Evading what?"

"The fact that you're not telling the truth. Seriously, Sloane. Do you think I'm that naive?"

"I don't know what you're referring to." She shook her head.

"This is exhausting." Georgina sighed. "What is your aunt's friend's name?"

"Huh?" Sloane hesitated, obviously stumped by the very simple question, as Georgina had expected.

Rule number two. Do not engage in prolonged pauses when pressed for details about your lie. If someone asked you your middle name, would you have to think about it?

"Your aunt's friend's name. What was it?"

"Sylvia."

"Sylvia what?"

"I don't know."

"She didn't tell you her last name?"

"No."

"Where was the house?"

"In Lake George."

"Come on, Sloane."

"Fine. I was with Luke."

"That was way too easy. Have I taught you nothing?" Georgina sat down next to her and poached a hunk of cantaloupe from her plate of fruit salad. "Why didn't you just tell me?"

"Honestly? I don't know."

"I would have been fine with not going. I'm not that sensitive."

"It wasn't that at all."

"Was it Hillary? I can keep a secret."

"Okay, first of all, you cannot keep a secret!" Sloane laughed, puncturing the tense mood. "But, still, that wasn't it either."

"Wait, you're not . . . are you?" Georgina's eyes widened.

"What?"

"Sleeping with him?"

"Are you out of your mind?" Sloane looked legitimately shocked. So Georgina could cross that hypothesis off her list. "I'm *married*."

"You wouldn't be the first married woman to screw another man behind her husband's back."

"Well, I'm not. Screwing anyone. I promise you."

"I believe you. So why lie about seeing Luke, then?"

"Like I said, I really don't know." Sloane bit into a slice of pineapple. "I guess I just didn't feel like dealing with any questions from anyone."

"I can understand that. Did you at least have fun together?"

"Kind of. Mainly we just caught up. It's been so long."

"You know he's still in love with you, right?"

"Would you stop? He is not!"

"Okay, Sloanie, whatever you say."

"Luke could have any woman he wants. In the world. I highly doubt he's been sitting around all these years pining after me."

"I didn't say he's been pining after you all these years. I just said he's still in love with you. Now. That you're back."

"That's the thing. I'm not back." Sloane buried her head in her hands.

"Well, do you want to be?"

"Hello, ladies." Hillary came into the kitchen and put an immediate halt to Georgina's progress with Sloane.

"Morning." Sloane smiled and looked up at the oven, which read nine o'clock. "This is late for you."

"I know. Can you believe it? Ten hours of sleep, and I feel like a new woman."

"What should we do today?" Georgina slid the rest of her orange juice toward Hillary, who accepted it gratefully.

"I'm thinking it's a beach day." Hillary sliced an English muffin in half and placed it nook and cranny side down in the toaster oven. "It's supposed to be eighty-three and sunny. Can't argue with that!"

"I'm game, as long as we party tonight," Georgina added. "We only have a few more days until the men get here and cramp our style." She watched Sloane's face dim when she mentioned the husbands' arrival.

"Sounds like a plan." Hillary smeared raspberry jam on her English muffin and then split it between two plates, setting one at her place and the other in front of Georgina.

"Thanks, Mom!" Georgina giggled. Remarkably, Hillary had a knack for understanding exactly what she needed. "What's for lunch?"

"Why don't I pack us a picnic? That'll be fun!"

"Will you adopt me?" Georgina chewed and spoke simultaneously.

"Only if you close your mouth when you eat! Sloane, you in?"

"Huh?" Georgina could tell that she was distracted and hadn't really been paying attention to their conversation.

"Of course Sloane is in for a day at the beach, right?"

"Yup. Absolutely." Sloane nodded vaguely.

Georgina couldn't help but wonder what she was thinking about. More precisely, about whom she was thinking. Luke? Eddie? The two of them? She couldn't put her finger on what was going on with her best friend, but it definitely wasn't nothing. As she tried to decipher Sloane's mood, she thought back to her liquor-fueled diatribe about marriage being bullshit, the one she'd filched from Georgina. Was there something more to that?

"And then where to tonight? Back to that place we went last time?" Hillary asked innocently.

"Nah, I'm over King Neptune's," Georgina answered quickly, armed with the knowledge that Sloane wouldn't want to chance running into Luke or any of his friends, not when she and Hillary were around. Whatever it was they had to work out, they had to do it on their own, and Georgina was determined to step in and help in any way she could. It was about time she started acting like the friend Sloane needed her to be. The friend she had once been. The friend she desperately wanted to be once again.

"Me too," Sloane concurred, exactly as Georgina had anticipated.

"No worries. I always have something up my sleeve." Georgina grinned mischievously. "Remember what the mug says. . . ."

chapter 21

The doorbell rang just as they were finishing breakfast, and all three women widened their eyes and shrugged their shoulders to indicate their mutual surprise. Who would possibly be dropping in first thing in the morning without advance notice?

"Hold on a minute," Sloane called out, fastening her robe a little tighter around her waist. As she approached the front door, she heard a key turn in the lock and instinctively reached for the tall, heavy rain stick that was leaning up against one of the walls in the foyer. She wielded it like a baseball bat as the knob turned.

"Oh, for Christ's sake!" Sloane's aunt nearly fell backward at the sight of her.

"Aunt Annabel!" She released a sigh of relief along with the rain stick, returning it to its spot before hugging her aunt.

"You've nearly given me a heart attack!" She walked inside, with her palm still pressed to her chest, and dropped her purse on the entryway table like a ton of bricks. As per usual, she was bedecked in a colorful, billowing caftanlike dress with tangles of heavy beads around her neck. "You know that's possible at my tender age."

"I'm so sorry. I had no idea you were coming."

"Well, neither did I." She shook her head. "Turns out Gerome was a total dud. As soon as we got to Paris, he hightailed it to the closest McDonald's. I mean, can you imagine eating a Big Mac on the Champs-Élysées? Horrifying! That should have been all the writing on the wall I needed, but I let it slide. It wasn't until we got to Rome and he asked if we could go see Michelangelo's *David* that things really fell apart. Anyone with a brain knows *David*—in all his glory—resides in the Galleria dell'Accademia di Firenze." She put on her best Italian accent. "The Gallery of the Academy of Florence. You know," she translated.

"Of course." Sloane nodded. She had known the *David* was in Florence, but not his exact location. Though she dared not admit that to her aunt.

"He had a very tiny penis."

"*David*?"

"Oh God, no." She laughed. "His package is gorgeous. I meant Gerome." She held up her pinkie finger as a reference.

"And you didn't know this ahead of time?" Sloane cringed at her own question.

"Alas, I did. But when you're in love . . ."

"So you just left?"

"Of course! Once I'm done, I'm done."

"Well, good for you." Sloane thought about her own situation with Luke and Eddie. Part of her wished she'd inherited her aunt's black-and-white view of life. "I hope you can stay for a few days. Georgina will be thrilled to see you!"

"Oh, no, darling. I'm just here for a few hours. I wanted to see you girls and check in on how the renovations turned out. Very nice, don't you think?"

"I'd say that's an understatement. The place looks spectacular. Are you sure you can't stay for a while?"

"Certain. I'm catching a plane out of Albany in a couple of hours."

"To where?"

"Honolulu." She followed Sloane into the kitchen. "I wasn't even sure I'd have ten minutes to stop in."

"Well, I'm so glad you did." Sloane cleared her throat. "Look who's here!"

"Annabel!" Georgina leapt off her barstool and rushed toward Sloane's aunt with wide-open arms.

"Darling!" They embraced like long-lost relatives. "Let me have a look at you." Annabel held Georgina at arm's length. "Absolutely stunning, as always."

"I could say the same! You haven't aged a day since last I saw you."

"Aren't you a love? And my very favorite person in the whole wide world, which is saying a lot." She squeezed Georgina's shoulders and then turned to Hillary. "You must be Sloane's friend from Brookline."

"That's right. I'm Hillary and it's so nice to meet you." She extended her hand. "Thank you so much for allowing us to stay here for a few weeks."

"Nonsense." She ignored Hillary's hand and pulled her into a hug instead. "It's my pleasure. I only wish I could spend more time with you gorgeous girls."

"You're not staying?" Georgina frowned.

"She's leaving for Hawaii this afternoon. Can you believe it?" Sloane envied her aunt's spontaneity, although she didn't think she'd ever be able to live that way. Always packing up for the next adventure. Never sure of where she was headed next. Or with whom. Georgina, on the other hand, could relate to Annabel more than anyone. In so many ways, she was a younger version of Sloane's aunt.

"I'm jealous!" Georgina chimed in. "That's one place I've never been."

"Well, next time you'll have to join me." Annabel smiled genuinely. Sloane could totally envision the two of them jaunting off to Hawaii together without the remotest concern about leaving anything or anyone behind.

"I would LOVE that!" Georgina's face lit up like that of a child who'd just been dropped in the center of a toy store and been told the sky was the limit. "Can you at least come with us to the beach today?"

"I wish, but this visit is a short one."

"Georgina, why don't we go upstairs and get our stuff together, so Sloane and her aunt can have some time alone?"

"Um, okay." Georgina was, quite obviously, not a big fan of Hillary's suggestion, as was evidenced by her failure to move an inch, even as Hillary began to walk toward the stairs.

"Come on, let's go," Hillary urged. "Maybe you can help me pick which wrap goes best with which bathing suit." Sloane grinned appreciatively at Hillary.

"Sure, yeah." Reluctantly, Georgina followed Hillary, but not before giving Annabel a kiss on either cheek. "Don't you dare leave without saying good-bye. Promise?"

"You have my word." Annabel smacked her on the rear end playfully. "And *that* is worth its weight in gold."

Once Hillary and Georgina had retreated to their bedrooms, Sloane brewed two cups of coffee, dousing her aunt's with a shot of whiskey at her request, and then they meandered into the family room, where they sat facing each other on either end of the sofa.

"So, tell me what's going on."

"Nothing too exciting. We've just been hanging out and relaxing." Sloane sipped her coffee.

"That's not what I meant." Annabel narrowed her eyes. "What I'm interested in is what's going on with you. As in why are your shoulders up to your ears? And why does your jaw clench every time Georgina speaks?"

"Really? I hadn't noticed." She avoided eye contact with her aunt.

"Bullshit."

"Aunt Annabel!"

"What? You've never heard me curse before?"

"Obviously I have; it's just . . ." Sloane trailed off as she maneuvered her body awkwardly in her seat.

"Just what? You don't like when it's directed at you, huh?" She smiled now and moved closer to her niece, placing one weathered hand on Sloane's leg. "Talk to me, darling. Tell me what's going on in that clouded head of yours."

"I don't know." Sloane looked down, noticing the deep crevices that ran horizontally from the base of her aunt's pinkie to the base of her thumb.

"If you're worried I'll say something to your mother, I assure you my lips are sealed."

Sloane hesitated. "I miss Amy. More than usual. I'm not sure why I expected anything different, but the house and Lake George have brought so many old memories to the surface."

"I can understand that."

"And they're good memories. You know? Nothing bad or anything like that. I just . . ." Sloane started to cry softly and her aunt inched closer again, this time wrapping her arm around Sloane and allowing Sloane's head to rest on her shoulder.

"You just what, darling?"

"I just miss her. I miss her so much." Tears tumbled down Sloane's cheeks.

"Of course you do. We all miss Amy terribly." She rubbed Sloane's back gently. "I was hoping some time with your friends would offer you comfort, help relieve you of the terrible burden you've been carrying around since she passed away."

"So was I." Sloane took a deep breath and wiped the dampness welling in the corners of her eyes with the sleeve of her robe.

"But it's not?"

"Not really. Somehow I feel more distant from Georgina and Hillary than I ever have." Although, were they really to blame for this? Or was it that reconnecting with Luke had been all the outlet she'd needed thus far? Not that she'd run crying to him about Amy. Still, though, he'd offered her an escape: pockets of time where the furthest thing from her mind had been her sister's death. She wasn't sure whether to feel guilty or grateful for that.

"Well, that's a real shame."

"I mean, Georgina hasn't so much as mentioned Amy's name. Can you believe that?"

"I can, actually." Annabel nodded sagely. "Can't you talk to her?"

"I suppose I could."

"You just don't want to?"

"It's not that I don't want to. But I feel like the ball is in her court on this one."

"I see."

"I'm sorry."

"Sorry for what?"

"You came all this way, and I'm dumping my problems on you."

"Don't be ridiculous! Your problems are my problems, Sloane."

"Well, thank you." She turned to face her aunt again. "I'm so happy you're here, even though it's too short."

"Me too." Annabel checked her watch.

"Can't you stay a bit longer?"

"If only I'd known that you were upset, I wouldn't have made plans to travel."

"I'll be okay."

"Will you?"

"I will," Sloane reassured her, even though she wasn't certain of it herself.

"Well, then I'd best be going soon."

"But you haven't even been here for that long!" Sloane protested.

"I know. I know. And I feel just awful about that. Don't want to miss my flight, though. You understand." It wasn't a question. While Sloane adored her aunt, there was no doubt that when the going got tough, she got going.

"I understand," Sloane confirmed, even though her instinct was to grab on to her aunt's caftan, or whatever you called it, and never let go. Either that or to ride her caftan tails all the way to Honolulu.

"Before I go, let me remind you of one thing." She cupped Sloane's cheeks with her hands.

"What's that?" Sloane awaited whatever philosophical nugget of wisdom her aunt was prepared to impart.

"Remember what I told you about this house. Enter broken. Leave fixed."

"I wish."

"Don't wish, my love. Wishing is the work of fools. Just open your heart. Open your heart and trust."

chapter 22

Although Hillary tried to focus on the shoreline, she couldn't take her eyes off the little girl playing nearby in the sand. Even though it was like watching a rerun of the same sitcom over and over and over again, laugh track and all. First she would walk down to the water's edge, her miniature feet trudging through the sand. Then she would check over her shoulder to make sure her mother and father were a captive audience. They'd beam at her, offer an encouraging wave, and she'd beam back. She'd scoop up some water with her bucket, race back up to where she was constructing her makeshift sand castle, and pour the water over a dry area of sand. She'd fill her bucket to the brim with the damp sand, smile up at her parents once more, and—after they'd encouraged her with the smallest hand motions to pat the sand down—she'd pack it in real tight. Once she was satisfied with her work, she'd flip her bucket over in one seamless movement, tap, tap, tap the bottom of it, and then lift it up to reveal the next in a long line of identical bucket-molded shapes.

Ultimately, they'd all explode into boisterous laughter, clapping and cheering for a job well executed. And then the whole routine would start from the beginning.

It was almost addicting to watch, really. More than once, she'd wanted to break into applause with them, but she was too embarrassed to let on that she too had been a captive audience and it wasn't even her child. Eventually, though, she couldn't contain herself anymore and when the little girl's row was complete, Hillary permitted herself a congratulatory woot.

"She's very determined." The girl's mother smiled at Hillary.

"I'm impressed." Hillary smiled back. "She's absolutely adorable. What's her name?"

"Isla. Isla May."

"Gorgeous. And so unique."

"Isla we just loved. Found it in a baby book by chance. And May was my maternal grandmother's name."

"And how old is the lovely Isla May?"

"Three going on forty-five!" The woman struggled to sit up in her chair and Hillary noticed she still appeared to be carrying some baby weight around the middle.

"Oh boy! Is she your only?"

"For now." She rubbed her stomach.

"You're pregnant again?"

"Yup, halfway there." She wiped the perspiration off her forehead with the back of her hand and took a swig from a large bottle of water she'd pulled from an ice-filled cooler.

"Well, you look great."

"Thank you for saying that, but please—look at these cankles.

With Isla no one could even tell I was pregnant until I was seven months along. But this time it's completely different. I blew up like the Goodyear Blimp the minute I read the positive pregnancy test." She exhaled, which seemed like a workout in and of itself. "Let's just say this bambino wasn't planned."

"So it's a boy?"

"It's a boy! And that's a good thing, since I'm not sure Daddy would have been able to handle all the estrogen if there were three ladies in the house." Daddy nodded in agreement and then spotted Isla toddling a few inches too close to the lake for his liking. He took off after her, swooping in and cradling her in his burly arms before hoisting her into the air and spinning her around until they both collapsed onto the sand, giggling and dizzy.

"And you said he wasn't planned? Wait, before you delve into the depths of your personal life, I'm Hillary." She extended her arm. "I don't mean to be nosy."

"I'm Jill. And it's totally fine. I'm the one who brought it up in the first place!" She watched as her husband and her daughter frolicked in the waves. "Can I be completely honest?"

"Of course." This wasn't new to Hillary. Wherever she went and without fail, complete strangers would divulge their deepest, darkest secrets to her without even knowing her chosen profession. If nothing else, it served to prove that she'd gone into the right line of work.

"I wasn't sure I wanted kids at all."

"Really?" Hillary was intrigued. Typically when people confessed their feelings or indiscretions to her, they weren't about something so directly connected to her own life and her own issues. There might be an admission of alcoholism or an extramarital affair.

Possibly even drug use or—worst of all—some kind of physical or emotional abuse. But never, not once, had someone with one child in tow and another on the way declared she wasn't sure she'd wanted children to begin with. Within the first five minutes of meeting her no less. It was almost exhilarating, if not encouraging, to hear that she wasn't the only woman who felt that way. At the very least, it was reassuring to be on the receiving end of such blatant honesty.

"Really. Derek had to push me."

"So he wanted kids?"

"Oh yeah, he's got three brothers and four sisters."

"There are *eight* of them?"

"Yup! And that was before reality TV." Jill swiped a bag of Cheerios from her bag and shoved a handful in her mouth. "Sorry, I can't go without eating for more than about thirty seconds. It's a curse. I'm going to be a whale by the time he decides to grace us with his presence."

"No, you really do look fabulous." It wasn't strictly the truth, but what was she supposed to say? Hillary had often wondered whether, if ever she did get knocked up, she'd be one of those exultant, glowing women who loved being with child or if she'd be one of those disgruntled, sweaty women who griped their way through all forty weeks. According to her informal tally, it seemed like the latter was more often the case. "Seriously, though, eight kids? I don't know how anyone could do that."

"At least not anyone in their right mind."

"Is your mother-in-law certifiable, then?"

"Amazingly, no. She's just Catholic."

"Ah. No birth control."

"Unless you count the rhythm method."

"I definitely do not."

"Neither do we. At least not anymore." She pointed to her stomach, which Hillary could now see was bulging, stretching the fabric of Jill's maternity bathing suit.

"Got it. I'm always a bit skeptical when people say their pregnancy was unplanned." How many teenage girls had come into her office through the years with swelled bellies the same as Jill's and tearstained faces, swearing up and down that it had been a complete mistake—they had no idea how it possibly could have happened? Only to reveal later that they had not used a condom or a diaphragm. They weren't on the pill, the patch, or any other form of birth control. *But he pulled out.* That's what most of them would say. Or, another of her favorites, *He told me he was wearing a condom.*

"What about you?" Jill turned the conversation quickly, unaware of Hillary's situation and thereby catching her off guard.

"What about me?"

"Do you have any kiddies?"

"No." Hillary cleared her throat. "I mean, not yet. We've been trying." She looked away.

"Sorry. I didn't mean to bring up a sensitive subject."

"Not at all. We're very casual about the whole thing."

"That's good. They say that's really important." She reached into the cooler again for another bottle of water and handed it to Hillary. "Nice and cold."

"Thanks." Hillary accepted it gratefully. She hadn't realized that her throat was parched.

"My friend Rachel and her husband, Jay, had been trying to get pregnant for six years when they finally decided to adopt. They'd tried everything. All the fertility treatments. Jay's a bigwig at some hedge fund in New York City, so you know they had the top-of-the-line specialists helping them. But still nothing."

"Wow."

"Right? So, get this. They end up adopting this stunning baby girl from Russia—all blond curls and blue eyes—and then Rachel got pregnant a week later. One shot the natural way."

"Just like that?"

"Just like that. Apparently, it happens a lot."

"Because they're relaxed."

"You got it." She drizzled the rest of the water from her bottle down the back of her neck. "Are you ready for the best part?"

"I think so."

"She was pregnant with twins!"

"Oh my."

" 'Oh my' is right. Can you imagine going from no children to three girls within the course of ten months?"

"Definitely not."

"So are you here with your husband?" Jill looked around as if he might materialize out of thin air.

"He's coming next week. Right now it's just me and a couple of friends enjoying some good old-fashioned female bonding." Come to think of it, where were Sloane and Georgina? They'd taken off for a walk along the beach over an hour ago. Of course they'd invited Hillary to join them, but from the looks on their faces she could tell they needed time alone, with any luck to work out some of their differences.

"That's awesome. You might as well enjoy it while you can." She heaved herself into a standing position. "Before long, you'll be puncturing a perfectly gorgeous day at the beach with the urgent need to get your child home for a nap." She waved Isla and her husband toward her and pointed at her watch to signal that it was time to get going. "It was so nice to meet you, Hillary. I wish you the very best of luck!"

"You too!" Hillary smiled as Isla bounded into her mother's open arms. "You have a beautiful family."

Long after Jill and Derek had packed up their things—oh, how much stuff there had been—and headed home, with Isla bouncing blissfully on her father's shoulders, Hillary still couldn't shake the image of her cavorting on the beach. Maybe it was the way her sparkling green eyes had glinted in the sunshine or how her corkscrew blond curls whipped in the breeze. Then there was the way her doll-sized features expressed every emotion as if it was magnified. Or maybe it was that Hillary had never witnessed a child look at her parents with such untainted adoration. Was she envious? She couldn't tell. But wouldn't that be a step in the right direction?

Typically, she was quite adept at self-analysis. But this was different. She'd asked herself if Isla could have been some kind of sign from God. Perhaps Hillary was meant to be on that very beach on that very day at that very time for the sole purpose of running into this little angel in her pink and white striped bikini. Perhaps Isla was meant to convince her she wanted kids of her own.

There was no doubt about the fact that Hillary would have delighted in romping around in the water with her. No doubt about the fact that she would have loved to be on the receiving end of Isla's running hug into her mother's arms. But those were just moments. Specks on the road map of life. Would she enjoy Isla just as much when she was wailing at three o'clock in the morning or regurgitating breakfast on her lap? And could she risk following in the footsteps of her own absentee mother? What if she suffered from postpartum depression like so many women do? Certainly she must be genetically predisposed.

Given how seriously Hillary took her responsibilities, it was hard for her to wrap her mind around being completely accountable for another human being. The child's path in life resting on how strong of a foundation you provided before sending him or her off into the world. Not that teenagers and drug addicts hadn't been doing it for centuries, but it was one thing to be a mother merely because you gave birth and another to really *be* a mother. Hillary's own mother fell strictly in the "because she gave birth" category.

And she simply couldn't do that to her own child.

Hillary sighed, knowing she'd have to face the music sooner rather than later, but not today. She closed her eyes and let the warmth from the midday sun cocoon her. Just as she was about to doze off, she felt a shadow across her face, and there was Georgina standing over her, ready to tip Hillary's bottle of water onto her head.

"Don't you dare," she warned, laughing all the while.

"I'll let you off the hook," Georgina crowed, revealing a wide, wicked smile. "But next time you won't be so lucky." She helped herself to a gulp of the water.

"Your phone rang a bunch while you were gone. Hope you don't mind I turned off the ringer. People were giving me dirty looks." Georgina's smile wilted. "Are you sure everything is okay?"

"I told you it's fine," she snapped. "Sorry, it's just frustrating. I think I need to change my number or something."

"Where's Sloane?"

"Taking a quick dip." She pointed toward the lake, but Sloane was already walking toward them.

"Did you guys have a nice stroll? You were gone forever."

"Lots to catch up on, you know." If Hillary didn't know, she could hazard a guess.

"Luke?"

"What? No. Why would you say that?"

"Just a hunch." She'd assumed Sloane had told Georgina ahead of time that she wasn't really going to visit with her "aunt's friend" yesterday. Or, if not, that she'd since come clean. Hillary hadn't said a word about her suspicion to Georgina, but she was a smart girl, especially when it came to the intricacies of manipulation. The funny thing was, Hillary wouldn't have cared in the least if Sloane had been going to see Luke. She trusted Sloane enough to know that she wasn't doing anything illicit. It was the fact that Sloane didn't trust her enough to confide in her that irked her. And made her think there was something more to her relationship with Luke than an innocent reunion between old flames.

"Well, your shrink-o radar is off on this one," Georgina corroborated.

"I'm not a shrink. I'm a family counselor."

"Whatev."

"I'm ravenous, ladies, what about you?" Sloane sat down in the chair next to Hillary and touched her arm with her cold, wet hand. "Sorry we were gone so long."

"No worries. And, yes, I'm starving. Good thing you guys finally came back or I would have had to eat everything myself." Hillary lifted the lid to the picnic basket and handed Georgina three plastic cups and the thermos of fresh iced tea she'd brewed. "You take care of that."

"I can do that!" Georgina handed one cup at a time to Sloane, filling each to the brim.

"What else do you have?" Sloane's stomach grumbled. "See, I need food!"

"I have a tuna on wheat, turkey and Swiss on rye, and ham and American on white."

"Ham, please." Georgina raised her hand.

"I'm good with either of the other two," Sloane added.

"Wanna split them?" Hillary asked, peeling off the plastic wrap.

"Definitely!"

"I also made some fruit salad and there's a bag of tortilla chips and salsa in here somewhere."

"You're the best, thank you." Sloane smiled appreciatively, before taking a generous bite of her sandwich.

"Yeah, thanks, Mom!" Georgina cheered.

And this time, Hillary didn't wince at the designation.

chapter 23

Of course Georgina hadn't mentioned Amy yesterday. Why would she after all this time? And, more to the point, why did Sloane still expect it of her? Maybe Hillary was right. If she hadn't accepted Georgina for who she was by now—shortcomings and all—then she ought to either start, learn to speak her mind, or come to terms with the fact that their relationship had always been destined to fail at some point when it came under too much pressure. Kind of hard to digest after fifteen years of friendship. Fifteen years of vacillating between the highest highs and the lowest of lows. All for naught?

They'd walked for nearly two hours up and down the beach. Poor Hillary had been completely sidelined by their disappearing act, but Sloane eased her guilty conscience by remembering how much time Hillary and Georgina had been spending together when she wasn't around. In fact, she hadn't realized until yesterday that it was irritating her on some level that they'd bonded so easily. As sure as she was that two plus two equaled four, she'd been equally assured that Georgina and Hillary would clash and then butt heads for the duration of their vacation. Evidently she'd been wrong, as quite the opposite had happened.

Not only was it the last thing she'd seen coming; it simply didn't make sense. She was each of their best friends. They were not meant to be each other's. For this reason, it had felt satisfying to have Georgina all to herself for such a substantial chunk of time. She'd also wanted to chitchat about Luke without Hillary around.

The guilt flooded her brain in waves. *Why was Luke constantly on her mind? Why was Eddie never on her mind? Why was she trying to hide her feelings from Hillary? Fear of being judged? Fear of admitting the truth? What if she'd married the wrong man? What if she hadn't and Luke was a mere distraction getting in the way of her repairing things with Eddie? What would that lead to? Was this what a midlife crisis felt like?*

As always, then it all came back to the most important question of all. The one she could never and would never want to escape. *What about Madeleine?*

The thing was, Luke made her feel alive. He made her realize that she hadn't felt engaged in her own life in way too long.

Still, there was Eddie. Her husband, lest she forget. Eddie, who had graduated from UMass Amherst with an over three grade point average. It was a state school, but a good one. And he was successful in his career. The family insurance business, but he did well nonetheless. That said, he wasn't someone who was driven by a burning ambition. For anything. He wasn't someone who invested hours into analyzing stock market statistics or someone with a penchant for political debates. Above all, he definitely wasn't someone who devoted even a minute to scrutinizing his relationships—marital or otherwise. They existed, and as long as nothing was glaringly wrong, there was no reason to rock the boat. Or to even think about swaying it.

She'd given a lot of thought to telling Eddie about Luke. To coming clean about their past together and the romantic feelings that still lingered. But then what? Then she'd have to stop seeing him. And she wasn't ready to do that. Would she ever be truly ready to say good-bye to Luke?

Sloane opened her eyes. She'd been mostly awake for at least an hour, but had relished the chance to lie there and relax, drifting between her thoughts and the short spurts of slumber that cannibalized them. Her cell phone rang, urging her to sit up and grab it off the nightstand.

"Hello?" she answered groggily before realizing she didn't recognize the number.

"May I please speak with Sloane?" The woman's voice was courteous but professional.

"This is Sloane. Who's this?" It sounded like a receptionist at her dentist's office. Had she made an appointment and forgotten?

"Hello, Sloane. This is Serena."

"Oh, hi." She was alert now, if not a little surprised to be hearing from Serena at eight thirty in the morning.

"I'm Luke's assistant."

"I know who you are." Sloane was about to laugh, but she'd learned by now that Serena didn't do humor. Seriously, though, did she really think Sloane was that unaware? Perhaps Luke's other friends were too fancy to recall the names of his staff members. Sloane would never be that person. She was half tempted to tell

Serena that not only did she know her name, but she also could tell her what she'd been wearing on the two occasions they'd met. And she might very well have if not for the distinct impression that said information would serve only to creep Serena out or instill her with more power than was necessary.

"Right. Luke asked me to call and see if you're free to join him on his boat for the day."

"Did he forget how to dial a phone himself?"

"Not to my knowledge. He's very busy, tied up on other calls."

"I see." Was this girl for real? Not to her knowledge? Sloane had to wonder if Serena had ever cracked a smile or, God forbid, giggled at anything. Was she that glum of a person or did she just take her job *really, really* seriously? Had Luke instructed her to always act unwaveringly sober? "I'll have to ask my friends."

"Luke wanted me to tell you the invitation is just for you."

"And the dozen other people who work on the boat?"

"It'll only be me and the captain today. He's let everyone else know they can remain behind."

"Oh."

"So can I let Luke know it's a yes?"

"Does anyone ever say no to him?"

"No."

"I didn't think so." Sloane hesitated, feigning that she was actually considering her reply, for her own benefit and Serena's. "Okay, I'll come."

"Excellent. I'll let Luke know."

"What time?" Sloane was already calculating how long it would take her to get ready and whether she should wake Georgina to enlist her help.

"A car will be there to pick you up at ten."

"Oh, wow, okay. Thank you."

"You're welcome."

They hung up and Sloane took a deep breath before revealing a wide smile. A whole day alone with Luke—what an unexpected treat. Maybe she'd finally be able to start answering some of those pressing questions that had been haunting her for too long.

Sloane had been the first to rise by a long shot and when she'd left the house at ten, Georgina and Hillary had still been fast asleep. She'd poked her head into Georgina's room, to see if she could procure wardrobe approval from her, but she'd looked practically comatose, so Sloane had decided to leave her be. Hillary, on the other hand, had rustled a bit when Sloane cracked her door, but then rolled onto her side and resumed her faint, albeit perfectly rhythmic, snoring. So Sloane had resorted to leaving them a note, detailing where she was going, how long she'd be gone, and that it had been a last-minute invitation. She'd even encouraged them to take her car wherever they wanted and said that she'd be back in time for dinner.

They'd been out late the previous night. Georgina had found a dive bar on the other side of town, one they'd never been to before. The band had been raging, as had the crowd. Drinks had been sucked down and refilled at warp speed and they'd all been significantly buzzed when a cute guy Georgina had picked up earlier in the evening had offered to drive them home. Not their most responsible decision ever, but Hillary had seemed fine with it, so Sloane had relented. She hadn't exactly been in a position to get behind the wheel herself, so the decision had been between hottie Ben or a cab. Hottie Ben had won. Unfortunately, he'd then lost when Sloane had said he wasn't invited in. She had, however, had the wherewithal to pay for his cab ride back to the bar, since he'd driven them home in her car.

The black limousine Luke had sent for her pulled into the parking lot of the marina and Sloane could see Serena waiting to greet her. As soon as they came to a stop, the driver hopped out and opened Sloane's door, taking the beach bag she'd brought with her and handing it to the other woman.

"Oh, I can carry that myself." Sloane wasn't used to this sort of treatment and she wasn't sure she liked it.

"I've got it." Serena nodded, gripping the bag tighter.

"Okay." Typically Sloane would have protested, insisted that since Serena was already holding other things, it was really fine for her to let Sloane manage her own tote. But when Serena was certain about something, she was certain. And who was Sloane to get in the way of protocol?

"Beautiful day, don't you think?" She followed Serena down the dock to the *Edwina*.

"Yes." Serena pursed her lips. "Here we are."

"There she is." Luke came onto the deck through a sliding door and Sloane's heart began to gallop, as a red flush spread across her cheeks. It was too early to blame it on the summer heat.

"Hey, you." He folded her into a hug and then took her by the hand.

"I have a great spot all set up for us. Come on." Luke led her up the stairs to the second level and around the other side of the boat, where there was an outdoor living room arranged with a couch, a coffee table, and two chairs, all facing the lake. On the coffee table was an ice bucket with a bottle of champagne tucked inside, two glasses, and a spread of cheese, crackers, crudités, hummus, and chips, along with a few other unidentifiable dips and spreads.

"This looks amazing." She sat down on the sofa.

"You look amazing." He grinned gluttonously, as if he might devour her in one bite, and then lowered himself into the seat next to her.

"Such a charmer."

"Only to you."

"Ha! As if I'm expected to believe that."

"Believe whatever you want."

"Okay, seriously. I know you know I'm married. I know you have a zillion women knocking at your door. So why even say something like that?" Sloane had shocked herself with her brazenness. It was just that if she was going to find answers, she needed everything on the table. Now or never.

"Because it's the truth." His expression was serious.

"So you've been pining after me all these years?" Sloane smiled and tilted her head to one side.

"Not exactly." He cracked a smile too.

"I didn't think so." She tried to mask her disappointment.

"But I wasn't the same after you left that summer." He looked solemn again.

"Really?"

"Well, for one, you left without saying a proper good-bye."

"I thought our last night together was a pretty great finale."

"No argument there, but it still wasn't a proper good-bye."

"I'm sorry." Sloane bowed her head. She remembered it like it was yesterday, specifically deciding not to bid Luke a final farewell, because she'd wanted to go out with a bang. Literally. "You could have called."

"It wouldn't have helped. And you were already back with Eddie. I'd have seemed desperate."

"So?"

"You know I don't do desperate." He laughed easily and draped his arm over her shoulder.

"Of course, what was I thinking?" Sloane laughed with him.

"I was in love with you."

"You thought you were. We were young." Sloane took a deep breath. She couldn't focus on anything beyond his words. He'd loved her. He'd been *in love* with her. Suddenly she felt like either the luckiest or stupidest person in the world. If she'd gone to him at the end of that summer, to say good-bye on her last day in Lake George, would he have let her go? Or would he have persuaded her to stay? Would her life's path have been entirely different?

"I was in love with you, Sloane."

"How do you know?"

"Because I've never had that feeling again. For anyone."

"Never?"

"Not until now." He turned toward her.

"Wait, what?" Sloane stood up.

"I didn't mean to upset you."

"I'm not upset, I . . ." She sat back down, unsure of what to say.

"I know you're married. I know you have a daughter. I know all of it, Sloane." Luke took her hand in his. "I just can't let you go again without telling you how I feel. I won't."

"I'm sorry. I'm really at a loss for what exactly to say here."

"If you don't love me too, just tell me. I'm a big boy. I can take it. But if you do, Sloane. If you do, I'm asking you to be honest."

"Is this why you called me here today?"

"Yes. No. I don't know." He sighed. "Can you tell me you don't love me?"

"Luke, I . . ." She paused. "I can't deny there are feelings there."

"Then that's a start." His face flooded with relief, which Sloane knew—at least in part—was a gut reaction to having evaded rejection. Luke Fuller did not get rejected. By Sloane or anyone else. Whether in his personal life or his business dealings.

"But I'm still married." Instantly she felt both sorry for betraying her husband in this manner and annoyed by his existence at the same time. As if he was the lone roadblock standing in the way of her leaning forward and pressing her lips to Luke's at this very moment and kissing him the way she felt so desperate to. But the logical part of her knew that it wasn't just Luke—part of the attraction she felt toward him was that he represented everything her life at home wasn't. But shouldn't she face up to her responsibilities, rather than waltzing around pretending she was still a carefree young adult? She felt so conflicted.

"Are you happy?"

And there it was—the question she had been running from for over a year. "I don't know."

"Are you happy when you're with me?"

"Yes."

At that, Luke's eyes seemed to shine even brighter. "Well, then?"

"It's not that simple. I have a life in Brookline. I love Eddie. And Maddie is my everything."

"If you really love Eddie, then why are you here with me?"

"I'm not sure."

"I can make you happy, Sloane. I really believe that. But you need to figure things out for yourself first."

"I will. I promise. I'm not trying to lead you on."

"That's my girl." He wrapped his arm around her again and squeezed her close. "Now let's go have some fun, okay? That's what the rest of today will be about. Good old-fashioned fun." He smiled down at her adoringly.

"Sounds good to me."

"I thought it would." He jumped up. "Last one to the Jet Skis gets thrown in the water!"

"Then watch out!" Sloane pushed him aside, shrieking as he tried to catch up with her. Could it really be this simple? Was this what happiness felt like?

chapter 24

Hillary sat on the back deck with her knees to her chest as she gazed at the morning sun rising over the lake. For hours she'd been coiled in the fetal position in a dark green Adirondack chair, which was, deceptively, more comfortable than it looked. She'd been rudely awakened once again at three a.m. by the shrill peal of Georgina's cell phone and had been unable to fall back to sleep. In part because Georgina's phone had continued to ring; first it had been at five-minute intervals. Then ten, twenty, and, finally, on the half hour until six o'clock, when Hillary had finally decided to get out of bed and head downstairs to brew a cup of coffee and have some time to herself before the other women awoke. Hillary had no idea how Sloane could sleep through the incessant chiming. Certainly Georgina could not have, given her proximity to the phone.

Still, she couldn't blame her insomnia entirely on the phone calls. Prior to being roused, she'd had a strange dream. She'd been expecting—around seven months along—and overjoyed about the whole thing. *That* had been the strange part. It wasn't the first time Hillary had dreamed of being pregnant, but—up until this point—those fantasies had played out more like nightmares, in which she'd been trying desperately to get the baby out of her belly or resolve how she was going to give it away before Greg figured it out. To anyone else these thoughts, or manifestations, whatever they were, might have seemed drastic, even cruel. But Hillary knew better. She understood how the unconscious mind worked. Of course she'd never attempt to abort her pregnancy—on her own or otherwise. Of course she wouldn't give her child to a stranger. Or try to hide from Greg that they were about to become parents.

It would never come to that point because she could far more easily and ethically ensure that she didn't get pregnant in the first place. Well, the ethical part was debatable, since she was well aware that it was unconscionable to delude Greg in this way. Her husband. The man who loved her more than anyone or anything in the world.

And why was it that she couldn't confide her deepest, darkest secret in this man who adored her unconditionally? She didn't have an answer beyond utter fear. Beyond being steeped in guilt and stifled by self-hatred for having lied for so long. She'd never kept anything from him before, much less something so earth-shattering. She'd never thought she was capable of betraying him so profoundly.

They'd always had a strong, solid relationship. One based on communication and trust. But what if he didn't understand where she was coming from? What if he said that not having kids was a deal breaker? What if he hated her for being so cold and callous, not to mention calculating? What if he equated her to her own mother? What if he left?

At some point as she'd tossed and turned, eager to glean a few more hours of sleep, her thoughts had turned to Isla, the little girl at the beach. She'd been so darling. She'd let her mind wander to the ruffled dresses she could buy her and the itty-bitty Mary Janes. Not to mention the hair bows and the manicures they could have together. Side by side. Mother and daughter. Hillary knew as well as anyone that pink tutus and sparkly ballet slippers did not a parent make, but perhaps the rest would come naturally. Perhaps if she dived in headfirst, she would figure it all out.

She'd remembered that a few months earlier, when she'd been in line at her local bagel shop in town, there'd been a group of women gathered around a table rallying their parenting woes like a Ping Pong ball—back and forth, back and forth, until someone slammed down a winner. The first woman had complained of a colicky baby who spit up everything he ate. The second woman had griped about a three-year-old whose diva demeanor made Mariah Carey look like a kitten. The third woman had then come in with the kicker, declaring that not only was her son dyslexic, but he was also allergic to dairy, gluten, and most fruits, with the odd exception of kiwis. For the next ten minutes—Hillary had taken a seat near them so she could hear the conversation in its entirety—the three of them had bounced grievances off one another at warp speed. Until finally, they'd all turned to the fourth woman—who'd been silent to that point—and collectively raised their eyebrows. She'd looked new to motherhood, still with a swollen postpartum belly. Hillary had watched her face morph from rapt attention to fear of being put on the spot. She'd waited for her to burst into tears or to engage in their table tennis game of "my kid's more challenging than yours." But she hadn't. She'd just smiled serenely, shrugged her shoulders, and said, "I'm just figuring it all out as I go along."

Her friends had shared knowing smirks. One had even rolled her eyes when she wasn't looking. Hillary had finished her bagel and left, wondering which of those women she'd end up like. Would she be the perpetually harried mom, whose child carried on in the middle of any well-populated public space, wailing louder and louder as if only to spite her? Or would she fall in with the rare breed of unruffled mothers who toted stocked diaper bags, ready to produce clean tissues for snotty noses and an array of snacks to sate the most ravenous of appetites at a moment's notice?

Hillary sighed, still unable to envision herself proudly pushing a pram down the sidewalk wearing a perma-grin without a care in the world outside of her precious newborn. Even if a part of her had started to warm to motherhood, she still couldn't envision it for herself. And how could she proceed with such a life-changing event if she couldn't even fathom it in her imagination? How on earth could she expect herself to deal with the reality and the possibility that her mother's mental illness would prove hereditary? So she unraveled her legs, stretching them out in front of her, and stood up to do the same with her arms, rotating side to side at the waist in order to relieve the cricks in her back. Then she walked back inside to fill her coffee mug, only to find Georgina pacing the great room and whispering urgently into her cell phone. As soon as she saw Hillary, she ended the call without warning.

"Would you believe it was the wrong number again? Completely ridiculous." She tilted her head to one side, ostensibly inspecting Hillary's face for a reaction. "You look tired."

"Probably because I was up all night."

"Oh yeah? A lot on your mind?" Georgina dropped herself onto the sofa, burrowed her head into the armrest, and draped her legs over the back side in one fluid motion. "I didn't sleep that well either."

"There's a shocker." Hillary sat down next to her. Enough was enough. "Do you think perhaps it was because your cell phone didn't stop ringing all night?"

"Was it?" Georgina avoided eye contact.

"Georgina." Hillary's voice was stern. In many ways, dealing with Georgina was like managing her patients, the teenage ones.

"Hillary." Georgina feigned a sober expression, which cracked into a smile after a minute. "I told you it was a mistake. For whatever reason, they don't seem to get it. Maybe I'll change my number today."

"I don't believe you." There, she'd said it. If there was one thing she'd learned through years of practicing family counseling, it was to be direct and to the point. She probably should have said something sooner, rather than letting this farce continue.

"Fine, you're right. It's way too nice a day to spend running errands! Should we go back to the beach?"

"Georgina, you know that's not what I meant."

"Huh?"

"Those calls. The ones you've been receiving at all hours of the night are not a mistake."

"I don't know what you're talking about." She shook her head defiantly. Another move that reminded Hillary of her teenage patients.

"I think you do." She inched closer and placed her hand on Georgina's leg. "Can you talk to me? Maybe I can help."

Hillary had considered only briefly the extent to which Georgina could be in trouble. She just hoped whatever was provoking all these urgent and excessive calls wasn't illegal. What if she was on the run for having committed some sort of crime and Sloane's family was harboring a fugitive? Would the authorities assume that Sloane and Hillary had been willing conspirators? The idea seemed preposterous, cinematic even, but when it came down to it, how well did she really know Georgina? For that matter, how well did Sloane know her after all this time? She'd said herself that she hadn't seen Georgina in years and that their communications via phone and e-mail had been scant at best.

Still, what could she have done? She didn't seem the type to rob a bank, not to mention that Sloane had said Georgina was set for life financially, thanks to family money. And she certainly hadn't killed someone. What else could be so bad?

"I highly doubt you can help me."

"So you admit it's not a wrong number?"

"I didn't say that." Georgina cleared her throat and began fidgeting with the tassels embellishing one of the throw pillows on the couch.

"Fine, then let me answer next time your phone rings."

"No!"

"Why not?"

"Because it's private."

"What's private?" Hillary leaned forward. "Georgina, you have to talk to someone. If not me, then Sloane."

"Yeah, right."

"She's your best friend."

"She can't know about this." Georgina squeezed her eyes shut. "Sloane cannot know about this."

"Why not?"

"Because . . ." Georgina opened her eyes and Hillary noticed that they'd welled with tears. "Because then she'll really believe I'm an awful person."

"That's not true."

"Yes, it is. Trust me. You don't know her the way I do."

"Well, then let's have it, Georgina. I assure you this isn't my first rodeo. Whatever your situation is, I have heard worse." As she spoke, she fervently hoped it was true.

"I don't know."

"This is my job. You can't hold this in indefinitely. Talk to me, please."

"Fine. You really want to know?"

"Yes." Hillary nodded decisively.

"I had a baby. Okay? Is that what you wanted to hear? Happy now?"

"If you're going to make light of the situation, I'll find a better way to spend my time. I just thought it might help for you to talk to someone."

"It's the truth," she whispered, her voice quivering now.

"I'm sorry, but I don't understand." Hillary tried not to let her expression show how stunned she was. One of the worst things a counselor could do was register obvious emotion.

"Just over a year ago, I had a little girl. Zara Rose. She's got red hair like I do." Georgina's voice splintered at that point.

"Where is she now?" Hillary had so many questions she wasn't sure where to begin and she also knew how important it was not to toss them off rapid-fire at Georgina just when she was starting to open up.

"In England."

"With whom?"

"Hugh. And my mom."

"So they're the ones who've been calling?"

"Yup."

"Is everything okay with Zara?"

"Oh, yeah. She's perfect." Georgina smiled sincerely.

"Then what's the issue?"

"I kind of took off without saying good-bye."

"I'm going to need more of an explanation than that."

"When I found out that Sloane was on her way back to Lake George, it felt like a gift. I needed an out. Somewhere I could go to get away from my life. From Hugh. Even from Zara. I know that sounds terrible."

"No, it doesn't. Not at all. Every mother needs a break. It's completely natural."

"Is it natural that I'm not going back?" Georgina looked Hillary in the eyes for the first time since her confession and Hillary could see the intense fear welling up inside her.

"What do you mean you're not going back?"

"I have no plans to return to London. At all. I left a note saying I'd be home in a week or so, but when Hugh saw that most of my stuff was gone, he sort of figured it out. Smart chap."

"No wonder you brought so much with you."

"Yup."

"I see." Hillary scolded herself for not having been more observant. Georgina was a stubborn nut to crack, but Hillary might have figured out sooner that there was so much cracking to be done.

"So now what do you think of me? Mommy of the year, huh? Who would even believe me in the role of someone's mother? Poor kid."

"It's not my place to judge you. Georgina, everyone has their own stuff to deal with. Everyone makes mistakes."

"This isn't a mistake, though. It's best for everyone."

"How so?"

"You haven't noticed I'm not maternal material?"

"Just because you like to have fun doesn't mean you can't be a successful parent too."

"It's not about that at all."

"Then what is it?"

"I never meant to get pregnant in the first place. I never wanted a child. I've known my whole life that I'm not cut out to be a mother. It finally occurred to me that she'll be better off without me. That's what dawned on me when I learned about Sloane coming to Lake George for a few weeks. It was my chance to escape. All I'd be good for is screwing Zara up."

"I doubt that. And what does Hugh say?"

"Obviously he wants me to come back, but I just can't do it. I can't. He can love her enough for both of us. He's good at the parenting thing."

"Not everyone is a natural from day one. It takes time. Surely you've learned something in a year."

"I haven't exactly been around much. I'm a wanderer, Hillary—

I need to move from place to place. Check in at home occasionally and then hit the road again. Only now, I'm not sure about the checking in. I think it would be too confusing."

"For who? You? Or Zara? Don't you think she needs you?"

"She may think she does, but—as I said—I know she's better off without me." Georgina sniffed. "And you want to know the irony? My own mom is a better mother figure to Zara than she ever was to me. By a long shot."

Hillary wondered whether her parents would be that way if she and Greg had children—improved versions of their former selves. Second-chance parenting. "Still, she's not Zara's mom. Only you can fill that role."

"Only genetically speaking. And I think we both know genes do not make a mom."

"True." How many times had Hillary said practically the exact same thing to her patients—those who'd been adopted or abandoned by their mother or father.

"I know what you're thinking, whether you say you're judging me or not. Who does something like this, right? Only someone rotten inside."

"Actually that's not what I'm thinking."

"Well, now you know my little secret."

"Not so little."

"Please don't tell Sloane." Georgina's eyes watered again. "I can't take any more stress at the moment."

"Georgina, you can't keep this from her forever."

"I don't know about forever. But I can't tell her now. You have to *swear* to me you won't either. She'll side with Hugh and she'll be furious with me. Sorry, even more furious than she is at me about not being there when Amy died."

"So that's why you were missing in action last year."

"That's why."

"She'll understand eventually."

"I don't know." Georgina was crying softly now. "The thing is, Hillary, Sloane used to look up to me. Even if it was for all the wrong reasons, she did. I'm not as ditzy as I come across sometimes, you know?"

"I can see that."

"Sloane always envied the fun I had and we were such a good pair together."

"What do you think would happen if she found out about Zara?"

"She certainly wouldn't have anything about me to admire anymore. But more than that, I don't want her to be disappointed in me. To see me for the loser I actually am."

"You're being too harsh on yourself."

"Oh yeah? Try this on for size. Woman in her mid-thirties, whose good looks are dwindling. Single. Abandoned her child. No home. No friends. Glamorous, huh?"

"I'm your friend."

"Oh God." Georgina's hand flew to her mouth. "I've been entirely insensitive. Here you are trying to get pregnant and I'm yammering on about walking out on a child I didn't even plan on having. Lovely, aren't I?"

"It's okay."

"No, it's not. I'm a selfish cow."

"You're not the only one." Hillary hunched down in her seat.

"Right—as if you've been selfish a day in your life."

"You'd be surprised." Hillary took a deep breath.

"I doubt it." Georgina stood up and Hillary followed. "I'm going to take a shower. Maybe we can talk more later?"

"Of course."

"Thank you." She pulled Hillary into a tight hug.

"Any time." Georgina started toward the stairs. "Georgina?"

"Yeah?"

"Your secret is safe with me for now. But trust me when I tell you this. You can run, but you can't hide forever. At some point you'll be more desperate to confide your secret than to keep it." Hillary swallowed a lump in her throat. "Even if you think Sloane is going to be upset, you have to trust her enough to tell her the truth. If she's really your best friend, she'll forgive you."

"You're right. I know you're right."

"Then you'll tell her? Sooner rather than later?"

"I'll tell her." Georgina nodded reluctantly.

"Soon?" Hillary couldn't help but press.

"Yes, but just not today. Okay?"

"Okay." Hillary sighed, knowing full well she should take her own advice and tell Greg her secret before the ramifications became too steep to anticipate, much less endure. Just not today.

chapter 25

She'd spent another whole day with Luke on his boat. Neither Georgina nor Hillary had made any mention of her absence, and, come to think of it, they'd both been acting out of character when she'd arrived home. Georgina had been unusually reserved and hadn't expressed so much as a modicum of interest in her time spent with Luke. Typically she'd have peppered Sloane with a litany of questions, attempting to pry every last detail out of her until she'd been rendered breathless. Hillary, for her part, hadn't been reticent, but she had been overly defensive of Georgina, even when Sloane had lightheartedly mocked her for stubbing her toe on the kitchen island for the fourth time that week.

Why did it feel like the tables had turned, leaving Sloane alone on one side with Georgina and Hillary sandwiched together like the best friends of the trio? Of course Sloane couldn't let them know that it bothered her that they had become so close—what kind of a person got upset that her good friends had become friends? So, instead, she'd kept to herself, waiting to speak until someone else initiated conversation. Something must have been in the air, because none of them were particularly chatty and they'd all gone to bed early. Had she been the only one to notice the tense mood? Or worse, were they discussing it together behind her back?

Either way, she'd welcomed the extra sleep and had awakened feeling refreshed. In her dreams she could be who she wanted to be without any of the work required to make difficult changes in her life. In fact, there was no scenario too convoluted for her to make sense of once her unconscious had taken over. And she'd explored many of them in the past week or so. But surprisingly she hadn't dreamed of Luke last night.

She'd been nervous going back out on the boat with him on the heels of their last conversation. But this time, Luke had called to invite her rather than Serena. He'd promised no love talk. He'd said he just wanted to spend the day with her, sweep the demons from their minds, and have another dose of good old-fashioned fun together. Sloane had been amused by the turn of phrase considering that Luke didn't do anything the old-fashioned way. There wasn't so much as a roll of toilet paper that had been on the boat for more than a New York minute.

The angel on her shoulder had encouraged her to rebuff his offer—enough was enough, her conscience seemed to be telling her, shaking her haloed head, but the devil had nodded so vigorously, reminding her that there was absolutely nothing wrong with enjoying a day out on the water with a good friend. Her devilish side had triumphed. And she'd boarded the *Edwina* promptly at eleven o'clock before they'd set off for lunch at Christie's, a casual steakhouse boasting the best views of Lake George and the tastiest salads and burgers around. They'd split steamed clams, a crab cake sandwich, and a large slice of cheesecake from Northwoods, purveyor of the creamiest and probably most calorie-laden cheesecakes known to man—each bite so decadently luxurious it quite literally melted in your mouth like a warm chocolate soufflé.

After that, they'd cruised the lake for hours, sometimes lying next to each other in complete silence. That was the thing about Luke; he didn't feel the need to fill empty space with idle chatter. He reminded her of Hillary in that way. When they hadn't been sun-bathing, they'd gone for a dip in the water to cool off.

As the day had started coming to a close, Luke had wrapped her in a towel and then himself. They'd taken a seat on the back deck, sipping frozen margaritas and snacking on a spread fit for at least three times as many people—cheeses, crackers, fruit, tortilla chips, hummus, and some kind of fried fritters that Sloane could easily have eaten the entire plate of by herself. They'd talked again about Luke's brother, Teddy. Finally he'd been located by a friend, Abe, at a dive bar in Manhattan's Greenwich Village. According to Abe, Teddy had been high as a kite and wasted off his ass. He'd taken him back to his apartment and called Luke to let him know he'd do his best to keep Teddy there and sober for as long as possible, but they both knew that once Teddy's belligerence kicked in, there was little any one person could do to confine him. Apparently Abe had ended the call by saying, "I'm really sorry, dude. But I'm kind of scared of him."

Luke, despite what he'd told Sloane previously, had stepped in to save the day. He'd sent a car service with two security guards to make sure Teddy didn't try to run off. Teddy had then been driven back to the facility in Connecticut to resume his lifelong battle against drugs and alcohol. It had been a heavy ending to such a light day, but Sloane didn't care, because it had only made her feel that much closer to Luke. She couldn't help but wonder if that was what it would be like if they were married. They could ride the ups and downs of life together, side by side, no hill too steep to climb, no drop too sharp to free-fall hand in hand.

The next morning Sloane came downstairs to find a note in the kitchen from Georgina and Hillary saying they'd gone for a walk on the beach and would be back in under an hour. She opened the refrigerator door and grabbed the orange juice, a carton of eggs, two slices of Swiss cheese, and a container of ripe cherry tomatoes. Hillary had been doing most of the cooking, which was a welcome contribution, but Sloane was happy to have breakfast alone for once with the morning newspaper and her thoughts. Just as she was about to crack the first of two eggs into a frying pan, her cell phone rang with an unrecognizable international number flashing on the caller ID.

"Hello?"

"Sloane, is that you?" The line was fuzzy and she could barely make out the woman's words, much less identify the voice behind them.

"It is. May I ask whom I'm speaking to?"

"Oh, thank goodness. It's Vivienne." Sloane searched her brain to match a face with the name.

"Vivienne who?"

"Vivienne Fielding."

"I'm so sorry! It's been so long. How are you?" Sloane had met Georgina's mother on only a handful of occasions, and each time she'd fallen in love with her just a little bit more. That wasn't to say she would have wanted Vivienne Fielding as her own mother, but she was an absolute whirlwind of everything fabulous as long as she wasn't responsible for raising you. Sort of like Sloane's aunt. Actually, it was a shame she'd never introduced them.

"Not good. I wish I was calling under happier circumstances."

"I see." Sloane had a sudden Amy flashback. "Are you looking for Georgina?"

"I am, in fact."

"Well, she's out for a walk right now."

"So she *is* with you. I knew it! Hugh didn't think she'd dare go that far, but I know my Georgina. Damn her." Sloane overheard her speaking to someone else in the background. "Where exactly are you living now, my love? Did I hear Boston?"

"Well, I live in a Boston suburb, but we're all at my aunt's vacation home in Lake George right now." This was one of the strangest and most unexpected conversations she'd had in quite a while. Why was she so desperate to locate Georgina? She certainly wasn't someone who reliably stayed put for any great length of time. Neither of them was—a common trait between mother and daughter. "Is there something I can help you with?"

"Yes, you can tell Georgina that if she doesn't return Hugh's calls or phone me by tonight, I . . . I . . . I don't know. Just let her know that if she knows what's good for her . . . No, no, here's what's going to happen. I'm going to have her father freeze her trust fund. That should get her attention, since nothing else seems to."

"Um, okay." Sloane had never heard Vivienne sound so stern or, dare she say, motherly. "I don't mean to be nosy, but is there a reason you're in such dire pursuit of her?"

"Well, obviously, the baby, Sloane."

"What baby?"

"*Her* baby. Zara. Well, I guess she's not really a baby anymore."

"Excuse me?"

"Georgina's daughter, Sloane. You know."

"No, actually I don't." Sloane squeezed her eyes shut as a tumult of emotions swirled around in her chest, threatening to tear her open from the inside as it escalated. How could she? Who was she? Sloane didn't know *this* Georgina. For her to have a child and not tell her? It was so far out of the realm of possibility . . . except that apparently it wasn't.

"For God's sake." Vivienne sighed, as if she'd finally reached her limit in parenting such a wildly volatile child, never mind that she had barely been present for any parenting duties during Georgina's youth. "Sloane, I'm at a loss for what to say. She's left Zara behind, and, from what we can tell, she has no immediate plans to return. Hugh and I have been calling her every day, over and over. Poor man is up to his ears in poopy nappies. She left him with absolutely no warning."

"I can only imagine." Sloane tried to pull herself together in the wake of Vivienne's shocking news. Although "shocking" didn't even really do it justice. "You can be sure I'll pass along the message."

"You're a gem, Sloane. You were always such a good girl."

"Thank you." If only Vivienne knew.

"And remember. No phone call, no money. Georgina is allergic to the word 'budget.' "

"Got it."

Once they'd hung up, Sloane walked into the great room, sat down on the sofa, and stared at the wall in front of her. She'd lost her appetite. It couldn't be true. Georgina couldn't have gone through forty weeks of pregnancy—and how many months of motherhood?—without telling Sloane. Her best friend. What a joke, right? Real best friends didn't withhold life-altering information. Real best friends didn't look you in the eye and lie again and again and again. Even if she had never asked her outright, "Hey, don't suppose you had a baby and forgot to mention it?" it went without saying that Georgina should have shared the news of the birth of her child with her. Either way, it was the deepest sort of deception.

Sloane was practically panting with anger, ready to pounce as soon as Georgina came through the front door. There was no stopping her now. Every lingering emotion she'd felt for the last two years was hissing to the surface. She had allowed Georgina to crash her vacation with Hillary, willing to give her time to open up about why she hadn't been there last year for Sloane, and *this* was how she repaid her? She was a ticking time bomb waiting to detonate.

She stayed in the same spot for thirty-five minutes, completely silent and motionless, watching the clock as the second and minute hands made their rounds. And then it happened. She heard the key turn in the lock and Georgina's rowdy laughter spilling into the house, as if she didn't have a care in the world.

Hillary followed Georgina into the room, and it was evident on her face that she immediately sensed that something was wrong.

"Are you okay, Sloane?" Hillary approached her.

"Yeah, you look kind of pissed." Georgina started toward her as well.

"Don't come near me." Sloane pointed a stiff index finger at Georgina.

"What's got you so cranky?"

"Well, let's see." Sloane shot up to her feet so she could come as close to Georgina's height as possible. "I just had *the* most fascinating call from your mother." Her voice was trembling.

"Oh." Georgina's face turned pale.

"How's your daughter, Georgina? What's her name again?"

"Zara," Georgina mumbled, and looked at the ground.

"DO NOT TALK TO ME!" In her rage, Sloane was pretty sure she had screamed louder than she ever had before.

"Okay, Sloane, let's try to relax." Hillary went to touch her arm, but Sloane jerked it backward.

"Relax? Did you hear what I just said? Georgina has a child! She has a fucking child who she just fucking failed to tell us *anything* about. That doesn't strike you as completely fucked-up?" Hillary diverted her eyes away from Sloane's. "No. Do not even tell me . . ."

"I knew." Hillary nodded.

"You have got to be kidding me." Sloane flailed her arms in the air. "You told *her* before telling me? Oh, wait, I'm sorry, you didn't actually tell me. I had to hear it from your mom! Imagine my fucking embarrassment, Georgina, when she assumed that I knew. Because why wouldn't she assume that? Who would keep something that big from their best friend—that's what you call me, right? Your best friend? So, educate me. Who would not tell their fucking best friend in the whole wide world that they were pregnant? Or keep it a secret that they've given birth to a little girl?!"

Georgina didn't say anything.

"And you." She turned to Hillary now. "I can't believe you had anything to do with keeping this from me. Why didn't *you* tell me once you knew? You're *my* friend. What's your excuse? How could you feel more loyalty to Georgina than to me?"

"Sloane, I just found out yesterday." Hillary maintained her composure like the professional she was, which served only to fuel Sloane's ire.

"Sure, you did. How do you expect me to believe anything either of you says now?"

"She's telling the truth," Georgina interjected.

"Of course you'd defend her." Sloane shook her head vigorously. "And by the way, Georgina, since Hillary is your new favorite person, don't you think it's a little insensitive that you couldn't give a shit about your own child when Hillary has been trying so hard to get pregnant? I mean, she has quite literally been devoting years to something you've just shit on. You are so goddamn inconsiderate and selfish, I don't even know who you are anymore. I'm disgusted." Sloane practically spit out the last part.

"I understand." Georgina was crying quietly now.

"I'm not done yet. You know something, Georgina? I came here pretty pissed off that you hadn't bothered to call me once. Not one time when Amy died. Can you even imagine what that felt like? To have the person you're closest to, the person you spent your entire life growing up with and looking out for, stolen from you at such a young age?" Sloane swallowed a sob. "She was everything to me and you didn't care at all. You didn't care one fucking bit. All you cared about were your own problems. That's who you are, Georgina. Well . . . I hope you end up alone with no one by your side to love you."

"You don't mean that." Hillary tried to cut in.

"Like hell I don't." Sloane wiped away the tears that had started running down her cheeks involuntarily and dashed toward the front door. Before leaving, she paused, took a deep breath, and, without turning to look at either of them, said softly, "I'll be back in a few hours. Georgina, I'll expect you to be gone by then."

Twenty minutes later, Sloane found her car stopped in front of Luke's gate. One of the staff buzzed her in, and by the time she'd reached the house, Luke was waiting for her outside. She ran toward him, collapsing into his arms, weeping uncontrollably.

She tried to speak, but nothing that came out made any sense. He just held her close to him. Then he lifted her face with his hands and started to kiss her, parting her lips with his own.

"Wait! I can't do this." Sloane pulled away and put a little distance in between them. "It's moving too fast. I have a husband and a daughter to think of."

"I want you to come away with me, Sloane." He whispered in her ear, "Please, come away with me."

chapter 26

After Sloane stormed off, Georgina had immediately withdrawn to her bedroom, leaving Hillary standing alone in the middle of the great room feeling like she'd just been soaked to the bone by a torrential monsoon of emotions. Sloane had been suppressing her anger at Georgina for more than a year, and by this point, there hadn't been much Hillary could have done to help Georgina and Sloane resolve their feud in an amicable manner. If she had a dime for every time she'd reminded her own patients that bottling things up was never an effective approach to a relationship, she'd be a zillionaire by now.

Still, people dealt with things the way they needed to—it had to feel right for them. She had learned this the hard way with her own father. Hillary recalled how when she was younger, he'd grunt and grimace at her mother's profound incompetence, muttering expletives under his breath loud enough to reach anyone within earshot. Sometimes, she'd even eavesdrop, crouched into a ball outside the door of his home office. He'd be speaking in an urgent but hushed tone about how utterly incapable her mother was of existing in the same world as everyone else. How he was sick and tired of having to look after her like she was an invalid. But he never said anything about it to Hillary's mom. He never let on what a burden she was, because—in reality—he didn't allow her to be much of a burden where he was concerned. Work was his sanctuary and he spent as many waking hours immersed in it as possible.

Until the one afternoon when everything had changed for them. Hillary had returned home from high school to find her father's new Jaguar parked in the driveway in the middle of the day. She'd had a sense of foreboding as soon as she'd seen it, since he rarely ever came home before ten o'clock, and ten was an early night. Hillary had walked into the house, unbeknownst to either of her parents, and she'd overheard her father railing at her mother, detailing every irresponsible thing she'd ever done like the litigator he was. In his chilling voice, which Hillary had witnessed only once before, in the courtroom, he'd boomed insults and threats, calling her stupid and lazy, and telling her she ought to pull it together if she expected him to stay married to her.

Hillary had been terrified by the sounds of his unbridled rage, unsure whether to stay and save her mother or to flee to their neighborhood park and cry her eyes out on the swing set. She'd picked the latter. And, as she'd sat there, staring at a colony of ants creeping single file into an almost invisible hole, she'd thought about how organized they'd looked. It was teamwork at the most fundamental level. If one of the ants had decided to scurry off in a different direction, surely the head ant would *communicate* that this sort of behavior was troublesome.

Next she'd gazed up at the sky, watching intently as a flock of birds had aggregated and then flown in intricate patterns, looping above, under, and around one another. She could only assume these configurations made sense to them. Wasn't that all that really mattered? That whomever you chose to soar through life with—be it a significant other, a family member, or a friend—was someone who got you. Someone who understood what made you happy. And sad. Someone who both spoke and listened. Someone who did not bury his or her grievances beneath a polished surface.

If all those ants and all those birds could function together in harmony, why was it sometimes so hard for fully grown adults to do the same? Weren't human beings supposed to be the evolved ones? First her parents, now Sloane and Georgina.

Hillary had figured out how her parents operated a long time ago. In public they dressed up in their finest suits and most extravagant ball gowns, wearing their handsomest smiles and shrewdest smirks, having learned to adjust their own moods according to whomever they were speaking to at the moment. Of course in the privacy of their own home, there was none of that. The morning following a swanky event, one of those very same gowns could be found crumpled into a ball, perhaps torn at the edge where her mother had safety pinned it at the beginning of the evening. Not because she didn't have other gowns to wear or because she couldn't afford a new one. But because—simply stated—the action of driving into town to the tailor was just too much for her mother on an average day. There wasn't enough medication in the medicine cabinet to render that task an easy one for her.

As Hillary's father had once told her, "Going to the supermarket for your mother is the equivalent of you or I planting and growing all that food ourselves." It had been the one and only time he'd acknowledged that there was a problem, and though she hadn't exactly grasped the complexity of the concept back then, his words had eventually become the most concise means of explaining her mother's very obvious deficit.

She knew that if her father hadn't been so hell-bent on keeping up appearances, they'd have been divorced long before Hillary had been old enough to speak. But even now that they were older and her father had made a name for himself so prominent no one could ever take it away from him, he still remained her faithful husband. Well, maybe not entirely faithful. Perhaps it wasn't only about what other people thought. Maybe he liked having a wife who wasn't constantly vying for his attention. A wife who didn't care if he played eighteen holes of golf instead of nine. A wife who—although she would never have dinner on the table— wouldn't ask twice about where he was going if he wanted to dine out and, in that eventuality, whom he would be dining with. When Hillary's mother wasn't unknowingly threatening to burn down the house, Hillary supposed she wasn't much of a nuisance to her father at all.

It was impossible to say what would happen with Sloane and Georgina. In many ways they were more alike than either of them cared to admit. Would all this be water under the bridge eventually? Would they go back to being the "best friends" they once were or the "best friends" they'd become? Just as men and women in relationships grew apart, so could girlfriends. While there were some bonds that were everlasting when people were fortunate enough to develop at the same pace and in the same directions, still there were other cases where no matter how close you'd once been or hoped you could still be, there was little left in the relationship to salvage. The same person who got everything about you and then some in high school or college might very well have transformed into someone you wouldn't actually want to be friends with if you'd met her as an adult. Or worse, she might have remained stagnant, while you had been busy defining yourself beyond football games and fraternity bashes. And sometimes, even when both parties were determined to revive what they once had, the writing was too big and too bold on the proverbial wall. Too much had been said. Too much had remained unsaid.

Hillary moved slowly toward the open French doors leading onto the back deck and inhaled a blast of fresh air in the hope that it would revitalize her. She wasn't sure where Sloane had gone, but she was sure of one thing. Sloane would be okay. She had Eddie. She had Madeleine. And apparently she had Luke as well. That discussion was for a later date. Right now she needed to talk to Georgina. To tell her that she understood her, perhaps better than Sloane ever could. To open up to her and admit her own secret, the one that had been scorching a hole in her heart.

She turned back toward the stairs and ascended in the direction of Georgina's bedroom. There was loud music thumping inside, a song she'd never heard. She knocked twice and waited. Nothing. She knocked again a little louder. Still nothing.

"Georgina, are you in there?" She was pounding now, fearing the worst, though she couldn't let her mind go there.

"What is it?" Georgina finally cracked the door open, barely revealing her mottled, tearstained face.

"Can we talk?" Hillary smiled sincerely, indicating that she came in peace.

"Funny thing. I'm not really in the mood to chitchat." Georgina disappeared into the room and in the next instant Hillary followed her. She hadn't expected Georgina to be quite that transparent in her desire for help and companionship.

"Okay if I come in, then?"

"Do what you want." Georgina crept onto her bed and tucked herself under the covers.

"Great, then. I will." Hillary crawled over Georgina and—to Georgina's obvious surprise and discomfiture—tucked herself under the covers right next to her.

They sat quietly together for what felt like an hour. It had started to pour outside, as the weatherman had predicted on the previous evening's news, and the rhythmic pitter-patter of raindrops pelting the roof was somehow soothing.

"I'm sorry," Georgina finally said, breaking the silence.

"I'm the one that's sorry." Hillary looked at her and then, realizing how preposterously close they were, threw back her side of the bedspread and rearranged herself to be facing Georgina.

"That doesn't make any sense." Georgina shook her head and Hillary noticed anew how naturally beautiful she was, even after she'd had a good long cry. "I'm the one that lied about having a child.

Sloane was right. And I should have been more considerate around you, what with . . ."

"I'm on birth control." The words fell out of her mouth and, to both her disgust and delight, she felt instantly lighter.

"Yeah, sure." Georgina laughed incredulously.

"It's the truth."

"What do you mean?" Georgina leaned forward, her attention clearly seized by the staggering news.

"I mean that every day, for three weeks straight, rain or shine, I pop one of those little blue pills, wash it down with water, and protect myself from getting pregnant."

"But why? I don't get it."

"Because I'm not sure I want to be a mom."

"And Greg doesn't know?"

"Nobody knows."

"Holy shit."

"Yup. What do you think of me now?"

"I think I love you."

"Oh yeah?" Hillary laughed despite herself. "And why is that?"

"Because you're almost as fucked-up as I am."

"Hey, now. Let's not go that far."

"So you just changed your mind one day?" Georgina slid her legs out from underneath the covers and crossed them in front of her.

"Nope. I never went off the pill in the first place. I told myself I needed more time to think about it. That I'd do it in a couple of days. But then days turned into weeks, weeks turned into months, and months turned into three years this summer. I know it's beyond awful." Her eyes filled with tears. "The worst part of all is that Greg would make the best father in the world."

"And you would make the best mother in the world."

"See, that's where you're wrong."

"No way."

"Way." Hillary nodded. "Just because I can throw together a mean picnic basket doesn't mean I have the maternal gene. A child needs more from her mother."

"I hear you there, and I can't even throw together a mean picnic basket, but I don't believe you. I'd venture to say I've never known someone as well suited to be a mom as you are."

"Strike two."

"Tell me why."

"To be honest, I'm not sure. I thought it was all about the timing. That when I was ready, I'd feel ready. You know?"

"Not really."

"Right, well, that *ready* feeling never arrived. I guess, in large part, it's because of how I was raised—or not raised—by my own mother. As I mentioned, she was deeply depressed. I suspect maybe she suffered from another kind of mood disorder too, although it's never been diagnosed. She was always so sad. What if that's me ten years from now?"

"You're not depressed, though."

"No, not now, but it can be genetic. And as a child, I was given to bouts of what they called 'the blues.' "

"Probably because you had crap parents."

"Maybe, but it's impossible to say. With all of the hormones coursing through your body during and after pregnancy, who knows? Don't get me wrong, I'm happy for my life, but—in truth—my mother and father never should have had me. According to my father, my mother's problems didn't surface until after I was born. What if that happens to me and my unborn child? What if I get post-partum depression and it never goes away?"

"And you haven't talked to Greg about your concerns at all?"

"Not really. I brought it up once early on, but he doesn't see it. He says I'm nothing like my mother and could never be. He doesn't think there's anything to worry about. He sees only the best in me. I know he'd tell me we have no idea what the future holds and that having a child is worth the fear I'm feeling."

"You're kind of a bitch, huh?" Georgina was looking and acting more like herself again, having been distracted from her own despair by someone else's harrowing issues. "Just kidding."

"You're right, actually."

"Obviously no judgment here."

"Can I ask you something?"

"Sure."

"Do you miss her? Zara."

Georgina's expression turned solemn, as if on cue. "Yes."

"Then why not go back to London?"

"Just because I miss her doesn't mean I want to be a mother."

"But you are."

"Only by relation. If I stuck around, I would just end up screwing up that little girl."

"I've never met another woman who knows how I feel. Or at least not one who will admit it."

"That's the thing. There are so many people out there who have kids for their own selfish reasons or because they think it's the next natural step. I'm not that person. And I've never been apologetic for not wanting to be."

"Until now."

"Until now."

"What if she needs you one day?"

"She'll find me, I guess." Georgina thought about this. "What about you? Will you ever tell Greg?"

"I have to. It's already gone on way too long. I can't believe I've been keeping such a horrible secret from him."

"If he loves you as much as you say he does, I bet he'll forgive you."

"Would you?"

"I don't know."

"He might leave me."

"He might."

"Then I'll have to come live with you."

"Oh, you haven't heard? I have no home."

"Home is—"

"Please do not say 'where the heart is.' " They both laughed.

"I was going to say 'where you make it and with whom you make it.' "

"I like that. And you." She gave her a warm smile.

"Weren't planning on that, huh?"

"Well, you know what they say. The best-laid plans . . ."

"Are bullshit?"

"Exactly."

chapter 27

Come away with me. Those four weighty words had been orbiting in her head on repeat for the past twenty-four hours. And the kiss—it had been so brief, so delicate. And with it had come a moment of such surprising intimacy. She almost felt as if she'd dreamed it. Almost. She'd had to close her eyes and indulge in that moment countless times since, if only to convince herself that it had actually transpired. Then, immediately feeling incredibly guilty, she'd tell herself it wasn't romantic. That she'd done nothing wrong. It was a peck. She hadn't initiated it and she'd stopped it as quickly as she'd realized what was happening. Also she'd been in distress and he'd been comforting her. Still, in her gut she knew it was terribly wrong.

There hadn't been any inappropriate physical contact after that. Luke had taken her hand in his and led her outside onto the back deck, but she'd dropped her palm from his grasp as soon as they started walking. He'd sat with her in silence for nearly an hour until Serena had disturbed their solitude in order to remind him of a meeting he'd been running fifteen minutes late for. Luke had offered to reschedule, to spend the day with her, to whisk her away on the boat, but she'd refused his overtures, preferring not to be any more of a burden than she'd already been. He'd been disappointed, she could tell, and had insisted that if she wouldn't let him stay, then she should at least spend some time by his pool, allowing his staff to pamper her. She'd spent a few minutes saying it wasn't necessary, but it was clear he wouldn't take no for an answer and that he hoped she'd be there when he got back. He'd kissed her chastely on the forehead before leaving.

When Sloane had returned to her aunt's house, Georgina and Hillary had been gone. Not surprisingly, there'd been no note. Still, she'd figured they couldn't have gone far without a car. Although that's what she'd assumed last time, only to find out later that they'd made the brilliant decision to hitchhike to the beach. Fortunately, she'd been too furious with them to spend much time speculating on where they were. And anyway, they were two grown adults perfectly capable of making their own decisions—far be it from her to tell them how to lead their lives.

She'd spent the rest of the day at home, scrutinizing what Luke had said. She'd analyzed every word with the precision of a surgeon, wanting to determine which direction would repair her heart, broken since Amy's death. Did her future happiness lie with Eddie? Or with Luke? Losing her sister had taught her that you never knew how many days were left for you, so you had to create your happiness whenever you had the chance. The only lesson she could take away from Amy's premature passing was to make each day count as if it were her last.

When she'd finally decided to go to bed around nine o'clock, physically and mentally sapped—and with three unreturned calls from Eddie—she'd been unable to sleep. For one, she'd still had no word from Hillary or Georgina. Maybe Georgina had finally decided to listen to her and had booked a plane ticket back to London. Or, rather, called Daddy so he could send a private jet. Hillary, on the other hand, she would have expected to return to the house by now. Had she sided so definitively with Georgina that she'd left too? Concerned, Sloane had scurried out of bed and down the hall to make sure that their stuff was still in their rooms. It had been. So she'd returned to her own room again, tucked herself under the covers, and closed her eyes.

But sleep hadn't come. Only Luke's words on their endless loop through her brain, traversing from one side to the other and back and forth again, until she'd been forced to sit up, turn on the light, and own up to reality. The reality that Eddie would be arriving the next day. Whereas she had intended this break to help her figure out how to improve the stalemate in their relationship, after spending the day with Luke yesterday, she now felt more unprepared to figure things out with her husband than she had been on the day she'd left him at their front door. The day he'd bidden her farewell with, "I love you so much, Sloane. More than you'll ever know." Why weren't *those* the words she was so desperately clinging to?

She'd heard Georgina and Sloane roll in well past midnight. There'd been a squall of laughter and stage whispers, followed by a chorus of shushing from both of them. *How considerate.* Coming completely awake, she'd bristled, arms folded across her chest, sitting up in her bed, as alert as an owl. As they'd bumped their way through the house, sounding more like a stampede of bulls than two slim women, Sloane had continued to seethe. But when their charge had finally come to a close with a cacophony of doors slamming, she'd had enough. With remarkable restraint, she'd refrained from bolting down the hall, storming into their rooms, and giving them a piece of her mind. Unfortunately, there hadn't been a piece of her mind to spare.

Now, in the bright morning light—when she'd hoped against hope that everything would suddenly make sense, that all of her confusion, anger, and fear would have dissolved into nocturnal obscurity—Sloane felt no less encumbered. Hillary and Georgina had been avoiding her by nursing their hangovers with large steaming cups of coffee on the deck, while Sloane had been darting around the house in an attempt to tidy things up for the men's arrival.

Sloane had overheard Hillary telling Georgina how excited she was to see Greg, how she'd missed him so much over the course of the last two weeks. Georgina had replied that she was ecstatic to finally meet him. Sloane had rolled her eyes for no one to see. She checked her watch. They'd be there any minute. Her vacation had come to a screeching halt, just as her life was on the precipice of something chillingly transformative.

After running things over and over through her mind all night, she had concluded that when Luke had asked her to come away with him, she might actually have gone if he'd been leaving at that very moment. She suspected that, given how betrayed she felt by her friends, she could have left everything behind in a dizzying blur, promising herself she'd let her family know what was happening as soon as a travel plan materialized on the fly. It wouldn't have been right, on so many levels. At some point, she would have owed an explanation to Eddie—and there was no good explanation for running off with an old flame, even if you were feeling hurt and confused. So at the very least, she was grateful that her rational mind seemed to have returned to her in the light of a new day. Still, she suspected she couldn't trust herself anymore and that fact was both exhilarating and deeply troubling at once.

She'd have to spend the next week with Georgina and Hillary, despite what had emerged. Of course Hillary's choice to withhold information didn't come close to Georgina's colossal deception. It was still impossible for Sloane to process. Wait until she told Eddie. She'd considered calling him in the middle of the night to say she was coming home. She'd been just about ready to pack up her things and jump in the car, back to a life of simple contentedness. But there'd been something holding her back. It felt like she still had something to work through here at the lake before she returned home.

Just as Sloane was slipping two pieces of bread into the toaster, the front door opened and she heard Greg's familiar, friendly voice booming from the foyer.

"Anyone home?" he bellowed as Hillary came bounding in from outside.

"Honey!" She threw herself into his open arms, nearly toppling him.

"Hey." Eddie smiled, folding Sloane into a warm and welcome embrace. She was struck by how comforting his arms felt around her. How she was actually happy to have him there now that he'd arrived.

"Hey." She smiled back, letting him kiss her on the lips. The same lips that Luke had parted with his own exactly one day earlier. It occurred to her then that she was just as much of a hypocrite as Georgina—still, she couldn't stop herself from feeling conflicted. Perhaps she had simply reached a point in her life when she no longer wanted to hide from her feelings.

Moments later, Georgina danced into the room. "Eddie, my love!" She squeezed up against him in a tight embrace.

"How are you, Georgina?" He laughed at her exuberance.

"I've been better, actually." She glared at Sloane when he was looking the other way.

And Sloane bit her tongue. Clearly, their skirmish of the day before hadn't tortured her too severely. Or perhaps Hillary had eased her concerns away with her counselor-speak. What with them being besties and all.

"Sorry to hear that."

"Thank you." She looked at Sloane again, warily this time, which she could tell Eddie immediately picked up on.

"Greg, this is Sloane's friend Georgina. The one I've been telling you about."

"Only glamorous things, I hope!" Georgina tittered.

"Wonderful to finally meet you, Georgina." He went to shake her hand and she kissed him three times on alternating cheeks instead, which he seemed to take great delight in. "Hey, Sloane. Thanks a million for having us here. I sure am ready to relax after a hellish week at work." He sighed. "I may very well hate summer school as much as the students do."

"Well, come on in, then, and let's get everyone settled." Sloane was about to give the men the grand tour, when Hillary cut in.

"Come on, honey, I'll show you to our room." Hillary reached for Greg's hand and dragged him awkwardly up the stairs.

"Okay, Eddie, we're this way." Sloane motioned to him as she trailed behind Greg, leaving Georgina alone.

As soon as they'd reached Sloane's bedroom and closed the door behind them, Eddie asked, "What's wrong?"

"Why?"

"Because I know you. And the tension down there was off the charts."

"I don't even know where to begin." She slumped onto the bed in a despairing manner.

"If this is about us . . ."

"It's not." She was quick to reply, a reaction that instantly pacified Eddie.

"Good, then come over here." He pulled her onto his lap and started stroking her back. Then kissed her again. This time like he meant it.

And before she knew what she was doing, Sloane was making love to her husband for the first time in as long as she could remember.

———

"That was amazing." Eddie rolled onto his back a while later, with his hands supporting his head and elbows out to the side. Sloane had often joked that it was the standard postcoital male position—satisfaction and pride combined. "I've missed that. I've missed us."

"Me too." Sloane curled her body into the fetal position, facing him. It had felt amazing, which didn't happen terribly frequently for her.

Typically whenever they had sex—at least in the last year— she'd been in such a rush to have it done with that she never let herself become immersed in the first place. But this time, her orgasm had come fast and strong, so much so that even Eddie had been surprised. Perhaps it was all the pent-up sexual energy from the time she had spent flirting with Luke. Or maybe it was how good Eddie looked—tanned and toned—just the way she liked him.

She wasn't lying when she'd said she missed him. The truth was that she hadn't realized just how much she had missed him until he was right there in front of her. No matter what old feelings Luke had stirred up in her this summer, Eddie was still home to her. He was still the person she relayed the details of her day to. He was still the one who listened to her gripes about her mother nagging her to gain weight or cut her hair. He was still the father of her child. He was the one she had chosen. Then how could she have felt such a wild attraction for Luke when they were alone together? It was all so unsettling as well as perplexing.

"I'm really glad to hear you say that." Eddie kissed her again on the lips. "I'm gonna go hose off. Wanna join me for round two?"

"You should be so lucky," Sloane flirted playfully, surprised at how natural and right it felt. "Go ahead. I'm going to go down and eat something. I'll shower after you. And then what? Should we go into town and I can show you around?"

"That sounds great. With the others?"

"I don't think so."

"Even better." Eddie smiled widely.

"Wait until I tell you what's going on with Georgina. You're never going to believe it."

"I bet I will. I've heard all of your Georgina stories. How bad could it be?"

"Let's just say she's outdone herself this time."

"Doesn't sound good." Eddie walked toward the bathroom, his tight tan ass exposed. "Greg said he wanted to do a big dinner here tomorrow night. You know, cook for everyone as a thank-you for hosting them," he called over the running shower.

"That sounds great. Why don't we pick up the fixings while we're in town," she called back.

"My thoughts exactly." He peeked out from around the bathroom door, taking in every inch of her naked body. "Mmmm, you better get downstairs or I'm going to pull you in here with me."

"Go!" Sloane laughed, pointing toward him. "I'll be back up in a few."

———

They'd managed to avoid the others on their way out. On the drive into town, Sloane had told Eddie all about the call from Georgina's mother. The child she had known nothing of. The betrayal she'd felt when she learned that Georgina had confided in Hillary before her. And, finally, their massive falling-out, during which Sloane had harangued Georgina for having been conveniently missing in action when Amy died. After all—and Sloane had thought about this relentlessly since discovering the secret Georgina had been keeping from her—Georgina could easily have called her without revealing that she'd been pregnant or had a baby. Her daughter was merely an excuse for her selfishness, not an explanation.

Eddie had alternately nodded and shaken his head at everything Sloane had relayed. By the time she'd finished chattering away, he'd had nothing to add, aside from a simple, "Unbelievable. She really is something." In characteristic Eddie fashion, he hadn't asked what Sloane was going to do about it. Whether she planned to forgive Georgina—or Hillary, whom he hadn't bothered to defend the way she'd expected he might have. He hadn't suggested Sloane was wrong for even a minute. He'd only supported her and agreed with her, which was exactly what she'd needed him to do. She'd never felt happier to have Eddie on her side, so much so that she hadn't thought about Luke once in the last hour, which was approximately fifty-four minutes longer than she'd gone in the past two weeks.

After they'd hit the butcher's, the seafood shop, and the bakery, Sloane and Eddie were ambling hand in hand along the main drag in the center of Lake George, oblivious to their surroundings. So oblivious in fact, that she nearly walked right into him.

"Hey, Sloane." She looked up to find Luke's penetrating brown eyes focused on her to the exclusion of the man by her side.

"Oh, um, hey." Sloane's heart began pounding against her rib cage as seemingly every sweat gland in her body released its floodgates. She was instantly transported back to the chaste kiss they had shared, but this time, all she felt was disgust. Disgust for her transgression and for the disastrous path she could have gone down and thankfully had not.

"Hi, I'm Luke." He extended his arm toward Eddie. "Sloane and I—"

"We met through Georgina," she cut in. "Sorry, yeah, Luke is an old friend of Georgina's from what? Ages ago?"

"Something like that."

"Well, it's great to meet you." Eddie shook his hand.

"Looks like you guys got some good stuff there."

"Yup. Just dinner. You know." Sloane couldn't look at him.

"Why don't you come?" This was Eddie. Poor, innocent Eddie.

"Sorry, I've got plans tonight."

"Oh well," Sloane answered quickly, though she couldn't help but wonder with whom he had plans.

"Actually I meant tomorrow night."

"Thanks, but . . ."

"Come on. I insist." Eddie opened the bag filled with crab claws and shrimp. "See, we've got plenty of food."

"Maybe he has plans tomorrow too, sweetie." She clutched Eddie's hand tighter.

"Then he can bring his plans with him." If Sloane didn't know better, she'd think Eddie had sensed the excruciatingly awkward

chapter 28

Once she and Eddie had returned home from town the previous afternoon with dinner in hand and a new dinner guest to announce for the following evening, things had quickly slipped back into a state of static discomfort. Sloane and Georgina had gone to great lengths to avoid each other, unwilling to meet each other's eyes, except when Eddie had announced the news about Luke—then Sloane had observed the instinctual register of shock on Georgina's face and the logical apprehension on Hillary's. It was a recipe for complete disaster and they all recognized it. The problem was, Sloane couldn't talk to either of them about it.

Why on earth had she told Eddie that she and Luke had met through Georgina? For one thing it was an outright lie. And keeping quiet about the sheer magnitude of the magnetic attraction she'd felt with Luke the minute they'd locked eyes at King Neptune's over a decade ago felt like she was betraying her husband all over again.

Yet Eddie was stable, committed, devoted—every praising adjective you could think of to describe the ideal husband. He was even sexy in the estimation of most women; sometimes Sloane could see it in their eyes. Had all this been a matter of deeming the grass greener elsewhere? Sloane was well aware that, from the outside, her life appeared to be rolling acres of the lushest lawn around.

Hillary had approached her later in the evening to ask if she'd wanted to talk, after they'd all fixed plates of food and segregated themselves—Hillary, Greg, and Georgina on the back deck and Sloane and Eddie at the kitchen table. Sloane wasn't sure whether the guys had picked up on the fact that none of the women had been able to properly enjoy their splendid feast. Poor Greg and Eddie, she thought. Here they'd assumed they were tagging on to the tail end of a tranquil respite, when in fact they'd vaulted headfirst into the lion's den. What must Greg think of the odd dynamic? Sloane had asked Eddie if he'd said anything to him, but he hadn't. Of course not—it wasn't what men did. If there was a problem, either they let it roll off their backs or they addressed it. Immediately. She couldn't remember a time when Eddie had griped about a friend, much less had a massive falling-out with one. On the other hand, toss a group of women in a room, and without fail, someone would be throwing down within a few hours.

Sloane hadn't been ready to talk to Hillary and made excuses to avoid the conversation for the time being. She'd come around some, asking herself what she would have done in Hillary's position. The likeliest answer was that she very possibly might have done the same thing—kept the secret and not gotten involved. In fact, it was really *Georgina's* fault for putting Hillary in the awkward position of having to decide what to do in the first place. It felt very comfortable to place the blame in Georgina's unprincipled hands. Every time she looked at her, a fresh knot of fury spooled in her gut.

Tonight, Greg and Hillary were taking care of the preparations for dinner, which Sloane had thanked them for, exchanging the slightest of smiles with Hillary. Greg had seasoned the steaks with his "special rub," touting its top secret ingredient—cinnamon— which naturally he could *never* reveal, despite the fact that they'd all watched him make it. Hillary was working on the crab claws and tossing a big salad with her homemade Dijon vinaigrette, having al- ready set out a platter of cheese and crackers along with a bowl of homemade guacamole and tortilla chips for dunking. Eddie was handling the alcoholic beverages. Sloane was pacing back and forth in the kitchen and from one room to the next, desperate to cast off as much of her nervous energy as possible before Luke arrived. And Georgina was draped across the couch in the great room with her feet up, laughing raucously at a rerun of *Family Guy*, which served only to anger Sloane even more.

She'd considered asking Georgina to lie for her in the event that how they'd met Luke came up in the course of conversation. She'd thought about walking right up to her and saying, "You owe this to me." But that would have given Georgina the upper hand. It would have shifted the power back to her. And Sloane didn't think she could bear that right now. At last she'd decided that if anyone made mention of it, she would act like it was her mistake, say something along the lines of, "Oh, I thought you'd introduced me to Luke. I didn't realize we all met the same night. Maybe you'd been talking to him first or something. Whatever." Sloane could not imagine that even Georgina would be cruel or stupid enough to mention anything about the fact that they'd had a relationship if it was clear that Eddie was unaware of their shared past. Not that she had anything to hide from that time in her life—she and Eddie had been on a break of sorts that summer. Still, she'd never bothered to tell Eddie about Luke. There'd been no point. Nor had she asked how he'd spent his summer as a single guy, even though he'd told her there'd been no one else. At the time, when he'd confessed she was the only woman he'd ever want, she'd thought she felt the same way about him. Maybe she had.

Sloane walked out onto the back deck, where Eddie was standing swigging from a bottle of Budweiser.

"Hey, sweetie." He took her in his arms and pulled her close. She leaned her head against his warm chest, savoring the familiar scent of him that she knew so intimately. "You okay?"

"I am now." She looked down at her outfit—a jean skirt and a plain white tank top with rubber flip-flops from the drugstore in town. For whatever reason, she hadn't taken any special care in getting ready. Eddie loved her best right out of the shower, with wet hair and no makeup at all. Suddenly, that was all that seemed to matter. Either Eddie's warm embrace had successfully calmed her or all that nervous pacing inside had done the trick. "Do you think I should go up and change into something nicer?"

"Absolutely not," he answered swiftly and definitively, which gave her a welcome boost of confidence. "You look beautiful just as you are." He kissed her on the lips.

"Oh, you have to say that." She laughed, trying to sound easy breezy, but she was anxious and hoped he wouldn't notice. Her uneasiness came from a different place than it had just a week ago. She wasn't anticipating Luke's arrival with guarded excitement or contemplating scenarios in her head about where the evening might take them. In fact, she'd have been perfectly happy, relieved even, if he'd called to cancel, so that she could spend the night alone with her husband. The man she'd been marginalizing for too long.

"No, I do not. And, still, I wouldn't change a thing. Not even your underwear. Unless you want to take them off . . ."

"Eddie!" She swatted his arm, even though she actually enjoyed it when he talked dirty to her. It had been a while. She also liked that Eddie seemed different, more self-assured than the guy she had left behind in Brookline two weeks earlier. It was subtle, but it was there.

"What? You can't blame a guy for trying!" As he was about to lean in and kiss her again, Sloane heard the doorbell chime from inside the house.

"I'd better go answer that."

"There are three other people here." He looked at her lustily.

"Yeah, but it's my house, or close enough."

"Okay, but I plan to have my way with you later." He slapped her on the rear end and followed her toward the front door. She took a deep breath before opening it, to find Luke standing before her proffering a chilled bottle of Dom Pérignon with a red bow, which Serena had most likely tied neatly around the neck.

"Welcome to our humble abode," Eddie announced. If only he knew how humble it actually was compared with Frog Hill Farm.

"Thank you for having me." He leaned in to kiss Sloane on the cheek, whispering in her ear how stunning she looked. Then he stood up straight once again, revealing an impish grin, and declared, "Let's get this party started!"

———

It hadn't been much of a party, despite the fact that there'd been plenty of liquor consumed. Hillary, Greg, and Georgina had sat at one end of the table, and, best efforts notwithstanding, Sloane, Eddie, and Luke had occupied the other end. There'd been some cross-conversation, mainly compliments to the chefs—Greg and Hillary—for the spectacular meal they'd prepared. The steaks had been so tender you barely needed a knife to slice them. The crab claws had been sweet and refreshing. And Hillary's famous upside-down caramel apple cake had been an appropriately tart and buttery final note.

Sloane had done most of the talking at her end of the table. She hadn't been able to stop herself from rambling on about everything from the weather to the food they were eating, even touching on a television show she'd watched a week earlier about dolphins. Who knew that they were closely related to the tortoise? Or that there were almost forty different species of dolphin? No one. Nor had they seemed to care. At one point she'd caught Luke staring at her with an amused smirk. He knew exactly what she'd been doing. Stringing words into sentences and sentences into thoughts in order to fill the unnerving silence that would have snuck up on them like a tiger pouncing on its prey had she not.

As the dinner was drawing to a close, most of them tipsy enough to have had their edges dulled, Eddie took the opportunity to start a benign conversation with Luke, as Sloane listened intently, ready to interject should the necessity arise.

"So, Luke, what line of work are you in?" He picked a cherry tomato out of his salad bowl and burst it with his back teeth.

"That would be real estate."

"Very interesting. Residential or commercial?"

"Commercial. Mostly hotels and resorts."

"Oh, wow, in this area?"

"Not really. We have some properties up and down the East Coast, but there are others all across the country. And a few years ago we went international." Sloane shifted in her seat. The only thing that Luke's global ventures reminded her of was his dinner with Georgina in Paris. Not her all-time favorite item for them to reminisce about.

"That's excellent. So you must do well for yourself."

"Eddie!" Sloane laughed. His authenticity, which used to make her cringe, was all at once undeniably endearing. If he thought it, he said it. Although, she realized with a start, even when Eddie was being critical, which he rarely was, he never came across as intentionally cruel. It just wasn't part of the fabric of his being.

"It's okay." Luke laughed too. "I do fine. It's a family business, so I can't take credit for building it, only for doing my best to maintain and grow it."

"Must be a big job."

"It's hard work." Luke nodded.

Just as Sloane was about to put the kibosh on their tête-à-tête, the doorbell rang.

"That's strange. I wasn't expecting anyone." She scanned the table and everyone shrugged their shoulders. "Maybe my aunt got sick of Hawaii. I'll be right back."

Seconds later, Sloane returned with their impromptu visitor. "Georgina, someone is here to see you."

"Hugh?" She shot up out of her seat as the glowing blush drained from her face. "What are you doing here?" Her body began trembling ever so slightly.

"What am *I* doing here? I could ask the same of you." Sloane spotted a pulsing vein ready to burst through the skin on his forehead. He was quite obviously furious, though his lyrical British accent belied his feverish conduct.

"Hugh . . . this isn't the time or place for this." She looked at him imploringly.

"It is now. You haven't given me any choice here!" He was having none of her nonsense, which gave Sloane a rise. Hugh practically grabbed Georgina by the arm and dragged her into the house as everyone seated at the table widened their eyes at one another and sat silently as Hugh and Georgina went at each other just behind the ajar French doors.

It was too much of a challenge to make out most of what they were saying without openly eavesdropping, but it was clear that there was more to Georgina's story, more even than the child she'd failed to mention—as if that weren't explosive enough in and of itself. There was something else Sloane should have remembered about Georgina. Just when you thought she'd outdone herself, she hadn't. There was always another bomb ready to detonate around the next corner.

When Georgina finally came back outside, there was no sign of Hugh. Her face was stained with tears and she approached them with her head bowed toward the ground.

"He's gone."

"Are you okay?" Hillary rushed to her side and tried to hug her, but Georgina's body was frozen stiff. "What happened in there? He didn't hurt you . . . ?"

"No," she inhaled on a sob. "He knows. He knows everything."

"Let's go find a private place to talk."

"No." Georgina shook her head vehemently. "I need to come clean once and for all. Really couldn't get much worse, could it?" She laughed bitterly.

"What is it?" Hillary stroked Georgina's arm. She recoiled, as if she didn't deserve the simple comfort.

"I don't even know how to say this, but Hugh figured out what I've been suspecting for a while. Somewhere deep down." She was crying harder now, and for the first time ever, it wasn't pretty at all.

"Just tell us," Sloane urged, eager for her to get to the point. She'd had enough of Georgina's histrionics to last her the rest of her life.

"Hugh is not Zara's father." Boom! They all fell silent at the revelation.

"Then who is?" Sloane couldn't deny she was curious, though it was probably some Euro-chic playboy she'd met along her travels.

"I, um . . ." Georgina couldn't get the words out. She didn't have to. All she had to do was look at him.

"You did NOT!" Sloane's head whipped around to face Luke, who had just connected the dots himself. Georgina nodded guiltily.

"Sloane, I . . ."

"Don't you dare say a word." She held up her hand. "I need you to just get the fuck away from me."

"Please, Sloane . . . ," she entreated pitifully.

"I said, GET. AWAY. FROM. ME."

Georgina ran into the house.

"You'll have to forgive me, but I think I need to excuse myself." Luke stood up. "Thank you for the beautiful meal. It's been . . ." What was there left to say? "I'm just going to go now."

"I think that's a good idea." Sloane couldn't even look at him. He could let himself out of the house. As far as she was concerned, Luke and Georgina deserved each other.

chapter 29

Still dressed in her sleeveless nightgown, Sloane draped a plaid wool blanket over her shoulders and descended the stairs from the back porch down to the beach below. Before stepping onto the sand, she shucked off her fuzzy slippers and pulled her hair into a loose ponytail. It was early yet, only seven a.m. if she'd read the wall clock correctly in their dimly lit bedroom. Eddie had barely stirred when she'd crawled out from under the covers, impatient to find some wide-open space where she could breathe and wade through her thoughts.

She'd been awakened an hour earlier by the shrill squawks of a flock of birds that had swooped past their window and, though it probably wasn't the case, sounded as if they'd been circling the house in search of something. After that, she'd lain in bed fully alert, her mind tearing frantically in diverging directions.

Everyone had turned in the previous night without so much as a word exchanged between any of them. Where to start? What else was there to say? Georgina had a secret child. The child's father was Luke, which meant Georgina and Luke had slept together while they were in Paris. Sloane wasn't sure which part throbbed more. That they'd had sex in the first place or that they'd *both* conveniently forgotten to mention the liaison to Sloane. Or was it the fact that their one-night stand had produced a daughter that was really gnawing at her insides the most?

And what if it hadn't been just a one-night stand? Maybe they'd each extended their stay so they could linger in bed, ordering heaping plates of room service to sate their rapacious appetites. Maybe Georgina had planned the whole sordid affair, short of bumping into Luke to begin with. Although, at this point, Sloane was reticent to put anything past her. She could barely claim to know her supposed best friend any longer.

Rationally, she knew that what Georgina and Luke had done fell into murky moral ground. Technically they hadn't truly done anything wrong. They hadn't cheated on a spouse or with anyone else's spouse. Still, wasn't there some kind of unwritten rule that you never—no matter how many years had passed or how many other boyfriends and girlfriends had come and gone—slept with your friend's ex or your ex's friend? Wasn't that an addendum in the relationship bible right under *Thou shall not have sex with your wife's bosom buddy*? No matter how nice her bosom was.

It wasn't like Georgina and Luke didn't have their fair share of suitors to choose from. They each could have had their pick of almost anyone. She laid the blanket on the sand and sat down, hugging her body to shield herself from the morning breeze off the lake, which at this time of day was as clear and still as glass. As the wind blew the escaped tendrils of hair off her face, Sloane tried to clear her head of the noise, but it was impossible.

Now that their secret was out, would Luke and Georgina sail off into the sunset together, a happy family of three? Sloane pictured them in a *Titanic* pose on the bow of his yacht, with Georgina cradling Zara, whose beauty was surely rivaled only by her mother's.

Sloane felt sick at the thought of how she would explain her reaction to Eddie. She hadn't even considered what she was going to tell him. Surely he'd figured out that Luke wasn't *just* Georgina's friend, if by nothing other than her reaction to the shocking news. He hadn't asked her anything last night, but he would. And understandably so.

As Sloane prepared to head back inside to make herself a cup of coffee, she heard footsteps coming up behind her. She turned to see Eddie in his faded boxer shorts and snug white T-shirt trudging toward her with two steaming mugs in hand. She smiled gently and he smiled back. But his was a guarded smile and she knew in that moment that he wasn't there to chat about Madeleine or their plans for the day. He needed an explanation. For so much more than the events of the previous evening. And he deserved one.

"Hey, early bird." Sloane slid over to make enough room for him on the blanket and he sat down beside her. She noted that he did not put his arm around her, as he normally would have. "Here. I figured you could use a little pick-me-up." He handed her one of the mugs.

"Thanks."

"You were restless last night." He gazed out over the water and Sloane did the same. Their bodies were almost touching, but the mere inch of space between them was defining. It said, *I am me. And you are you. We are not one.*

"I had a lot on my mind."

"Care to share?" He pressed his lips to his coffee cup and took a slow sip. "Be careful; it's hot."

"Well, it's complicated. . . ."

"I've got time."

Sloane inhaled a gust of sweet-scented air and exhaled, searching for the right words. "I actually met Luke at the same time as Georgina did. At this local bar called King Neptune's."

"Okay." He nodded but didn't look at her.

"I don't know why I told you he was her friend first. It just sort of slipped out."

"Doesn't seem like an important detail."

"I know. But, actually, it is." Sloane cleared her throat. "Luke and I dated that summer I spent here in college with Georgina, when you and I were on a break."

"Ah." Eddie was still staring straight in front of him.

"Then when I saw him again a couple of weeks ago, which was not my intention"—she decided to leave out the part about Georgina having orchestrated the whole thing, as it didn't really add anything relevant to her explanation—"it riled up some old feelings."

"And?" He turned to face her now, his expression unreadable.

"And nothing. I mean, I have to admit I wasn't thrilled to find out that Georgina had slept with Luke, lied to me about it, and that he's the father of her daughter. On top of everything else. But that's pretty much all she wrote." Or at least all she was willing to divulge. There was no sense in telling Eddie about the kiss. About how, eventually, she could have gotten tangled up in her feelings for him. As soon as Eddie had shown up on the scene, Sloane had realized that a dalliance with Luke would have been just that. It wasn't about Luke or what they'd once had. Sloane had been trying to figure out things for herself, and her involvement with Luke had been the most obvious manifestation of her issues. Any kind of long-term relationship between them would have been doomed before it began. And, at this point, the idea of having any further physical interaction with Luke was repugnant anyway.

"Good." Eddie was visibly relieved. She couldn't tell if he suspected there was something more to it, but even if he did, he seemed prepared to leave it at that, for which she was grateful.

Sloane rested her arm on his strong, toned leg and they sat in silence watching the first ripples undulate across the docile water. Until Eddie spoke up again.

"I'm glad you told me about Luke. Although that's not what I really wanted to talk to you about."

"Oh, okay." Sloane felt instantly uneasy and no less guilty for her transgression with Luke. They'd glossed over it. Case closed, as long as she didn't reopen it. It was unlike Eddie to initiate a serious conversation, though. In fact, she couldn't recall the last time he had. If ever he had. So she was determined to hear him out. "What's on your mind?"

"While you were gone, I got to thinking. A lot," he started. "This isn't easy for me. I'm sorry."

"Is everything all right?" She was more than apprehensive now.

"That's the thing, Sloane. According to what you said before you left, everything is not all right. And I'd been living, very happily, under the misconception that it was." He sounded so wise, so mature, so take-charge. Who was this Eddie?

"I see." She nodded.

"I love you, Sloane." He took her hand in his. "I love us. I love our family. I love our life."

"Me too." It was her gut response, though she realized it sounded silly in light of what she'd told him.

"No, you don't. Unless something has changed drastically since you've been here." He sighed. "I don't want to force you into a life you're unhappy with. I can't shoulder that responsibility, Sloane. And I love you too much to do that. If what you want is not to be with me, then I want you to tell me. I need you to tell me. We'll work it out."

"I . . . that's not . . . ," she stammered, and he held his hand up before she could formulate a cohesive response.

"Please, just let me finish." He looked at her now, really looked at her. The way he used to when they'd first started dating. "I won't like it. But I'll be okay without you. I've missed you terribly while you've been here. So terribly. It was like a part of me was gone. Still, I kept saying to myself, this is what it's going to be like if Sloane leaves. You'll have to get used to it. And you know what?"

"What?"

"It got a little easier each day. Not much, but a little. Inch by inch."

"Oh." Sloane didn't know what to say. She'd assumed he was going to arrive in Lake George and beg her to stay with him. Implore her to love him the way he loved her. They'd barely spoken in the two weeks she'd been there without him, and naively, she'd figured he'd been pining after her, while giving her the space she'd said she needed to come to her senses. Essentially kowtowing to her every whim, before considering his own needs and wants.

"Sloane, don't get me wrong. This is not my first choice by any means. But I won't be one of those guys like Dan Jenkins, who Andrea has less interest in than their family dog. I have more self-respect than that."

"I know you do." Sloane smiled affectionately at Eddie. She'd had no idea he was capable of such introspection or that he'd been observant enough to recognize that Andrea Jenkins did in fact treat their dog better than she treated her husband.

"I want to understand why you're discontented. If it's more excitement you need, I'll make it happen. If you want to go back to work, even teaching part-time, I support it wholeheartedly. But I need to know where your head is. And whether or not you're committed to rebuilding our marriage. For our sake and Maddie's."

"Eddie . . ."

"Don't answer now," he interrupted. "Just think about it, okay?"

"Okay."

"Let's take a walk." He stood up and extended a hand, lifting her to her feet. Then he shook the sand off the blanket and wrapped it around Sloane's shoulders, pulling her close to him. "I love you, Sloane. More than anything or anyone. I want to spend the rest of

chapter 30

Amy would have known just what to say to her. Just what to tell her to do. Even though she'd been the younger sister, Amy had been wise beyond Sloane's years. She'd been the person Sloane had called for everything from last-minute babysitting for Maddie—which Amy had never turned down, not once—to a question about a rash she'd found on her chest. Amy always had a practical approach to dissecting a problem, whereas Sloane's initial instinct was to freak out. It was one of the few ways their personalities differed.

Sloane stretched her legs down the length of the couch in the great room and yawned. After her talk with Eddie of the previous morning, they'd spent the day at the beach with Greg and Hillary. Things were perfectly pleasant all day, despite the fact that her exchanges with Hillary had been limited to idle banter. Apparently, according to Hillary, Georgina had decided to crash at a friend's pad. Translation: with whatever scumbag she'd met around town or at a dive bar. Sloane had asked Hillary if she knew whose pad she was at, surprised by the fact that she didn't really care if it was Luke's. Hillary hadn't known much, except that it was a new acquaintance, and she'd shown Sloane the address, which Georgina had given her "in the event that he's an ax murderer and I don't resurface tomorrow." It sounded like something Georgina would say.

When they'd returned home from hours spent in the sun, including a long walk on the beach and a short swim in the lake, they'd all been exhausted. Greg had grilled barbecue chicken, Hillary had baked a tray of asparagus, and they'd shared one bottle of white wine. Any more and they might have fallen asleep at the table.

As soon as her head had hit the pillow, Sloane had fallen into a deep sleep. And when she'd awakened at three in the morning, suddenly everything had seemed astonishingly transparent. She'd revisited a memory of Amy in her dream, reliving a moment when Amy was torn between two guys.

"But I love both of them." Amy had confessed her confusion over whether to date Dax Redgrove—a consummate bad boy sporting two ears full of piercings, a biceps tattoo depicting the devil rising from hell, and a permanent scowl—or Christopher Browning, whose idea of acting out was landing the lead role of Danny Zuko to Amy's Sandy Dumbrowski in their school production of *Grease*, despite his father's extreme preference that he play football or soccer instead.

Sloane had been a senior that year and Amy a junior. Sloane and Eddie had been blissfully joined at the hip for two years and counting, and Amy had made it abundantly clear on more than one occasion that she too wanted an Eddie. Apparently, even in the form of a Dax, who was as far from an Eddie-clone as possible.

"Well, which one do you love more?" Sloane had asked, unable to fathom Amy's dilemma. How could she not have a clear preference or at least a hunch as to which of them was better suited for her? For her own part, Sloane had never experienced any confusion in the way of men, if you could call the lanky, pimple-faced, hormones-pumping-through-their-veins man-boys that attended Brookline High School that. She'd known Eddie was the one for her the day she'd laid eyes on him. And no matter how many other guys had checked her out in her cheerleading uniform or asked her for her number behind Eddie's back, she'd never even considered it. Not once.

"I just don't know," Amy had lamented, falling backward onto the stack of fluffy white pillows propped against her hand-painted purple wrought iron headboard. "Dax is so cool. He's really into Pearl Jam and Mötley Crüe and he has no curfew. But, at the same time, Chris is so sweet. He brought me flowers from his mom's garden last week. And he invited me to their country club for dinner Saturday night. I don't know. . . ."

"If it was me, I'd go for Chris," Sloane had advised, without a doubt in her mind. She hadn't seen the allure of Dax at all. Sure, he was probably more electrifying than Chris was. And he got the fact that it was tacky to wear socks with boat shoes. Or to wear boat shoes at all. Still, those were unimportant details. Sloane was fairly certain no one had ever split up over a fashion faux pas.

"You're right. I know you're right," Amy had agreed, though Sloane had watched her chest deflate and a fragile veil of disappointment pass across her face.

Fifteen years from now, would Sloane look back on these weeks and worry she'd made a terrible mistake? No. Were she and Luke ever right for each other's future? No. Had seeing him again rekindled an old flame? Perhaps. But said flame was nothing more than a flickering spark. A flickering spark that had been extinguished along with the sentiment she'd *thought* she shared with Amy.

"But I love both of them" was no longer her truth.

Sloane opened her eyes to the bustle of Greg and Eddie bounding down the stairs, dressed and ready for a full day on the lake. She must have fallen asleep on the couch, drifting off and getting lost somewhere between her past and future.

"Shhh," she heard Eddie caution Greg.

"It's okay, I'm up." Sloane lifted the blanket. "I woke up early and must have dozed off."

"Are you sure you don't want to come with us? Last chance . . ." A week earlier, when Eddie had called to ask if she minded if he and Greg chartered a fishing boat while they were there, she'd thought it sounded like an excellent idea. An easy way to get rid of the men, so the girls could still have their time together. Of course now things were different.

"Not my thing. Is Hillary going?"

"Nope," Greg chimed in. "Apparently it's not her thing either. You two can have a wild party without us." He didn't look at her when he said it. Surely, Hillary had told him all that had transpired.

"Oh, okay. That's fine." Sloane wasn't sure how she felt about being alone with Hillary. She knew they'd have to talk eventually, but everything still felt so raw. The one thing she was thankful for was that Georgina wasn't around. She was sure how she felt about that. And it wasn't positive.

"So I'll see you later?" Eddie leaned over to give Sloane a kiss good-bye, and she wrapped her arms around his neck to hold him close for just a moment longer. "We shouldn't be home later than six," he whispered.

"I love you." She smiled affectionately. "And catch us some dinner!" she called after them.

"Oh, don't you worry. We're not coming home empty-handed!" Greg called back.

Just as the door closed behind them, Hillary came downstairs. "Did I miss the boys?"

"Just. I'm sure you can still catch them."

"Nah. That's okay." She walked into the kitchen and Sloane followed her. "Coffee?"

"Definitely, thanks."

"Omelet?"

"If you're making one, sure. But if not . . ."

"It's really no problem." Hillary reached for a frying pan, lighting a burner on the stove and placing it on top. Then she gathered a carton of eggs, two slices of cheese, a container of mushrooms and one of tomatoes, and a large yellow onion. "All this stuff good?"

"Looks delicious, thanks."

"Bacon and toast?"

"Nope, the omelet is perfect. I feel like I've gained twenty pounds from alcohol alone since we've been here."

"I know. Me too." Hillary cracked two eggs into the pan. "I'm detoxing as soon as we get home."

"Any word from Georgina?" Sloane couldn't help herself.

"Just a text saying she's fairly certain that Rob is not in fact a serial killer. Wait, I think that's his name, or did she say Rog?"

"Does it matter?"

"Good point!" Hillary laughed.

"I guess she didn't mention when she'd be gracing us with her presence again?"

"Nope." Hillary folded one side of the omelet on top of the other, flipped it expertly, and then slid it onto a plate. "For you."

"This looks amazing, thanks. You're not having one?"

"I'm not really that hungry."

"Oh, well, thank you. I didn't realize . . ."

"Sloane, I can't take this." Hillary pulled out the barstool next to her and sat down.

"Take what?"

"This." She moved her hand back and forth between them. "The awkwardness. It's awful. I'm so sorry for not telling you about Georgina's daughter. I know it's no excuse, but I felt trapped. On the one hand, she'd asked me to keep this huge secret. On the other hand, I knew it was going to be extremely upsetting for you to find out. I made the wrong choice."

"It's okay." What else could Sloane say? What was done was done. Perhaps Hillary had made the wrong choice. Perhaps Sloane was being oversensitive.

"It's not okay. I just hope you can forgive me."

"I can." Sloane smiled. "It's good to know you're not perfect *all* the time."

"Yeah, right. Far from it."

"Seriously, Hill? I've never once seen you make a misstep."

"About that."

"About what?" Sloane watched Hillary's expression turn dark. Something she'd never seen before. Please, God, she thought, what else could go wrong?

"There's something I have to tell you. And before I do, in the interest of complete honesty, I want you to know that I already told Georgina."

"All right." Sloane sighed.

"I don't know why. It just seemed easier to unload on someone who didn't know me so well. And, most importantly, someone who didn't know Greg. Someone who wasn't invested in us."

"What is it?" Sloane was anxious now.

"I'm on the pill."

"The birth control pill?" Sloane's eyes widened. It was possibly the very last thing she'd expected Hillary to say.

"Yup. The birth control pill."

"For how long? I don't understand."

"The whole time we've been trying. Even before that."

"Oh my God. Hill." Instinctively, Sloane pulled her into a hug and Hillary started to cry, her shoulders trembling beneath Sloane's embrace. "So I take it Greg doesn't know?"

"Right." She sat up straight again. "He's totally in the dark. He thinks it just hasn't been working."

"Wow." Sloane shook her head in disbelief. "But why? Don't you want kids? I thought you were desperate to conceive."

"That's the thing. That's what everyone thought. Thinks. Whatever. It's just assumed because I'm of a certain age and married to a great guy."

"So you don't want kids?"

"I'm not sure. I haven't really given myself the space to consider what I really want. All I know is that I definitely wasn't ready when Greg first broached the subject, but he was so sure, and then it was full speed ahead without any time to think. I'd been taking the pill back then and I just never stopped. I kept telling myself I would—soon. That I just needed one more month and then I wouldn't renew the prescription. Needless to say, that moment still hasn't arrived."

"Are you going to tell him?"

"I have to. The burden is too much to bear at this point. And something about this getaway has made me realize it's time to divest myself of the crippling guilt. More importantly, to own up to my own selfishness."

"I know how you feel."

"Luke?" Hillary had never been one to mince words.

"Yup, how'd you guess?"

"It wasn't hard. I've known for a while."

"I figured." Sloane covered her face with both hands.

"Did you . . ."

"Sleep with him?"

"Yeah."

"No. Thankfully."

"But you could have?"

"I don't think I could have gone through with it in the end, but the fact that I even considered it . . ." Sloane watched Hillary's expression for any indication of profound disappointment. Nothing.

"Isn't it amazing how we can lead such happy home lives, yet have this one thing that we can't let go of?"

"I'm not sure how happy I've been."

"But you and Eddie have always seemed so solid."

"We are now. Or, at the very least, we're working our way back. Ever since Amy died, things felt different."

"How so?"

"I don't know exactly. It's like I had all of these tumultuous emotions coursing through me and it created this barrier between Eddie and me, no matter how hard he tried to break through it. The problem was with me. I just didn't have the energy to invest in him and I let things slip between us. And when I saw Luke again, I started wondering what I was missing. Like, if I died tomorrow, would I have regrets? Would I have wanted to live life more fully? I think somewhere deep down it just seemed easier to start something fresh rather than the fix the problems that I'd let build up at home."

"I'd say your life is pretty full, no?"

"It is, but it's not always very exciting."

"Well, that's a different story. If you're thrill seeking, then being married with a kid and living in Brookline probably isn't your best bet."

"That's the understatement of the century!" Sloane crinkled her nose. "Can you believe he actually asked me to come away with him?"

"Luke?"

"Yeah. It sounds so ridiculous, even to me now."

"Well, I can't say I'm surprised. I've seen the way he looks at you."

"You have?"

"You'd have to be blind not to." Hillary thought for a moment. "What did you say?"

"Nothing. It's not exactly a realistic scenario."

"If it was, would you go?"

"I might have."

"Might have?"

"Oh, you didn't hear? Luke is the father of Georgina's child. Kind of puts a wrench in my nonexistent plan."

"I see."

"But it's not just that. I love Eddie. And when he arrived, I realized how much I actually need and want him as my partner. It was like I was seeing him through foggy glasses for too long, but the time here cleared some things away for me." Sloane paused in contemplation. "It's like I was broken when we first got here, but spending this time with you, and even Georgina, has helped me fill the holes in my life that were left after Amy died. Luke was never right for me. He was a distraction. A mere temptation. I guess I was happily surprised that reuniting with Eddie alleviated the last dregs of emptiness. I'm finally ready to recommit to our marriage."

"That's great. Sloane, I'm so happy for you." Hillary smiled genuinely. "By the way, I hope you know it's completely normal when you've lost someone to reevaluate your life."

"Is it?"

"Absolutely. Some people feel an obligation to change something drastic about themselves in order to make up for the fact that their loved one no longer can."

"Oh."

"Sloane, you can't live Amy's life for her. You can't do all of the things she might have done or worry about regretting that you didn't choose to live your own life like a rock star. And you wouldn't have been able to run off with Luke as a means of dulling the pain, even if you'd wanted to. It would have followed you."

"Why does it have to be so confusing? Why can't everything just be simple? Obvious."

"Because where would be the fun in that?" Hillary laughed and then turned serious again. "And I know what you mean about feeling broken. Being here with you and Georgina has set me on a healing path as well, and I bet she'd say the same if she was here."

"Maybe." Sloane shrugged. "Honestly, I'd rather not think any more about this."

"What say we clear our minds, then? Give ourselves a break and enjoy one of our last days of vacation?"

"That sounds perfect." Sloane smiled. "Thank you."

"For what?"

"For being a true best friend."

chapter 31

Sloane had been the one to call Luke this time. And she'd been entirely aboveboard about it with Eddie, telling him she needed closure—an opportunity to tie the tidiest bow she could fashion around the whole ordeal before walking away once and for all. He told her he understood and she'd believed him. There was no mystery when it came to Eddie. It had been one of the things that had made her pull away from him and now, as irony would have it, it was one of the things that was pulling her back.

She'd asked herself what she would have done if things had been reversed. If Eddie had reunited with a former flame and now, after she'd professed her unconditional love for him, he wanted a final chance to close the door on their relationship. Before she'd left for Lake George, she'd have maintained it would have been fine with her. Eddie had never wavered in his commitment to her. He'd never been the type of man to scope out other women, even if they were ten years younger than Sloane and significantly more endowed. It simply wasn't his style. And for that reason, it had never occurred to Sloane to be jealous of someone from Eddie's past.

Now, though, when she thought about Eddie with another woman, it made her stomach roil. He'd said he would be fine without her, hadn't he? And that had made her think. Really think. If she and Eddie split up, he'd have no problem finding someone else. All he'd have to do was visit the supermarket once or twice. Or wait for word to get around Maddie's school. The congregation of recently minted divorcées would assault him like the ravenous vultures they were, perched on standby for news of a freshly failed marriage, praying that their prey would be either passably attractive, rich, or—better yet—both. And while Eddie wasn't rich, he was gorgeous and fit with a healthy enough bank account. Beyond that, he was kind and generous. Sloane had been taking him for granted in the worst way, and that realization had begun to take an emotional and physical toll on her.

She'd always known that Eddie was special, that he was one of the good guys. In some measure it was what had cemented the bond between her and Hillary. Greg too was somewhat of a saint in the husband category. How many of their friends, they'd often mused, had spouses who left the house at six in the morning and didn't come home until nearly midnight, only to return to the office on weekends? Sure, in many of those cases, the men commanded hefty salaries that kept their lonely wives in the latest designer shoes and dresses. And many of those wives were content to spend their lives that way—corralling the kids when their nannies went home for the night and before they arrived in the morning, the rest of their time spent spinning on the ever-revolving hamster wheel of lunching, shopping, exercising, and treating themselves to the latest and greatest antiaging regimens. After all, their husbands expected them to look perfect, even if they weren't present often to actually look at them.

There were also the women whose husbands patronized them in public and, behind closed doors, served up a healthy portion of verbal abuse whenever they tried to assert themselves. Karen Milman had been one of those women. She'd been a longtime friend of Sloane's, her daughter Sylvie having been in the same Mommy and Me music class with Maddie and then in the same school with her since they were two years old. Karen had been an ambitious and successful attorney at the time. Prior to having two more kids within three years. She'd never been one to suppress her opinion or cower from confrontation. In fact, Sloane and Eddie had shared the belief that Karen was often a little too in-your-face, unwilling to view things any way but her own. Jonathan, her husband—a partner at one of the most influential law firms in Boston—had never been particularly friendly, occasionally barking at Karen when they were all out to dinner, but—in the same vein—Karen had always given it right back to him. Until something had changed. Something like a brood of three children under five and an unemployed Karen. Once she'd decided to take a leave of absence, swearing up and down that she'd return to work as soon as her littlest one was finally enrolled in school full-time, Jonathan had gained the upper hand and never lost it. And Karen had transformed, seemingly overnight, from the poster child for "I AM WOMAN, HEAR ME ROAR" to someone who said things like, "I'm so sorry I wasn't able to pick up your dry cleaning today, sweetheart. Can you please forgive me?" The power, which in their relationship had quite obviously been directly linked to the salary one commanded, had shifted entirely into Jonathan's court, as if he'd been biding his time until that day had arrived. Biding his time so he could hold over his wife whatever he damn well pleased.

For months, Karen had arrived with a tearstained face to meet Sloane for lunch or a playdate. There'd never been anything physical, at least not to Sloane's knowledge, but strangely, in Karen's mind, that had made it worse. Sloane would never forget sitting across from Karen over one final lunch, when the time had come that Karen said she couldn't take it anymore. She'd peered at Sloane through glassy eyes and confided, "You know, sometimes I wish he would just hit me. Because that would be undeniably wrong. And then I could nail his fucking ass to a wall and take him for everything he's worth."

As far as Sloane knew, Karen and Jonathan were still married. They'd moved to Washington, D.C., a few months later, when Jonathan's firm had transferred him with the promise of even more money to pad his already luxurious lifestyle. Karen had sent her a friend request last year on Facebook and Sloane had hoped to find a single Karen with a beaming smile. Instead, she'd been confronted by a visibly aged woman with one more child to her name in addition to a series of permanent frown lines. Sure, there were photos that, on the surface, painted the picture of a happy family of six. There they all were in the Bahamas wearing coordinated white button-down shirts and khaki pants, posing for a professional photographer to capture their "perfection." And then there was Karen, without her husband and kids, her arms wrapped around her mother and father. That had been the only snapshot she'd been smiling in. *Genuinely* smiling.

How lucky, Sloane thought, was she to have a man like Eddie? And it scared her to think how close she had come to losing him because she had selfishly been wallowing in her own dissatisfaction.

She dug her feet into the sand and hugged her knees to her chest. It was time to put the flirtation with Luke behind her once and for all. She'd asked him to meet her at one of the small local beaches in between her aunt's house and Frog Hill Farm. He'd suggested their spot. She'd said she preferred something different—neutral turf. Sloane wanted people around, if only a few. She wanted to be able to see the kids splashing in the water, shrieking with delight, and then running into their parents' waiting arms to be enveloped in the warmth of big dry towels—the family units, like the one she was so fortunate to still be part of. There couldn't be anything romantic about this meeting.

"There you are." Luke came up behind her.

"You scared the crap out of me." Sloane stood up and let him hug her briefly. Then she sat back down, motioning for him to sit beside her, which he did.

"Sorry about that. I thought you were down at the other end, so I parked there and walked. I hope you haven't been waiting too long."

"It's fine. My beach days are numbered, so I'm soaking it all in."

"I'm sorry to hear that. But I'm glad you called." He turned toward her and she noticed the dark circles under his eyes. Had he been losing sleep over his new kid? "Sloane . . ."

"Wait, let me." She cleared her throat, uncertain as to exactly what she was going to say. All she knew was that she needed to re-gain control of her life, and suddenly, it felt like there was no better time to start than now. "First let me say that I'm sure it was shocking for you to find out that you conceived a child with Georgina. I'm not sure, however, whether to say I'm sorry or to congratulate you."

"Sloane . . ."

"Please. Let me finish." Her voice was firm but not unkind. No matter how deeply Luke had hurt her, she could never hate him. "While it would have been my preference that you not screw my best friend, I realize that I don't really have the right to be angry at any-one. Of the three of us, I'm the only one who's married. Still, it didn't feel good to find out you and Georgina had kept such a big secret from me, especially in such a jarring way."

"It was one night and it didn't mean anything. . . ." He exhaled.

"What I was going to say is that I really don't care. I don't want the details. I've had enough of an opportunity to conjure the various scenarios in my mind." Sloane tucked a few stray hairs behind her ears and continued. "You should have told me that it happened, Luke. I may not have been thrilled, but the fact that you kept it from me and then pursued something between us feels wrong. Beyond that, it feels intentionally deceitful. I'm not that twenty-year-old girl you met in college anymore. I'm a grown-up and I expect to be treated like one." Sloane was well aware that her own words were steeped in the contradiction of how she'd regarded Eddie, but she'd owned up to the error of her ways. Had Luke?

"I understand." He nodded.

"That's really all I've got." Sloane shrugged.

"I don't know what to say. If I told you that I'd practically forgotten about that night with Georgina because it was that insignificant of a blip on my radar, would that make a difference?"

"It couldn't hurt." Sloane smiled, attempting to lighten the mood.

"It's the truth, Sloane. Without expounding any more than necessary, we were drunk. There was a leak in her hotel room ceiling, which had soaked the bed, and the hotel was sold out. I felt somewhat responsible since my family had just purchased the property, so I said she could crash with me, and . . ."

"Let's leave it at that."

"Fair enough." He locked eyes with her. "It doesn't change how I feel about you. It never did."

"What about your daughter?"

"I don't know, Sloane. I've given it a lot of thought. I just can't see how we'd work it out. I'm not daddy material."

"Oh." She wasn't sure why she was surprised to hear him say that. Or was it disappointment? Not that he didn't want to father Georgina's child, but that he didn't want to father anyone's child. Immediately, her thoughts turned to Eddie and what a truly devoted parent he was. There was no one more important to him than Maddie. He'd always said she was the apple of his eye. "So you don't want to be a part of Zara's life at all?" It was so strange to refer to Georgina's child—Luke's child—by name when she'd never so much as seen a picture of her, forget cradling her in her arms the way she'd imagined she would if Georgina ever decided to reproduce.

"Not in any regular way. Of course, I'll take care of everything financial. You know, private school, college, whatever. And of course I'd love to meet her, see her from time to time when I'm in London."

"Sure. That sounds nice," Sloane lied. It didn't sound nice at all. In fact it sounded downright cold. "Maybe you'll change your mind one day."

"Maybe. Though I doubt it. I know who I am, Sloane, what I'm capable of, and what I'm not. I also know that I still love you. The offer stands to come away with me."

"A week ago I might have said yes. But it would have been a grave mistake, if I'd actually gone through with it. I love Eddie. And I love our family. I could never leave Maddie."

"Georgina told me you'd say that."

"You spoke to Georgina?" It shouldn't have shocked Sloane that she'd get in touch with Luke, even before returning from whatever loser guy's house she was still shacked up at.

"Yeah. I saw her. She showed up at Frog Hill yesterday afternoon. Right after I got your text about meeting."

"She didn't happen to mention when she was coming back to the house, did she?" Sloane had yet to figure out how she and Georgina were going to move forward. *If* she and Georgina were going to move forward. At the very least, she knew they needed to talk. Honestly. About everything.

"Sloane . . ." Luke's expression was one of genuine confusion.

"What?"

"Georgina is gone."

"What do you mean gone?"

"She left this morning."

"For London?"

"She didn't say." He stood up and Sloane did the same.

"I don't understand." Sloane shook her head slowly.

"That's Georgina for you, I guess." He shrugged and then extended his arms toward her. "A kiss good-bye for old times' sake?"

"You'll have to settle for a hug."

"If I must."

Luke folded her into his chest and as they stood there, holding each other close, Sloane finally felt ready to let go once and for all.

chapter 32

Greg sat on the edge of the bed with his body hunched into a slouch and his hands covering his face. "I just don't understand."

"I know." Hillary's whisper was barely audible, even to her own ears. Telling him the terrible secret she'd been keeping had gone better than she'd expected. She'd been afraid he would scream, cry, and justifiably threaten to leave her. She suspected that the transgression she had committed was beyond the scope of forgiveness. But true to form, Greg had remained his levelheaded self. And for that, she would be eternally grateful.

Unless, of course, this was the calm before his storm.

"Well, can you maybe try to clarify for me why you've been lying to me for *three years*? Why I've been under the glaring misconception that you were trying to get pregnant? That *we* were trying to get pregnant?"

She'd confessed everything, except her feelings. For some reason, she hadn't counted on him desiring an explanation, at least not so soon. Instead, she'd expected a big reaction. An accusation. Something to punish her for her sins.

"I have no excuse for what I've done." Hillary sat down beside him and he quickly moved away from her. "I can only tell you that I was scared. That I *am* scared."

"Scared of what?" Greg looked up at her briefly, but as soon as their eyes met, he turned away.

"That I would be a terrible mother, like my own. I'm so afraid of the odds that I'll become deeply depressed—what if I was even worse than she was? And what if it wouldn't go away? I mean, what if . . ."

"What if what?"

"What if I was a failure? What if we got the baby home and I didn't like him? Or her. What if I changed my mind after it was born? What if I just wasn't any good? At being a mom."

"Everyone knows you'd be a great mom. You were *made* to be a mom, Hillary." He shook his head. "I'm sorry, but it just doesn't make sense. How could you not have told me any of this?"

"It makes sense to me. Growing up with a mother who can't take care of herself, much less you, isn't exactly a walk in the park."

"You're nothing like her." Greg paused. "Does this have something to do with that Georgina girl?"

"No, definitely not." There was a question she hadn't anticipated. "This has been going on since way before I even met Georgina."

"Right." He flinched.

"I'm so sorry, Greg. I love you so much, and—"

"You love me, but you've been deceiving me for three years? *Three years*, Hillary. Three years, I've been feeling sorry for *you*. Imagining the toll this must have been taking on you. I've been up until the middle of the night on the computer trying to figure out why everyone else can get pregnant except us. It's no wonder you've been unwilling to try fertility treatments." He flailed his arms in the air. "God, am I an idiot!"

"There was no way you could have known." She put her hand on his leg and he retracted it.

"Do you know what this has cost me, Hillary?"

"I can only imagine."

"No, I'm not sure you can, actually. I didn't want to tell you. . . ."

"Tell me what?" This was an unexpected turn. Had he been keeping something from her too? He wasn't the type to conceal anything. Although neither was she.

"I was demoted at work." He looked at her again, this time with a clenched jaw.

"What!? They love you. No one works harder than you do." It felt like someone was clamping down on her heart. He'd been demoted and hadn't bothered to share it with her. She was hurt, stung, and possibly the greatest hypocrite known to man.

"That's the thing, Hillary. I was so damn consumed with the burden of failing to conceive every month, as I said, staying up until all hours of the night reading every word of every website devoted to the subject, worrying about how it was affecting you, us, our future. It was like a second job, and I suppose my primary job somehow suffered for that." He shook his head. "And you know what? I didn't even care when they first told me."

"So this wasn't recent?" How long had he kept it from her?

"Six months ago."

"Six months ago!" She tried to touch his arm, but he recoiled again. "Why didn't you tell me?"

"Because *I* didn't want to burden *you*. As you may recall, I figured you were already beleaguered by our seemingly endless and fruitless efforts to try to have a baby."

"This is my fault." Hillary squeezed her eyes shut so the tears wouldn't come. She had no right to cry. She had no right to feel jilted or wronged. He had withheld this from her because she'd pushed him away, perhaps unintentionally, but that didn't matter. He must have felt it, somehow, because—in turn—he'd been unable to confide in her when it had mattered most.

Greg took great pride in being a professor. He took great pride in his students, his research. Unlike so many people going through the motions of their work life like robots on autopilot, Greg had a fervent passion for what he did and she'd robbed him of that.

"I'm not trying to place blame. My actions were my own. I'm just trying to figure out where we go from here." He exhaled. "What the hell am I supposed to do now?"

"I don't know." Hillary looked away so he wouldn't see her crying. She wasn't deserving of his sympathy and certainly not his empathy. "If you hate me, I understand."

"I could never hate you." Greg sighed. "But I am furious. And I damn well should be."

"I know."

"So, what? You don't want kids at all?"

"I didn't say that. We just need time to figure this out," she implored him, well aware that he owed her nothing.

"What I need is to go."

"Go where?"

"Back to Brookline."

"I'll come with you."

"No." His tone was firm, but not unkind. "I need to be alone. To think things through. I'll ask Eddie to take me." He stood up.

"You're leaving now?"

"I think that's for the best."

"Will you be there when I get home?" She braced herself for the answer.

"Yes, I'll be there. But this isn't going to be an overnight fix, Hillary."

"I know." Even though things were bad, she could feel her body release some of the long-held tension.

"It's going to take time. And understanding. On my part."

"Of course."

"And let me be very clear that I'd still very much like to be a father."

"I want that for you." She hugged his stiff body to her own and then cupped his face in her hands. "I want that for us."

chapter 33

Sloane raced up the stairs and flung open the door to Georgina's room to find the floor still littered with clothing and shoes, a pack of cigarettes on the dresser, and a bottle of vodka on the nightstand. Despite the vestiges of Georgina's presence, Sloane could tell she wasn't coming back. Not because Luke had told her so, but because her spirit had left the building.

She sat down on the bed, which—in a shocking turn of events—was carefully made up, as if Georgina had known she wasn't planning to return. All at once the tears came hard and fast.

"Hey, are you okay?" Sloane looked up at the sound of the voice, aware her face was mottled, to find Hillary standing in the doorway.

"She's gone," Sloane whispered.

"Who's gone?"

"Georgina. She left without saying good-bye."

"Oh, sweetie." Hillary sat down next to Sloane and wrapped her arms around her.

"I really wish Eddie was here." Sloane suddenly needed him more than she ever had. If her time at the lake house had taught her one thing, it was that, in the wake of Amy's death, she'd cut herself off from her emotions, the result of which had been her inability to connect with Eddie. The one person whom she should have relied on the most. Sure, Luke had reawakened something in her, allowing her to return to who she was before she'd lost Amy. He'd been a respite from the grief, a bandage to cover the wound, but never an enduring cure. Eddie was her life, and reengaging in their marriage was her priority above all else.

He'd called her from the car while she was on her way home from seeing Luke to say he was driving Greg back to Brookline. Immediately, she'd told him how much she loved him and how happy she was that they'd found their way back to each other. And she'd meant it. To Sloane's delight, she'd practically heard him beaming through the receiver and she knew, in that moment, that everything was going to be okay. That *she* was going to be okay, even without Amy.

"I'm sorry." Hillary sighed. "That would be my doing."

"Eddie told me that you and Greg talked, but he didn't offer any details. Are you okay?"

"Hard to say. I'm definitely relieved. I told him everything."

"*Everything?* About being on the pill? And not being sure you want kids?"

"The whole shebang. But talking to him was good. It made me realize that, with his help, I might be ready for this parenthood thing."

"And?"

"He was very angry, as was to be expected."

"I'm so sorry, Hill."

"It's okay. I think. I mean, I knew the day would come. I should never have let it go on so long." Hillary took a deep breath. "Greg was demoted at work because of it. He just told me, even though it happened six months ago."

"Oh no."

"Yup. Wife of the year over here."

"Don't be so hard on yourself."

"How can I not? I lied to him and pushed him away, which forced him to feel like he couldn't confide in me. Not to mention that I put his career in jeopardy."

"You had no way of knowing about that."

"As if that matters." Hillary raised an eyebrow. "I'm taking my lumps on this one no matter what anyone says. Though I do appreciate the support. And the fact that you're still willing to associate with someone as rotten as I am."

"Oh, Hill. So what now? Where did you guys leave it?"

"Well, fortunately for me, Greg is an amazing human being."

"Without a doubt."

"And an even better husband. He said he thinks we can work through it. Somehow."

"That's good news, right?"

"It is. I just hate it that he left so mad at me."

"I'm sure he just needs to process everything."

"I hope so." Hillary perused the room. "What are we going to do with all of Georgina's things? Doesn't she need them?"

"I guess not." Sloane shrugged. "It's vintage Georgina to leave a mess in her wake. She wouldn't be her if she didn't."

"Dibs on the leopard-print minidress draped over that lamp." Hillary laughed and walked over to the dresser. "This actually looks important."

"Let me see."

"It's one of those claddagh rings." Hillary placed it in Sloane's open hand and sat back down next to her.

"Oh, wow. I remember this. It was her maternal grandmother's. I can't believe she left it behind."

"Could she have done it intentionally?"

"You think?"

"Well, it's a traditional Irish symbol that represents love, loyalty, and friendship."

"Amazing." Sloane laughed softly. "No matter how maddening Georgina can be, then she'll go and do something like this. Maybe I'm a glutton for punishment, but I feel like she'll always play an important role in my life. Even though we've grown apart in so many ways, I suppose I've come to realize that I need her as much as she needs me. Perhaps in small doses." She paused, smiling now. "She's my oldest friend. She knows me better than almost anyone does. You know?"

"I do." Hillary nodded sagely.

"Although that's not to say that I don't cherish newer friends as well." Sloane squeezed Hillary's hand.

"Well, the feeling is mutual." She smiled. "I'm certain Georgina wanted you to hold on to this ring, Sloane."

"I hope so. And I will." Sloane slipped it onto her finger. "Until our next adventure . . ."

chapter 34

"Dinner's almost ready!" Eddie called up the stairs.

"I'll be down in a few minutes." Sloane closed her eyes as the aroma of grilled steak and cheesy gratin potatoes wafted into her bedroom. She'd returned from Lake George that afternoon feeling refreshed and renewed. Whole again.

It was their last night before Maddie returned from sleepaway camp, and Eddie had spent the morning leading up to Sloane's arrival gathering the fixings for a romantic dinner for two. He'd even set the smaller, intimate table on the back porch with white linen napkins and their fine china. As soon as she'd seen the expectant glint in his eyes, Sloane had decided not to insinuate that the fanfare was unnecessary and that she'd have been just as happy with Thai takeout, paper plates, and plastic cups. Instead, she'd run into his arms and hugged him as tightly as she could. She'd thanked him for helping her heal. For being the man that he had always been. The man whom, for a brief space in time, she'd forgotten why she'd fallen in love with.

"I'm popping the bubbly, so hurry up!" he bellowed as the clap of the cork echoed throughout the house.

"Coming!" Sloane walked toward the door, catching a stack of mail on the dresser out of the corner of her eye. On top, there was an envelope with her name and address scribbled on it in Georgina's chaotic handwriting. She grabbed it, immediately flipping it over in search of a return address, but—as expected—it was blank. She took a deep breath, filling her lungs with the courage to read whatever was inside, and then exhaled.

"Here goes nothing," she muttered, even though no one was there to hear her, and then tore open the envelope with her index finger. She unfolded the sheet of paper inside, which was sheathed in the tiniest red lettering. Sloane laughed, armed with the knowledge that it was challenging enough for Georgina to write that neatly in the first place, much less in such fine print.

My Dearest Sloane,

By the time you're reading this, I'll be gone, which is probably for the best, since I'm fairly certain you're not feeling terribly kind toward me at the moment.

If I was less of a coward, I suppose I would have said good-bye in person, faced the music, as they say. But I couldn't bear the thought of your profound disappointment in me.

You have every right to hate me. I don't even know how to begin to justify or even explain the many ways I've gone wrong. The many ways I've hurt you. Although you have no reason to believe me, I was gutted when Amy died. For your family. For her husband and kids. But mainly for you. I thought about calling so many times. I started e-mails and deleted them. I wrote a handful of letters that were shredded to pieces because they simply weren't enough. I know now that anything would have been better than radio silence. What can I say other than that I was horribly selfish? I was so consumed with the surprise of being pregnant—and by the time I found out, I had no choice but to carry the baby to term. I knew that if I was in touch with you, I'd have to tell you the truth about everything. And, somehow, I rationalized that not reaching out was better than the alternative, which was to own up to my mistake.

Of course, you tell one lie, it leads to another. I'm not looking for sympathy, but I do want you to know that I endured terrible pain in keeping news of Zara from you. I was well aware that you were already furious with me and that if I called about Zara so late in the game, you'd be even more furious. As well you should have been. So, again, I was a coward. I'm not proud of it, Sloane, but—in so many ways—this is who I am.

I never have been and I never will be the responsible, have-it-all-together woman you and Hillary are. And I could never begin to know how to be even half the mother you are to Madeleine. I hope she knows how lucky she is. Zara will never have the kind of mother she deserves and for that I am truly sorry. I'd love to be able to tell you that I'm headed straight back to London to raise her with Hugh, as he's so valiantly stepped up to do. Except I'm not sure I'm mother material. I do love nibbling on her sweet little fingers and toes, but that's not enough. She needs someone who is committed to her—through the best and the worst of times. I don't do "the worst of times" very well, as you already know.

Right now I need time to let the dust settle, as self-centered as that *probably sounds. I do hope, sooner rather than later, to return to Zara and Hugh—if he'll have me. You have inspired me to try, one day. And when that time comes, I hope that I'll be able to call on you as a mother and my best friend, even though I don't deserve it.*

I'm not proud of what I've done, Sloane. I'm not proud of the person I've become. And I've never forgotten that time in college when you said, "If I could be you and you me, I'd switch places in a heartbeat." It was quite possibly one of the greatest compliments anyone has ever bestowed upon me and I've held those words close to my heart ever since. Though I'd be willing to bet you don't still feel that way. The truth is, Sloane, if I could be you and you me, I'd switch places in a heartbeat.

The last thing I want you to know is that you have been the one constant in my life. The one person, through all of my rottenness, who's stuck by me. I am so grateful to you for that.

I hope one day you'll be able to find it in your heart to forgive me. For now, I'll leave it at . . . until we meet again, my friend.

xoxo, G

P.S. You might enjoy knowing that my parents have indeed lived up to their promise to cut me off from my trust fund until I return to Hugh and Zara. So it looks like I'll actually be working for a living. Gasp! The first step down a long path to becoming a grown-up. And to think I thought this day would never come. Life is full of surprises. The good kind and the bad.

P.P.S. I love you. Always and forever . . .

those secrets
we keep

EMILY LIEBERT

A CONVERSATION
WITH EMILY LIEBERT

Q. How did you come up with the story line for Those Secrets We Keep?

A. After my first and second novels, *You Knew Me When* and *When We Fall*, both of which dealt with the lives of two women as the main characters, I really wanted to try my hand at writing about three women. That said, I didn't want them all to be friends going in. In order to create an undercurrent of drama, I felt it was important for one of them to be the central focus—that's Sloane—and for her to have a friend from her past and a friend from her present who are coming together for the very first time. I also felt it was important that all three of them have strong plot trajectories of their own. So I decided to put them all in a vacation house for three weeks and give them each a big secret they were keeping, which would be revealed in a major way during the course of the novel.

Q. How did you conceive of the three main characters?

A. I knew that all three women needed to be very different, but—at the same time—be able to relate on some level. I wanted

Sloane, as the central character, to be a bit more neutral, the girl next door, if you will. Married with a child, but in a place where things in her life aren't feeling right. In turn, her old friend from college—Georgina—needed a big personality. I saw her as everything Sloane was not: impulsive, irresponsible, and unattached. In so many ways, you wonder why they ever became friends in the first place. On the flip side, you see how and why they complement each other; the purpose they fill in each other's lives. To add to that dynamic, there's Hillary, Sloane's closest friend from her married life, and she represents the type of person Sloane is drawn to as an adult. She's kind, reliable, and a great sounding board. She's also happily married with a successful career. Neither Sloane nor Hillary is based on anyone I've known in real life. Georgina, however, is loosely based on someone in my family!

Q. Why did you pick Lake George as the setting for the book?

A. For one, my husband and I got engaged on a motorcycle trip through Lake George, so it holds special meaning to me. It's also someplace that, while I've never actually stayed there for long, I've passed through many times, and I've spent time in the town itself. Since Sloane and Hillary live in Brookline, Massachusetts, and were looking for a getaway close enough to drive to, it was also a good fit for that reason. It's a real summer-vacation kind of locale and it's stood the test of time, which made it both possible and realistic that Sloane would have gone there growing up and also longed to return during a challenging time in her life.

Q. Each of the main female characters carries a secret to the house. What was your inspiration for deciding what the secrets would be?

A. This was the fun part! As far as Sloane, I wanted her secret to be something straightforward—something it would be easy for so many women to relate to: that feeling that while you should be content in your life, there's something holding you back from achieving true happiness. I also wanted her secret to be less of a secret and more of an issue that the reader understood from the start and could watch play out throughout the book. When it came to Georgina, I knew her secret had to be major and multitiered. She's the kind of person that, just when you think she's shocked you, there's another bomb about to detonate right around the corner. And with Hillary, her strong moral compass is so central to her characterization, I felt her secret needed to be something that made readers rethink everything they thought they knew about her. To ask themselves how someone so fundamentally good in every way could make such a poor and hurtful decision.

Q. Sloane and Georgina have a complicated relationship, which is only intensified once they're together. Is this something you've experienced personally?

A. I've never experienced the precise kind of relationship that they have. However, I do know what it's like to have friends from your past who, as close as you were with them many years ago, no longer necessarily fit in your life fifteen or twenty years later. I also know what it's like to still feel affection for those people. I have friends from high school and college that I'm no longer very close to today, but—in a way—they're family and always will be. There's a history that can't be erased, nor would I want it to be. They're people who could call me at a moment's notice for help and I wouldn't hesitate to leap into action, and I suspect it would be the same in reverse.

Q. The death of Sloane's sister, Amy, is an undercurrent that runs throughout the book. What inspired this decision?

A. As morbid as it may sound, I've always had a fascination with the ripple effects of a loved one's death—the void that it leaves in people's lives and the harsh reality that someone you love can be here one day and gone the next. It's been a theme, on varying levels, in all of my books. In Sloane's case, Amy's death was the catalyst for her questioning everything in her life. So often when loved ones pass away, we ask ourselves—am I living my life to the fullest? If I died tomorrow, could I say I was truly happy? This is a struggle for Sloane and very much at the forefront of her issues. She and Amy were extremely close and while her sister's death isn't necessarily something that affects her life every day on a practical level, as the loss of a spouse or a child would, it still has a major impact on her.

Q. Sloane is torn between two men for the majority of the book—her adoring husband and a rich, playboy-type ex-boyfriend from her past. Did you worry this would make her unlikable?

A. I think there's always the risk that when characters are considering stepping out on their significant others, it could make them at least somewhat unlikable to readers. I also think that it's something so many people have thought about at one point in time or another, so it makes Sloane relatable. People tend to show their character flaws at times of severe stress. She's at a real crossroads, not sure which path to take, and also questioning whether she chose the right path all those years ago. Just as she's at her most vulnerable, her first love bursts back onto the scene and he's everything she thinks is missing in her life—everything she desires, both physically and emotionally. Of course the timing of things can make them deceiving.

Q. *The ending of the book leaves unanswered questions. Was this intentional?*

A. Very much so. I'm a firm believer in not tying up endings with a pretty bow. That's not real life, especially since this book spans only a few weeks. When problems are that massive and such damaging secrets have been kept, it would be pretty unrealistic to have everything resolved that quickly. And the best part is that it leaves room for a sequel!

EMILY LIEBERT is the award-winning author of *You Knew Me When*, published in September 2013, and *When We Fall*, published in September 2014. She's been featured on *Today*, *The Rachael Ray Show*, and *Anderson Live*, and in *InStyle*, *People StyleWatch*, the *New York Times*, the *Wall Street Journal*, and the *Chicago Tribune*, among other national media outlets.

Emily is currently hard at work on her fifth book. She lives in Westport, Connecticut, with her husband and their two sons.